THE WORLD AS WE KNOW IT

"There are people in our lives whom we love, and lose, and unfailingly long for. They orbit our hearts like Halley's Comet, crossing into our universe only once, or if we are lucky, twice in a lifetime. This is a story of those kind of people—a tender, gentle, achingly beautiful tale that is impossible to put down."

—Jamie Ford, *New York Times* bestselling author of
Hotel on the Corner of Bitter and Sweet

"Joe Monninger beautifully captures the essence of childhood adventure and the sweet innocence of falling in love for the first time. Fans of John Irving, you have a new author to love."

—Lisa Genova, *New York Times* bestselling author of *Left Neglected*

"The beauty and brutality of nature unfolds in *The World as We Know It*—a touching tale of love, the wounds of loss, and the fragile complexities within the human heart."

—Beth Hoffman, *New York Times* bestselling author of
Saving CeeCee Honeycutt

"The combination of romantic love with ad   one-deep understanding of the wil   dent. . . . With echoes of Hemingv   nothing short of brilliant."

—Luan   author of
The Deep Blue Sea for Beginners

Praise for

ETERNAL ON THE WATER

"Henry David Thoreau meets Nicholas Sparks in this poignant love story rooted in the forests of Maine. . . . Monninger's keen eye for nature, subtle incorporation of indigenous myths, and use of symbolism make for a memorable story of love and courage."

—*Publishers Weekly*

"Monninger is a gifted writer, and readers . . . will relish this eloquently rendered tale."

—*Booklist*

"A touching love story immersed in the beautiful simplicity of nature and life lived in the present moment."

—Lisa Genova, *New York Times* bestselling author of *Left Neglected*

"Monninger is a brilliant writer. No one understands nature the way he does, under his skin and straight to his bones. He writes about new love with such tension, emotion, and the deep passion and understanding that develops between two people. The novel will keep you up all night. *Eternal on the Water* will be a classic."

—Luanne Rice, *New York Times* bestselling author of
The Deep Blue Sea for Beginners

"*Eternal on the Water* is a book that reminds you that joy and sorrow are inextricably entwined, that one means less without the other. . . . This luminescent story will never leave you. I adored it."

—Dorothea Benton Frank, *New York Times* bestselling author of
Lowcountry Summer

"*Eternal on the Water* is more than a heartfelt love story. It is a beautiful and searching exploration of the meaning of commitment and the majesty of nature, told in the strong, clear voice of a true believer. In these pages, there is much to learn of life, death, love, and healing. It's a book to savor and then to share."

—Susan Wiggs, *New York Times* bestselling author of *Just Breathe*

"*Eternal on the Water* is a compelling and poignant love story. Monninger's two characters, both strong and independent, meet by chance in the Maine wilderness and find in each other the depth of connection they have been searching for and the confrontation with mortality they have been dreading all their lives. Their celebration of life and their emotional parting will touch you deeply and move you to tears."

—Selden Edwards, critically acclaimed author of *The Little Book*

"Genuinely enchanting! If you ever went to summer camp, this book is especially for you!"

—Kaya McLaren, author of *On the Divinity of Second Chances*

Both of these titles are also available as eBooks.

THE WORLD AS WE KNOW IT

A NOVEL

Joseph Monninger

GALLERY BOOKS

New York   London   Toronto   Sydney   New Delhi

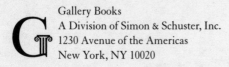

Gallery Books
A Division of Simon & Schuster, Inc.
1230 Avenue of the Americas
New York, NY 10020

First Gallery Books trade paperback edition October 2011

GALLERY BOOKS and colophon are trademarks of Simon & Schuster, Inc.

For information about special discounts for bulk purchases,
please contact Simon & Schuster Special Sales at 1-866-506-1949
or business@simonandschuster.com.

The Simon & Schuster Speakers Bureau can bring authors to your
live event. For more information or to book an event, contact the
Simon & Schuster Speakers Bureau at 1-866-248-3049 or visit our
website at www.simonspeakers.com.

Manufactured in the United States of America

10 9 8 7 6 5 4 3 2 1

Library of Congress Cataloging-in-Publication Data

Monninger, Joseph.
    The world as we know it / Joseph Monninger.—1st Gallery Books trade
paperback ed.
        p. cm.
    1. Brothers—Fiction. 2. Life change events—Fiction. I. Title.
PS3563.O526W67 2011
813'.54—dc22   2010051654

ISBN 978-1-4516-0634-8
ISBN 978-1-4516-0638-6 (ebook)

To Luanne Rice,
my dear friend through all the years,
all the pages . . .

The one red leaf, the last of its clan,

That dances as often as dance it can.

—*Christabel*, Samuel Taylor Coleridge

The
World
as We
Know It

PART I:

THE GREAT LAND

1

Years ago, on a cold New Hampshire day, my brother and I tried to skate to Canada. It was still early December and our first full snow had not yet fallen, and the rivers and lakes around us became pale green mirrors reflecting sunlight back to the sky. At night the stars reflected themselves also, and the moon rose above a second moon that appeared to rise from the earth and all its waters. In that same winter I recall hearing geese pass overhead late at night, their honking insisting they were *late, late, late,* and we listened from our twin beds in the attic bedroom, the windows frosted, the down comforters piled high on top of us by our parents in compensation for the lack of wood heat that made its way to us. In that same winter, as I remember it, the water glasses beside our beds turned to white plugs of ice each night so that, in the morning, we carried them downstairs to show off to our parents, proof positive of our suffering and heroism in sleeping upstairs. In the warmth of the kitchen, my mother pulled flapjacks off the stove—we were a family of enormous breakfasters—as the tick of the woodstove burned scraps from my father's carpentry shop. My brother and I proved our derring-do, our closeness to the eternal elements, as we watched the ice melt in the glasses as if they were fragile trophies we had brought back from distant lands.

We loved the outdoors, and we loved the sound of storms and rain on the roof, the protection under the eaves, the approval of our mother, who pretended concern over the frigid temperatures in our room, but who boasted to other mothers, women in the market, that her boys never got sick because they slept in the cold, naked except for boxers, and that they slept deep, full slumbers that carried them away each night and brought them back with the cock crow. She had that line from Dylan Thomas—she was a great reader, a volunteer librarian at the Joseph Patch library—but it was true nonetheless. We slept, too, beneath a map of Canada. It was not a typical map, not one of normal size, but one that my father had found in a thrift store, a map fifteen feet across and ten feet high that included little below the forty-seventh parallel. It had been exploded to that size for a conference on the northern forest that my father had heard about from fellow carpenters, and he bought it for fifteen dollars and tacked it to the rafters in our attic bedroom.

"A dream map," he told my mother. "The boys will never be trapped in their own heads with a map like that."

It was true. On certain nights he lay down beside us in one of our beds, my brother, Ed, curled on one side, me on the other, and we let our eyes roam together as other children studied clouds. My father loved the idea of Canada, its vast wildernesses, its freedom, its call to adventure. He liked to remind us, as we lay in bed, the wind whipping, the snow threatening to arrive any day, that the animals of the north had already returned to their hibernations, sinking into their blood and stupor, the great turtles asleep in the pond muck, the bright white polar bears leaping from ice island to ice island.

"Up there, near Churchill," he would whisper, pointing with his chin, "the sea ice has already closed in and the polar bears float away for the winter, traveling deeper and deeper into the northern seas. They crawl on their bellies and wait beside the seals' airholes, and then, when the bears time it correctly, they reach one great mitt down into the icy water and pull a seal through the hole so quickly that it occasionally shatters all the seal's bones. Did you know that, boys?

"And sometimes if the light is just right, they can see the seals approach the holes through the ice—dark, quick-moving things, like moths on a lampshade. And the seals see the bears' shadows, too, but they need air and they must come up and the bears are always waiting. But now and then the bears go after walruses and the walruses do something different. Instead of fleeing they hug the bears and jab their tusks through the bears' hearts, and they have found more than one pair of skeletons locked together forever, bear and walrus, gliding for eternity beneath the cold blue ice."

Such stories. Given the map and my father's interest, it was natural that we should decide to skate to Canada. For a week or more Ed charted the course. In the interval between lights out and sleep, he shined a flashlight on the area directly north of New Hampshire, moving the beam over the attic roof.

"See that river?" he asked me, pointing his flashlight and running it north and south. "And then that one? That water links to the Baker River right here. We can get on the river and just skate away."

"The Baker River runs south," I reminded him.

"Allard, in the winter nothing runs any which way. It's all ice. The streams are like ladders through the countryside. It's a great big skating rink."

And it was. In those first weeks of December, before the snow, we skated every day. On two pairs of secondhand hockey skates, we glided back and forth in front of our house, and followed the Baker River over to Beaver Brook then over to Turkey Pond. Cattails clogged the brook and the mouth of Turkey Pond during the summer, but in winter the grasses froze in place and we ran through them with our skates, the lacy ice brittle beneath us, the grass stems breaking like whips of light as we passed. We skated in the gloaming, the gray quiet of the afternoon, and it was impossible not to feel anticipation tinged with the desire for all things in the universe spiraling in our guts. We knew nothing, really, and yet we knew a great deal, and some small part of us, of our shared wisdom, understood that this winter gave us a paradise and that we skated in a quiet glory that sharpened itself against the warm white light that waited for us, against my mother's wonderful food and my father's quiet carpentry work. The sun is young once only, my mother said, quoting Dylan Thomas again, and this winter, as the poet promised, we were green and golden in our days.

It was on that first afternoon of snow—the snow that would reduce our world to a small hockey rink we shoveled clear daily—that I saw Sarah. I was skating beside my brother, Ed, the sky heavy with promise. We had scouted Turkey Pond and Beaver Brook, gliding like Dutch boys across the countryside. Seen from a distance, our progress appeared miraculous: two boys, both knotted in clothes, skimming the earth without apparent friction. Ed, squat and powerful, skated in a side-to-side motion, his thick legs pushing him off one blade onto the next, a beaver-shaped boy happy in his winter fur. He wore a backpack with our camping gear inside it because on this day we planned to make a foray up the Baker River. We did not know precisely if the Baker connected to any important streams, or if it would advance us on our journey, but we were young enough to believe Canada waited on the other end of a web of tributaries, that water, if we were patient, might lead us north to the heart of the *great land,* as my father called it.

We skated north. My brother led us along a spine of ice, the center of the river where boulders and logs sometimes interrupted our glides. Wind and currents had shaped the ice into burls and ridges, and we skated less effortlessly, the water humming deep below us. Both of us knew we entertained a fantasy; we never challenged it directly or promised too much to one another. We did not honestly believe we could skate to Canada, but with our father's prodding, and our own need for adventure, we continued past the Hewetts', the Benders', their river houses stately and large, built during the height of the New Hampshire logging days, their yards sloped to keep the river in its place during times of flooding. Had the people inside these houses chanced to look out on that dark afternoon, they would have been charmed by two boys pioneering the river, by the beautiful ribbon of black against the frigid pine trees.

The river tightened. The boulders became more plentiful. Our skating grew plodding. We did not know the river well this far up, and Ed, faithful to our adventure, pulled out a pair of binoculars and scanned the ice ahead of us. Only one lens worked, so he held it like a spyglass and swept it back and forth. As I waited for his report, I dug a 3 Musketeers bar out of his backpack. I opened it and split it in half. When he finished with the binoculars, he took the other half.

"Someone's up there ahead," he said, tucking the binoculars back in his pack.

"On the river?"

"Looks like it. They just went around the bend."

"What are they doing?"

He shrugged. "Let's go. We'll find out."

We went. The afternoon sky had grown brooding, the clouds lowering themselves as if to rest on the pines. Christmas was not far off, which meant we were approaching the longest evening of the year. We skated ahead, and as we went forward snow began to fall. I was aware of it completely only when I saw a blue jay snap onto a pine bough and scold us for a moment. Then I saw the snow, white and gentle against the green.

"It's snowing," Ed said. "Here it comes."

"So much for skating," I answered. "It will cover everything."

"We should turn back soon."

Then we came around the bend. The next thing that happened seemed strange and surreal and out of cadence with the afternoon. A girl stood in the center of the river, but she had obviously gone through the ice. She stood up to her waist in water. She was our age, twelve or thirteen. A dog swam in circles around her, and each time it put its paws on the thin ice, it broke away and made the hole wider. The girl did not call for help, nor did she seem particularly panicked. Her only interest seemed to be in getting the dog back onto solid ice. She lifted the dog and shoved it toward us, but the dog slipped back in and continued its nervous paddling.

We ran toward them as best we could on our skates. The dog circled her like a small planet around a sun. The girl wore a pink wool cap and a navy down jacket. As we approached, the dog began trying to climb on her, as if entreating her to do something, and she obliged it by holding it to her chest. After a moment it wiggled away. Its paws made no sound, but its breathing came in short *puhhhh, puhhhh, puhhhh*s.

We skidded to a stop about twenty yards away. The ice still felt solid under us.

"There's a current," she said calmly, her voice slightly froggy and deep, "and it's trying to pull me under the ice. I'm afraid to take a step. I'll go under if I do."

"Just hold on," I said.

"It's running toward you," she said. "It's strong. It's pushing at the back of my legs."

"Can you work your way to the bank?" Ed asked.

"I don't think so. I'm losing feeling in my legs. And I'm not leaving Natasha."

"She'll follow you," I said.

The girl shook her head.

"Let's go to the bank and work our way out," Ed said to me. "We don't want to be in the middle of the river if it gives way. And we don't want to add our weight to the ice."

We skirted diagonally across the river until we reached the western bank. Ice at the edge of the river snapped under our feet. It felt strange to walk on solid ground in skates. From this vantage point we could see the girl was not far out, maybe fifteen feet at most. But the ice trapped her in a perfect hoop. It would give way north and south, but on either side of her it was thick and wet and impossible to grab.

"I'll tie you off," Ed said to me, immediately coming up with a plan. "You're lighter. You should go out alone."

I nodded. Hundreds of nights gazing at the Canadian map had prepared me for this moment. Ed dug a rope out of his backpack, a thin clothesline we had retrieved from the basement. Of all the uses we imagined for it, this wasn't one of them.

Ed tied it around a thin pine and then knotted the other end to his pack. At first I didn't understand, but then I realized it would serve as a life ring. If she couldn't grab the thin rope, she might be able to hold on to the pack.

"Hurry," she said. "Please. I can't feel anything and Natasha is getting weaker."

Ed handed me the backpack. He sat down on the frozen river and kicked the heels of his skates into the ice. He looped the rope around his back the way our father had shown us when we worked with pulleys or heavy logs.

"I got you," he said. "Go on your belly. Spread out your weight as much as you can."

I did as he instructed, although later it occurred to me we might simply have thrown the bag to her. That would have allowed us both to pull her to safety. But so fully did I believe in my brother, I didn't hesitate. I fell onto the ice and pushed the backpack in front of me. I listened for the ice to crack, but all I heard was the rush of water beneath my knees. I was conscious of snow falling, the soft, dreamy silence of it as I snaked my way out to her. She had stopped trying to lift her dog, I noticed. She stood with her feet planted, afraid to move for fear of slipping.

"Almost there," Ed said.

The dog swam toward me, tried to climb onto the ice, then fell back into the current. I spread my body wide. I deliberately kept weight off my knees and hands, afraid they would puncture the ice and pull me through. As I neared the hole, I saw the water move rapidly against her. A *V* formed in front of her as it would for any rock.

Then things happened quickly.

The ice snapped beneath me and for a terrible moment I did not feel myself going through so much as the water climbing above the ice. It shivered across the ice like ants searching for sugar. "Look out," the girl said, but then the ice gave away entirely and I felt the cold sputter of my breath slam out of my chest. The skates pulled my feet down; I was aware, absurdly, of how they served as anchors, and it hardly mattered that the water was only four feet deep. Somehow, I decided, I did not want to die wearing a pair of skates. I clutched the backpack and felt the rope behind me begin to grind over the surface. I went headfirst into the current, and it pushed me sideways under the ice shelf in such a way that I felt I could glide, like the walrus and polar bear, forever southward along the river bottom.

I swung my feet down and tried to stand, to get air, but when my body uncurled, it slammed against the ice above me. I remained bent like a young Atlas, the weight of the world on my shoulders, the backpack floating away in the current like a dizzy black balloon. I grabbed at it and missed, and when I grabbed again, I felt the girl's hand in mine, pulling me toward her. With one final lunge I snagged the pack and held it in my left arm, and followed her arm closer to the hole. She pulled me toward her and I saw light and freedom and her face.

She had put her face under the water to see me. For an instant—the moment that bound us together—our eyes met. Then in the cold, black water of the Baker River, she pulled me forward until our lips brushed, and then we both exploded upward into the air and snow and my brother's screaming.

"THERE'S A CHANNEL," the girl said.

She appeared frightened and cold. Her face coated with mist and thin ice made her a creature more of water than land. I stared at her and it seemed as if I could see through her skin down into her organs and bones. The dog swam around us, a retriever mix I saw now, and it took me a moment to understand her.

"Where you went through," she repeated slowly, "you opened a channel."

"Come on, grab the backpack!" Ed screamed.

We did. Each holding a strap, we pushed to the edge of the opening, then fell upward onto our chests to get on the ice shelf, the bag between us. Ed pulled and I felt the bag slipping out of my hands, and I saw that the girl could not hold on, either. I told her to put one arm through a strap, while I did the same on the other side. With two good tugs, Ed had us within ten feet of shore. I knew quickly enough that we were saved. I used the tips of my skates to dig into the ice and help slide us toward the bank. The girl's jacket made a nylon sound when it went across the ice.

The dog opened the final channel. Bursting toward the shore beside us, she pushed past us and the last of the ice began to cave in. Ed edged into the water, but he was in no danger. I stamped a leg down through and found the bottom. The girl went on her knees and crawled the final yards to shore. She could barely move.

"Good, good, good," Ed said, yanking the rope fast now. "Come on, come on, we have to move. She'll freeze if we don't get her inside. So will you, Allard."

"Where do you live?" I asked the girl.

She lifted her hand and pointed across the river. Ed stood and tramped through the shore ice and grabbed her jacket. He smacked it hard, trying to get some of the ice off it, and trying to rouse her as well. He nodded at me. I knew what he wanted so I scrambled to my feet and helped lift her. Her eyes remained closed.

"We have to get you home," Ed said. "Now, right away. Come on."

He slapped her coat again, but when she started to walk, her movements lacked coordination. The dog, meanwhile, shook herself furiously, trying to get water out of her fur. Ed swung the backpack around his shoulders and detached the rope, then grabbed the girl by the elbow and tried to keep her going. She wanted to sit down. Her hat came off to one side and I saw she had beautiful blond hair, frozen in ringlets.

"No, no, no," Ed said, pulling her forward more quickly, "you can't sit. We have to get you warm. Come on. Allard, she's going under. We've got to get her home."

I only heard every third word or so. My body had begun to shiver in great, shocking tremors. I felt the cold in my ribs, felt it deep inside my brain. Ed slapped my jacket and tried to get the water off it. Then he got behind us and began shoving us back onto the ice toward the far shore. We skated like zombies, like two Frankensteins, our arms stiff, our legs impossible to bend now that the ice had formed on our pants. The dog raced ahead. Ed continued to shout at us.

It took all three of us fifteen minutes to skate back across the river where it was the thickest. Twice the girl stopped, terrified when the ice shifted or boomed in contraction. Each time we had to push her forward, shouting and warning her to keep going;

each time she reluctantly agreed. She hardly spoke. She managed, however, to tell us her house wasn't far. We knew the house. It had belonged to the Benders. New people had moved in, we had heard, but we didn't know the family. Obviously, this girl was part of them.

The sun disappeared. Whatever light we had now came from a thumbnail moon. The snow fell harder, and as we skated off the river, smoke from a nearby chimney drifted in folds of quiet light, its white haze pocked by kernels of sleet that turned the hillside to glass.

MRS. PATRICK — WE DIDN'T KNOW her name at the time—grabbed us at the door. She had seen us approaching through a large picture window and had, at first, thought how lovely that her daughter had made some friends. But then she saw the stiffness of our gaits and heard Ed yelling and slapping us, and she knew something had gone wrong.

She was large but vital, her hair dyed the red-orange of a robin's breast. Her eyebrows, too, had been painted to fullness and she wore a hooded sweatshirt that said IF MOMMA AIN'T HAPPY, AIN'T NOBODY HAPPY.

"My lord, what happened?" she asked at the door.

"I went through the ice, Mommy," the girl said. "Natasha broke through first."

"Oh, my God," Mrs. Patrick said to the girl, meanwhile grabbing her and pulling her inside. "Come in, come in, come in, you all look frozen."

"Natasha," Sarah said.

I had forgotten about her dog, but she hadn't. Mrs. Patrick opened the door wide to let the dog inside. We followed. Then she closed the door behind us. We stood on a small throw rug, our skates like cold bones on our feet, as Mrs. Patrick began undressing Sarah. She peeled off Sarah's coat and yanked off her hat. At the same time Ed began pulling off my clothes. As he worked, my hands and feet began to sting. As cold as I felt, I imagined Sarah must feel a hundred times colder. Occasionally when her mother yanked something free from her body, a thin coating of ice skittered to the floor.

"That river is just too tempting," Mrs. Patrick said to no one in particular, her hands furious on her daughter. "You're lucky these boys came along. I told your father about living next to water."

"It's a good river," Ed said because we loved the river.

"Natasha went through and I tried to help her," Sarah said, her voice stuttering with cold.

"I'm putting you in a bath right now," Mrs. Patrick said. "And you, son, what's your name?"

"Allard."

"You need to undress and we have a shower downstairs here. And your name?" she asked, speaking to Ed.

"Ed."

"Well, Ed, you help your brother. I'm impressed with you boys. You saved my daughter's life. My husband will be home shortly and I'm sure he'll be very thankful for all your help. Now come on, Sarah. I need to get you into a bath. I'm tempted to call the doctor, but you seem to be all right."

"I'm fine," Sarah said. "I'll be okay in just a minute."

Before Sarah went, she kissed each of us on the cheek. First Ed, then me. I had never been kissed by a girl before, unless our lips brushing underwater counted, and her nearness warmed my skin. She was beautiful and I knew that all my other desires paled beside my wish to stay beside her.

"Come on," Ed said to me, "let's get you thawed out."

Mrs. Patrick pointed out the shower, then went upstairs with

Sarah. Ed came into the bathroom with me. It was large enough to house the shower and a washer and dryer. A dog dish sat on a doormat partially under the sink. Ed helped me with the last of my clothes. Now that I was inside, I didn't feel so bad, but the cold still made me shudder and feel that something deep in my core had been lost.

"We've got to call home," Ed said when I stepped into the shower. "Mom will be worried. You okay in there?"

"My blood is coming back and it hurts," I said through the building fog. "But I'm okay."

"We did pretty well out there. I thought you were a goner for a second."

"We could have just thrown her the bag."

"I know. I thought of that later. Next time I'll remember what to do."

"You think we'll have a next time?" I said over the sound of the shower.

"Oh, sure. You always have to be ready for something like that. I'm going to go out and call Mom. Just stand under the hot water for a while. Make sure you warm up because we still have to get home."

I heard the bathroom door open and close. I turned up the temperature, letting the water scald me. It took a long time to heat me down to the core. As I was getting ready to climb out, I heard someone knock. Mrs. Patrick stuck her head in the door and called out that she was leaving me a pair of trousers to wear and a hooded sweatshirt. I looked to be about her nephew's size, she said, and he left these behind last visit. She also said she was making hot chocolate.

I turned off the water after I heard her leave. It felt odd to be naked in a stranger's house. I found a towel and dried myself. The corduroy pants Mrs. Patrick had left fit me fine. I pulled on the sweatshirt and went out and found Mrs. Patrick serving hot chocolate to Ed.

"How do you feel?" Mrs. Patrick asked. "You're Allard, right? That's an interesting name. Kind of old-fashioned, isn't it?"

"Yes, ma'am. It was my grandfather's name."

"And Ed," she said. "You don't find many boys with short, simple names anymore. I like Ed. It seems sort of dependable and safe. And your last name is . . . ?"

"Keer," Ed said. "Edward and Allard Keer."

"Dutch? It sounds Dutch."

"Yes, ma'am," Ed said. "Dutch ancestry, our mom says."

I sat and looked around. The kitchen was a large, comfortable room. Someone had built a breakfast booth near a sliding door that looked out on the backyard. The booth formed a natural center to everything. Sitting in its half circle, it made me wonder why every house didn't have one. A large woodstove pushed heat from the far wall of the kitchen. I felt comfortable sitting in the room, and I knew Ed did as well.

Mrs. Patrick gave us hot chocolate and cinnamon toast that she cooked on a little grill on the woodstove. The smell of cinnamon filled the room. She asked us general questions: who we were, where we went to school—we didn't, we said, we were homeschooled—and what the neighborhood was like. She was still talking when I heard a dog's collar jingle and Sarah stepped into the room.

She wore striped socks and a terry-cloth bathrobe over a bulky cable sweater. Her hair was up in a towel, which left her high, sharp cheeks exposed. Her eyes were deep blue. Her body hinted at that of a woman's, but she was still a girl. Natasha was at her side. In the warm lamplight, I saw that the dog was devoted to her. When Sarah crossed the kitchen, her socks gliding on the wooden floor, her posture perfect, the dog clicked beside her, her claws ticking on the wood. Sarah put something in the sink, turned the faucet on, then shut it off. I could not take my eyes off her. She came and sat beside me, her mother handing her a hot chocolate, and I inhaled her shower odor, the scent of her shampoo and soap, the wet tendrils of her hair sometimes dropping small drips onto her shoulders and the seat between us.

"Well, all safe and sound," Mrs. Patrick said. "No harm done, I suppose. Now, tell me what happened. I have it in bit and pieces from Sarah. She was standing in the water when you found her?"

Ed told the story. I remained quiet while he explained our idea of skating north, our plan to meet one river leading into the next and to ascend them like so many ladders of ice until we reached the *great land*. Mrs. Patrick listened as she sipped her hot drink, her eyes intent on Ed. Meanwhile, I concentrated on Sarah, her nearness making me nearly sick with nerves.

"That's an incredible rescue story," Mrs. Patrick said when Ed finished. "Thank you both for being there."

"We might have done better," Ed said, "if we had simply thrown your daughter the bag. We put Allard in danger when we didn't have to."

"You saved my life," Sarah said in her scratchy voice. "If you two hadn't come along when you did, I wouldn't be here right now."

Mrs. Patrick reached to Sarah and held her hand.

How had we landed here? How had my life changed so dramatically in a single day? It was a strange and wonderful afternoon. Mrs. Patrick wanted us to wait for a ride, but Ed explained we needed to get going. She offered to drive us, then realized she did not have a working vehicle. Her Subaru was in the shop, she said. To compensate, she made sure we had enough dry clothes to keep us warm. She also made us promise to stay away from the river, despite the fact that we had skates. After a few minutes of discussion, we clumped into two old pairs of enormous boots her husband had left near the woodstove. Then it was time to go.

At the doorway, Sarah thanked us both again. She kissed our cheeks. When she stepped back, she smiled at me. Then we stepped out into the quiet night, our skates slung over our shoulders, the bright white of new snow catching the falling moon.

2

"They're the lottery winners," my mother said later that night at dinner. "So that's where they moved in? The old Bender place. That's one mystery solved."

She served lentil soup out of our large Dutch oven, her ladle pulling out steam with each bowl of soup. Snow had continued to fall. I was glad to be inside and happy enough to listen to Ed's retelling of the rescue story to my mother and father, but I felt impatient, too, to get away and contemplate Sarah.

"Who is?" my father asked. "This family Ed is talking about?"

"They must be," my mother said. "Ginny at the market told me they had moved in here somewhere recently. The timing makes sense. Apparently it was big, but not one of those gigantic jackpots."

"How much?" Ed asked.

"Eleven million," Mom said. "That's what I heard."

Ed whistled.

"That's not gigantic?" my dad asked.

"Or maybe it was seven million," Mom said, sitting as she finished serving. "I'm not positive."

"Either way, it's a lot of money," my father said. "On the river here, especially."

He stopped for a moment. It was time for a blessing. We were Quakers, so that meant, at least as we practiced it, that we did not have organized prayers. Instead, we remained silent to collect our thoughts and give thanks.

Tonight my mother spoke in her soft voice. "It's our first snow today and I am reminded of how beautiful the world is around us. I am grateful for my boys' safe return, and for their courage in helping a young girl in a difficult situation. We are adjured to build a house beside the road and be a friend to man, and my sons practiced the best of that this afternoon. We welcome winter this quiet evening, and we welcome this new family into our community. May we all be warm and have sufficiency, and may the animals be safe in their dens and burrows. Amen."

"Amen," we intoned.

"They won the lottery?" I asked as soon as the meal began again.

"According to the local gossip," Mom said, passing a plate of rolls. "Ginny's aunt is a realtor at Baker River Realty. She said she had been contacted by a family and they wanted waterfront property, but it was more the husband's idea than the wife's. They're from southern New Hampshire, down around Manchester, but they wanted to move up north here. The rumor was they had won the lottery. I guess they paid for the house in cash, just like that, one check and bingo."

"Why here, though?" Ed asked.

"Because it's a pretty valley," my father said. "And it's quiet and peaceful. They have to live somewhere, I guess."

"When you think about it, it's sort of a compliment," Mom said.

"Allard has a crush on Sarah," Ed said plainly, and I didn't hold it against him because he didn't do it to taunt me. "She's the one we saved."

"Well, if he does, that's fine," Dad said, "although I don't think anyone can fall in love in a single afternoon."

"And why not?" Mom asked. "I fell for you as soon as I saw you."

"Yes, but I was especially dashing," Dad said, smiling. "I had a full head of hair and I looked like a young Zeus, you said."

"Just the beard," Mom said. "No lightning bolts."

"What would you do with that much money?" Dad asked, changing the topic.

"Not a thing," Mom said. "I'm happy with our life."

"I'd go out West and go camping," Ed said. "Or maybe go to Canada."

"How about you, Allard?" Mom asked.

Before I could answer, someone knocked at the door. We all looked at one another to see if someone knew who it might be. As a rule the people of Warren did not pay visits on winter nights. A glance around the table informed us that no one expected company. Ed, who handled so many of our family obligations of this type that we occasionally joked about his being our butler, slipped out of his chair and went to answer the door. We did not move our silverware. We listened to the door crack open and Ed's voice rise in greeting.

A moment later Ed returned with a large man in his wake. Sarah walked behind him, carrying a plastic bag containing our clothes, although I didn't know that at the time.

"Dad, Mom, this is Mr. Patrick," Ed said. "And this is Sarah."

"Just Charlie," Mr. Patrick said, his voice loud and slightly watery. "Just Charlie Patrick."

I did not look at Sarah too closely, for fear my parents would see too much. I observed only that she wore a bulky sweater and a pair of faded jeans. As a result of my feeling shy about Sarah, I studied

Charlie Patrick closely. He was, for starters, more than large. He was easily six feet seven inches and broad. He wore what appeared to be a new plaid wool parka, and the plaid seemed to stretch as wide as a movie screen. He had soft blond features and a chin that gave his movements a wattle slowness. More than anything else, he struck me as a *dude*. The jacket, for instance, seemed a recent purchase, probably from L.L. Bean, and while it successfully captured the idea of life in northern New Hampshire, it lost in its newness any degree of authenticity. My mother popped up and offered them both a bowl of lentil soup, which Charlie accepted on their behalf with no hesitation. He pulled off his jacket and revealed more plaid, this time green, underneath a pair of suspenders as wide as a pair of croquet wickets.

"Boys," Charlie said, his voice filled with emotion, "before I sit, I want to shake your hands. You've earned our eternal respect and gratitude for what you've done earlier today. I've come up with a little thank-you that I hope you'll accept in the spirit it's given. Of course, no gift could compensate you for rescuing my little girl, but this token from Sarah's mother and me, well, it's just a little something to make tangible how much we appreciate what you've done."

Solemnly, he shook each of our hands and handed us two envelopes. Then he sat down. Sarah remained standing at his shoulder.

An envelope from a lottery winner was enough to set my mind racing, even with Sarah in the room, but as my mother filled two soup bowls, my dad thanked Mr. Patrick and answered for us.

"I know I speak for the boys when I say they would never accept a gift for doing a service to a neighbor. Boys? Isn't that true?"

Ed looked at me. I nodded and passed him my envelope, which he placed on top of his own and handed to Charlie Patrick. Charlie took the envelopes back grudgingly, and Sarah patted her father's shoulder.

"That's just a shame," Charlie said, shaking his large dragon head. "It really is, but I understand and I appreciate your position. I do. Well, do you boys like the Red Sox? I can get us tickets to sit on the Monster Wall. How would that be? Maybe you'll permit me that little luxury. Let me see what I can arrange. I need to say thank-you somehow. The Patrick family has had a run of luck lately, so we'd like to share some of that with these boys. I mean, what happened today, when I think of it . . ."

He choked up. My father asked me to go get another chair for Sarah. I placed the chair next to Charlie Patrick and she sat. Her father composed himself.

"I'm an emotional sort," Charlie said, pulling the bowl of soup toward him. "In my field—I am a high school guidance counselor— it makes some sense, I suppose. Empathetic, you know. But I think people get uncomfortable when a big person gets emotional. People always favor Jack in the Beanstalk story, not the giant. When you think about it, the giant is always made out to be a fool. But it's Jack who sneaks in and steals the hen that lays the golden eggs. The giant is living a peaceful life until Jack comes along. . . ."

"Are you still planning on being a counselor?" my father asked.

"I just stopped this fall. I was down at Trinity High School. I guess it doesn't make much sense to hide it. We're lottery winners. We won last spring, fourteen million dollars. I bought a Powerball ticket when I went out to get some milk. Isn't that the craziest thing? Worked for years, my wife, Mrs. P we call her, she worked, too. And then one day, just like that, poof. We're rich. Of course, we didn't get all that money, but we did just fine. Taxes. We paid our share. Now, I'll be honest, we are looking for a simpler life. I may be doing a little part-time counseling at the high school here. I'm negotiating that right now. It's getting too crowded down around Manchester. Let's face it, Manchester is northern Boston, really. Up here, you still have the old flavor of the state. And we can be a little more anonymous."

"What a story," Ed said. "What did you feel like when you realized you won? I've never met anyone who won something like that."

"He lost the ticket," Sarah said.

"I did," Charlie said, his voice amazed at his own mistake. "Lost it after I knew we won. Can you believe that? I was so concerned that I not lose it that I put it away someplace safe, then immediately forgot where that was. A doctor friend of mine said it's an amnesic reaction to traumatic news. He said sometimes killers forget up to sixty percent of their murder scene. They call the police and they have a knife in their hands, and they say, 'Hello, my wife is dead and I don't know what happened, but I have a knife here and there's a lot of blood.' He says it happens all the time."

"So where did you find the ticket?" Mom asked.

"We went on lockdown. My wife made us all sit down and calm ourselves, and then she put tape over the toilet and over the doors and over everything. At first I thought she had lost her mind. But she wanted to make sure we didn't inadvertently chuck something out or flush it. You know. It took us a day and a half to find it. It was in a book I was reading. I must have placed it there for safekeeping. I still don't remember putting it in there."

"Then Mom took it and she put it in a small change purse and taped it to her wrist until we could get to the Lottery Commission on Monday morning," Sarah said.

"That's our story," Charlie said, digging a spoon into the soup. "I'm sure we stirred up some gossip coming here. That's just a fact of life for us now. You know, you can't complain to anyone when you win something like that, but it does have its downside. It isn't always easy. We get solicitations constantly, and many of them are from excellent causes. But you can't fund everything. . . ."

"I can imagine there are a lot of hurt feelings," Mom said, blowing on a spoonful of her soup. "A lot of misunderstandings."

"And when you do give, it's never enough," Charlie said, sipping the soup. "Delicious soup, by the way. Lentil, right?"

"Yes," Mom answered.

Charlie ate. Sarah took a spoonful or two. We resumed our meal. Afterward, my father offered to show them his workshop. We often gave this small tour to visitors because my father made instruments, double basses, that were reasonably famous in the music world. He sold four or five a year, depending on the market, each costing between $7,000 and $10,000. He had placed close to twenty instruments in the major symphonic orchestras around the country over the years.

Built along Ed's body type, my father was square and solid, a man who walked on the flat of his foot. He had dark hair, turning gray, with good shoulders beneath his neck, and hands that appeared rough and common until you saw them move across wood. His workshop—a converted two-horse barn with a large, nickel-plated Franklin coal stove in the middle—was the kind of space that made visitors stop and silently evaluate their own lives.

For one thing, it was orderly to a degree that promised a better, less chaotic world. Each tool, scores of them, hung from its own hook. Without inspecting a thing, one understood that every tool held a fine edge, that nothing shoddy would be permitted to leave this space, that music wrung from the lumber stacked scrupulously on racks blossomed organically from the soil and water that sent up trees. The shop smelled of wood and sawdust and woodsmoke. The halves of instrument tops—spruce, primarily, with willow bottoms, or sometimes maple or poplar, depending on the sound a bassist sought—were glued in butterfly patterns, translucent and wavy with the slightest shift of light. People smiled at seeing the shop, smiled as they might at a clean, tidy British country house, and most ran their hands over the wood after first getting permission from my father.

"It's just beautiful," Charlie said, turning around to see every aspect of the shop. "You must be very proud. And you sell the instruments around the country?"

"Around the world," I said, because I was proud of my father and he didn't like to boast. "Mostly to Europe, but now Japan and China are buying quite a few."

"Is that so?" Charlie asked. "Well, that's just marvelous. Where did you learn to build these . . . ?"

"Double basses," Dad said. "They're the big brother to the cello."

"Double bass. I don't know much about music. Sarah plays the violin a little, don't you, honey?"

"A little," she agreed.

"I learned from an uncle," my father said. "I was his apprentice."

The next thing—a thing we did often when we gave a tour—was to play one of the instruments. Visitors rarely know how deep and sonorous a double bass is when played alone. My father had a double bass ready to deliver, and he pulled off the cloth cape—fashioned by my mother, made of black felt with the initials of the purchaser stitched at the bottom—to reveal a perfect instrument. Sarah sat down on a stool and we leaned the double bass against her.

Sarah Patrick. How beautiful she looked! How lovely she appeared as she accepted the bow from my father, allowed him to position the bass between her knees, how she reached up and placed her thin fingers on the strings. The instrument was comically large for her, but I saw her take a moment to compose herself, and then, with intricate care, even though she had never played a bass before, she drew the bow across the raised bridge.

She stopped immediately, astonished that such a sound—loud and deep, the voice of trees, my father said—could be created by such a simple stroke. Then she smiled at all of us, and we laughed, and her father encouraged her, and my mother went back to make coffee, and Sarah ran the bow across the strings again. This time she nodded as the notes came out, and she went back and forth, gauging the sound, and when she ran the bow against the strings once more, the sleeve of her sweater rose up along her arm. And that was when I spotted my name, written in dark ink across the back of her wrist, a bracelet that she had placed there herself. ALLARD, it said. FOREVER.

3

IN FEBRUARY OF THAT WINTER my father bought seventy-eight acres of mountainous woodlands from the Dice Mill Paper Company. The great pulp mills of New Hampshire had disappeared, one by one, leaving behind enormous smokestacks and derelict outbuildings, which senators and congressmen visited for photo ops to declare the mills would be replaced by federal prisons, or state-run casinos, with incentives for new businesses that took up residence there. But a century of industry is not so easily replaced, and the Dice Mill Paper Company sold off its holdings under bankruptcy protection, and my father, always watching for lumber, swung a loan through Northway Bank and became a sizable landowner.

He bought the acres for the antique spruce, poplar, and willow, which, he said, had become increasingly rare. Working with the county agricultural agent, he walked the land a dozen times before making a final purchase, marking selected trees with orange tape. He liked to stand in front of a particular tree and try to see an instrument inside it. The ideal spruce, he said, was an arrow pointed at heaven.

Ed and I went with him. Clattering on the beaver-tail snowshoes my father picked up at yard sales, we all walked the land together, passing through the late-winter light, the air a stab each time we breathed. Apart from the wood he might find on it, he liked the feeling of having land. Later on he would say during our late-night surveys of our Canadian map that the land belonged to us as much as to him.

"Hold on to it," he'd say, his whiskers rubbing against the clean pillow shams, his eyes up at the map. "Don't be fooled that there is something better than land. There isn't. The land will belong to you both. Don't divide it. Don't fracture it. Cut it judiciously. Walk it often and let it seep into you. If all else goes wrong in your life, you can always retreat to it and survive."

At the tail end of the month, we made plans to take out wood. Along the creek banks, my father discovered a stand of spruce that he particularly fancied. Because the desired trees grew on slanted creek beds, and because we would have to tow the logs between other trees, my father contracted with Lester Hawkins, an old-time New Hampshirite, to bring his pair of oxen onto the site and drag them out that way.

ON CUTTING DAY we woke early, the sky still gray. The temperature had risen during the night, though, and when we entered the kitchen, my mother had the back door open. The air felt good, but my father remarked that it wasn't quite spring yet, and she slowly closed the door.

"I used to love fall," she said to no one in particular. "All that mortality and pangs of loneliness, but now, it's spring for me. I must be getting old."

"You're not old," my father said. "You're still the young girl I stole from your family."

Then he started humming a tune and he grabbed my mom and made her dance a two-step around the kitchen. She protested, of course, and made a big deal about putting down her coffee, but then she obliged him by allowing herself to be led like a buffing machine around the floor. When he let her go, he went outside to check that he had all his saws properly sharpened and prepared for cutting. He was a happy man. He had work to do and breakfast to come.

Mom cooked us a lumberjack meal, complete with bacon and flapjacks, and she tucked away log-roll sandwiches, which she made from leftover pancakes filled with peanut butter. She liked the idea of her men going off to the woods to work and she liked, I'm certain, the quiet house she would have to herself afterward. As she cooked, she told us she intended to run into Plymouth, she had a doctor's appointment, and then, if she had time, she planned to go to a new bookstore she had heard about, the Readery.

We felt happy and bracketed by our parents' good moods. It was that kind of day. When the phone rang, my mother picked it up on the second ring, her voice merry.

"Friend or foe?" she asked, obviously enjoying herself.

She listened for a moment, then looked over at me. "It's Sarah," she said, her hand covering the mouthpiece. I felt my heart beat a little sideways and I had trouble eating. I had thought of Sarah constantly since our meeting in the river, but she felt as remote as the great land we studied each night on the map.

"No, sweetheart, that would be just fine, I'm sure. They'd love to have you. And your dad, too, of course. They'll be leaving pretty soon. . . . Well, it's going to be a long day, so you might want to bring your own vehicle. Do you know where it is? . . . Do you have snowshoes? . . . That will be fine then. . . . Yes, that's perfect. You'll make a day of it, I'm sure."

My stomach did a heavy roll up near my chest.

"That," my mother said when she hung up, her spatula glinting in the early light, "was Sarah Patrick. The Patricks caught wind about our cutting day, some sort of connection to Lester Hawkins, and she and her father would like to come and watch if it was okay. I said it was."

"The more the merrier," Ed said.

I tried to regain my composure, but the idea that Sarah intended to spend the day with us paralyzed me. If anything, I felt a nervous sort of eclipse, as if Sarah stepping across my pale light changed the world. I made an excuse to get up and go to the sink and rinse a fork, secretly checking my image in a mirror my mother kept on the inside of the nearest cupboard door. My only hope for reprieve—though I did not really want a reprieve—was the possibility that my father would nix having company, doubtless citing safety issues. But when he returned and sat down to his stack of pancakes and side of bacon, he nodded and proclaimed them welcome.

"A day in the woods is good for anyone," he said. "Besides, we can always use another set of hands. We're lumberjacks today, boys."

So it was settled. An hour later, when we pulled up to our land, Charlie Patrick and Sarah greeted us. To my astonishment, Sarah stood behind the pair of oxen, a driving stick in her hand. The oxen—Tom and Jerry—wore an ash yoke and appeared drowsy in the morning light. Lester Hawkins, wearing camouflage trousers and large rubber boots, stood talking to Mr. Patrick. Lester looked small beside Mr. Patrick, and bony, too, as if he were a tool Mr. Patrick might select and strap against his thigh. But I knew Lester, knew his prowess with a bow during deer season and his ability with animals—two years running he won the Littleton Ox Pull. He lived well out along Hastings Road, the last house before Holiday Mountain, and he presided over a farmyard of animals, a native back-to-earther who believed in self-sufficiency.

"Morning, morning," my father said to everyone. "Are we ready to drag out some trees?"

"We'll cut a little trail as we go in to the stand," Lester Hawkins said, "is my suggestion. I was just talking it over with Charlie, here. Maybe set up a little woodlot that you can get to when you like, up here, close to the road. A landing. How's that sound? Them trees will dry nice if you put them in the sun. Be ready for working up whenever you like."

I watched Sarah. I did not take my eyes off her. She looked beautiful that morning, her face already flushed red with cold, her eyes bright, her striped scarf knotted close under her chin. She wore a plain black watch cap. Twice our eyes met and I had to look away each time. Whenever she moved her arm, I tried to see her wrist, hoping it still carried my name in ink. But for the most part, after saying hello to both of us, she ignored us and concentrated on the oxen. She seemed to know what she was doing—which made no obvious sense—until Lester Hawkins explained.

"Sarah's your driver today," Lester said. "She's been taking lessons through 4-H and I've got a young pair of steers coming along. She's been driving them and they aren't half as experienced as Tom and Jerry here. I figure she'll work them while we get the hooks on and get the trees down. Oxen will go all day, don't you know? Better on slant ground, too. Better than a horse. Hell, I wouldn't drive a horse for this kind of work if you gave him to me. Take a pair of oxen any day. More sure-footed by yards."

We filled a heavy wooden sled Lester had brought with him—with our saws and chisels and axes and lunch boxes, and a bale of hay for the oxen—and followed my father into the woods. The sun had already cleared the surrounding mountains, and light glinted everywhere. Sarah walked beside the animals, her shoulder nearly tucked into Tom's neck, and she whispered and spoke to them as they trudged along. The team wore bells, tiny sleigh bells, which gave our progress a festive sound. Ed and I ranged off to the side, showing off our skills in snowshoes a little, while Mr. Patrick and Lester followed the sled ruts, their voices filling the quiet morning. Ed and I called out animal tracks as we came to them—we prided ourselves on our ability as trackers—and halfway to the tree stand we startled an ermine that ran like a wild furred inchworm across the forest floor and scattered up a tree.

"Tough little varmints," Lester said of the ermine.

"We should be able to catch a peek soon," my father said, his excitement evident. "Not far now."

Twice we stopped to cut down beech saplings to widen the trail. Sarah watched us patiently. When we finished, she started the oxen again with a clicking sound. She tapped her driver's stick against their chests and necks if they started to go off line, but she did it gently, almost reluctantly, and I watched each movement that she made.

"Here we are!" my father eventually called, his arm waving at a dense spruce grove. "I'd like a good five of these and maybe leave the rest for somewhere down the road."

"That's a deer yard," Lester said. "I bet they hole up there on the cold days. Probably most nights, too."

"It is," Ed said. "We looked it over. They left a lot of hair on the branches from rubbing and whatnot."

"They say fairies gather with the deer," Lester said. "Leastwise, that's what I always heard."

Sarah backed the oxen off in the direction we had come to keep them out of the way while we felled the trees. Lester told me to help her feed them, which would have troubled me under normal circumstances—I wanted to be with the men cutting trees—but because it was Sarah, I went along without protest. She expertly turned the oxen and poked them down the trail they had just made. The pair smelled of barns and hay.

"When did you learn to drive oxen?" I said when we stopped the pair a hundred yards away. "Did you just pick it up?"

"I love animals," she said, tying them off to a young pin oak. "My father heard about Mr. Hawkins and he thought I might like it."

"Well, you seem like you know what you're doing."

"It's the training they've received. Mr. Hawkins puts the young ones in yokes when they do just about anything. Then they learn to work together."

That was about the extent of my conversation. I wanted to say more, to be bright and interesting, but my head felt as empty as a jar. I grabbed the bale. Sarah told me to hold on a second while she broke it in half. For a second we worked shoulder to shoulder. I felt my hands grow shaky and nervous. She slipped out of her gloves to get a better hold of the twine that bound the hay, then she tugged it down and unleashed it. The hay fell apart like a dinner roll flaking under butter.

"Not too much," she said as she shook some out for Tom. "They have work. We should put half the bale back in the sled."

"Okay."

"You lift that and I'll feed them. Let me just break a little more off here."

She did. When she finished, I swung the half bale back onto the sled. A few strands of hay stuck to my jacket. I dusted them off and went back to watching the oxen. She gave the animals hay by the handful, talking to them quietly. I was so involved with watching her that the sound of the chain saw starting sent a mild shock through my body. I heard the men calling to each other, and when I turned, I saw my father limbing the lower sections of the first spruce tree.

"Do you remember our kiss?" Sarah asked when I turned back to the oxen.

"Our what?" I asked, although I remembered every molecule of it.

"Our kiss," she said. "The one underwater."

I looked at her and nodded. "But we didn't really kiss," I said.
She looked at me.

"We're destined to be married," she said, her hand still passing
hay to the oxen. "Meeting like that, well, it doesn't happen all the
time, you know."

"I know."

"You saved me, but I saved you. Do you know how rare that is?"

"I guess it's pretty rare."

"I told my mother and she says only one in a million people
meet and fall in love and live happily ever after. She said outside of
storybooks, it hardly ever happens."

"That's probably true," I said.

"Don't ever be afraid to talk to me, Allard. I'm going to know
you better than any person on earth, so you might as well accept it."

"I don't know about that. Maybe so, I don't know."

She looked up at me. I knew we were going to kiss again and
we did. We kissed gently, neither one of us quite sure how to
proceed, our hands at our sides. Once, as we kissed a little deeper,
she brought her hand to my shoulder and the hay tickled my neck.
After a little we broke off and stepped back and our eyes met. I
wanted to kiss her again and started forward, but in that instant the
spruce tree began to fall. The saw gave a final zip at the wood and
we heard someone yell, "Timber" or "There she goes," we couldn't
tell, and the tree tipped forward and crashed down, yanking
branches with it as it came. When it landed, it thumped the ground
so hard that Jerry took a step sideways and Tom, anchored to his
partner, dragged a mouthful of hay across the snow and came away
with a white muzzle.

"She may be onto something," Ed said from his bed, his hands
under his head, his eyes on the map. "Crazier things have happened.

Mom says she's a terrific girl. She's gotten to know her from the library, you know, but she doesn't want to make a big deal of it around you. Sarah comes in and borrows books all the time."

"Sarah says we're going to get married. That it's our destiny," I said, my voice sounding odd to me. Her words had blocked me most of the day. I hadn't been able to get them out of my head.

"Well, why not? You like her, don't you?"

"I guess so, but it just seems so crazy for someone to talk like that. We're barely teenagers, for Pete's sake."

"Then maybe you *should* marry her. It would be an adventure, I guess. For me, marriage is out of the question. I'll be too busy exploring. I'll be working for National Geographic."

"I'll be with you."

"I hope you are," he said. "Just like we've always talked about. Our film company."

"The film company," I repeated almost like a prayer.

"Baker River Productions," Ed said, which was one of the names we intended to give to our wildlife-film company. It changed from telling to telling. "Animals as you've never seen them."

"A bird's-eye view of birds," I finished.

"Animals being animals."

He nodded as if to confirm his secret wish. I looked over and felt the love I always felt for my older brother. However confusing my feelings for Sarah were, I could envision the years ahead with my brother. We would travel the world, inseparable, daring and adventurous, probing the unseen world of animals. We would live, we said, in a mountain retreat, or maybe by the sea, and we would know how to crack whips like Indiana Jones, to throw knives like ninjas, to climb peaks impossible for other humans. We would be legendary, nearly mythical except when we returned to New York or Los Angeles to receive one award or another. Then we would wear tuxedos and invite our parents out to visit us in glamorous hotels, and we would shake our heads when we were called up to the stage, confess that we did the work because we loved it, and then, like superheroes, we would shed our clothes and head back out to the limo that would put us on a plane to some place even more remote, more challenging, than anything we had experienced to date.

That's what I thought about when I lifted from my pillow and gazed at my brother.

I could hear a light, freezing rain falling on the roof. It felt delicious to be in bed, to feel the ache of a day spent outdoors in the cold, yet to be utterly warm and tired and ready for sleep. We had dragged out five trees today, ten lengths in all, more than enough, my father had said, to keep him in excellent wood for his double basses for years to come. In all ways it had been a successful day, and by midafternoon it had grown warm enough to shed our jackets and work in fleeces. Sarah and I had not talked again directly, but her kisses still remained with me now, more perfect in memory than even the comfort of the bed and the droning wind outside. I couldn't remember being happier.

"You see," Ed said, "it's different for me. If I don't go out and travel and discover things, I'll bust. I really will. You're the same way, Allard, but only up to a point. I'm not saying that to hurt your feelings. We're just a tiny bit different, that's all."

"You're full of baloney," I said, though I wasn't sure he was.

"I'm telling you what I think, straight from the shoulder. I plan to spend, oh, I don't know, two hundred days a year out in the wild. That's no kind of family life. Think how Dad is almost always here. Think of that. Now imagine what it would be like if he were gone two-thirds of the year. It's different, is all I'm saying."

"You can't know what is going to happen," I said. "No one can."

"Well, of course not. But you have to play percentages. That's what Dad always says and he's right. You have to take in the law of averages."

"You like Sarah?" I asked, because that was the topic that interested me.

"She's great. I'm impressed that she learned to drive Lester's oxen."

"It makes me feel . . . when I'm beside her, I don't know. Like I sucked down a cold drink too fast, only different and not as painful."

"Love, probably," Ed said, his voice flat and factual. "You know Romeo and Juliet were only a little older than we are right now and they're the most famous lovers in the world."

"But that's a story."

"Everything is a story. If it didn't happen right in front of you, then it's a story."

"I kind of know what she means," I said, a little dreamy and drugged with sleep. "It's like we're destined to be together. Like she walked right into my life and knew she belonged there."

"You got it bad."

"I don't know what I've got."

"Those trees coming down were intense. I liked that a lot."

"I know," I said. "And Dad was really happy."

"Dad is pretty much always happy. That's because he likes his work. That's his secret."

"What did you think of Mr. Patrick?"

"He's like a big Labrador retriever, but you got to like him. They're not the average family anyway."

We talked for a while longer, mostly about our film company, places we wanted to visit, adventures we expected to have. Ed said we needed a video camera, a good one, one with a tripod and a zoom lens, and that started a long, sleepy discussion about which animal should be our first topic.

Ed had heard about a man over in Hanover who had raised a bear cub and set it back free into nature, and he thought that might be a good subject. I voted for squirrels, which I said were so common that no one spent any time thinking about them, and that made Ed consider the possibility of filming an underwater documentary on an average New England river, such as the Baker, and showing people the kind of diversity that lived there. The trouble was, he said, underwater photography required more equipment and that could be a problem.

As he talked more, his voice, my brother's voice, sent me slowly up into the map. I floated, riding up, entering the Great North, hearing the wind and watching the white bears ride icebergs out to sea. I kept going up and soon I was surfing the winds, and yet I was still in bed, still under a half dozen blankets, the weight anchoring me even as the winds pushed me through clouds and into a snow as soft and white as down.

Sarah waited for me there, and we held hands and drifted, and my brother's voice became a thin, long string, and we were kites, Sarah and I. My brother remained on the ground, pulling us gently to make us ride the currents higher, and finally the string snapped and we flew away together, our bodies creating perfect holes in a fleecy cloud, our hands forever locked, our flight joined by geese hurrying northward, their hearts full and pumping, a million years of adaptation waiting to be released in the spring flush of northern rivers.

4

My father's acreage made him slightly drunk with wood over the next couple years. In addition to storing willow and spruce for his instruments, he started talking about building a large structure, and he began to study mortise joints. Stick building—using standard two-by-fours—held no interest for him. He conceded that the two-by-four had liberated the common man by giving him the means to build a dwelling without aid of a second pair of hands, but a mortise joint, he said, required a community to fashion properly. And that suited him.

My mother fed his new passion by carrying reference materials home from the library for him, ordering from inter-library loan a shotgun blast of books on woodworking.

We had turned fourteen and sixteen that fall, and early the following spring, in the afternoons after lessons with my mother—we read *The Hunchback of Notre Dame* and studied French cooking under her tutelage—we climbed into my father's roomy Ford 150 and traveled around to study local covered bridges. Often Sarah would join us. She had started to spend more time with us on weekends and occasional afternoons. And now, when she wasn't helping Lester or the local 4-H, she was part of our field trips. My father contended that covered bridges were the university of mortise joints, and as we puttered around, he spoke at length about the simple complexity of covered bridges.

"A bridge like that . . . a covered bridge," he said, shaking his head, the bright, fragile spring framing his profile beyond his open window, "it's a testament to an entire way of life. Shipwighting, really. Did you know, boys, that the *Mayflower,* the boat everyone makes such a fuss about, is now part of a barn in England? Not many people know that. The reason for the *Mayflower* being used for a barn, you see, is that a barn is a ship turned upside down. That's all it is. You use the same techniques in building with mortise and tenon joints. And it's the same technique used in constructing the old covered bridges. You learn to make a proper mortise and tenon joint, and you've learned a secret no one can take away from you."

He talked in great loops as he drove, and Ed, Sarah, and I listened, our pleasure at being with him, at having the spring air rushing in through the cab, sharp as an apple. After an hour or so, seldom more, he'd pull over next to a wooden bridge—sometimes in Vermont, sometimes in New Hampshire.

"Wood to wood," he said, his eyes scanning the quiet interior, a six-battery flashlight pointing out the workmanship like a man spraying graffiti with light. "Imagine the satisfaction, kids, as the builders felt the oak peg go in, just so . . . knowing the whole thing, each runner and timber, had been carved and hollowed to perfection. No room for error. And yet, they also knew the oak peg would swell in spring and bind the frame tighter, then would relax in winter . . . just a notch off its belt, so to speak. A bridge is still a living thing in some important ways."

On certain bridges, he encouraged us to draw the interior. "To sketch a thing is to see a thing," he said, and so on those spring afternoons, Ed, Sarah, and I sat against one wall and sketched the opposite one while my father hoisted himself up along the beams to get a closer look.

"The trees," he said one afternoon, "are always checking and seeking light. Even dead, the light is still in them, calling them to straighten. Do you see? They yearn for the sun even now. That's why you have to leave a little give."

One afternoon on the drive back from one of the bridges, he asked Ed and me, "What do you say, boys, do you think we're ready to build ourselves a barn?"

"Yes, sir," Ed said. "I think we are."

I nodded.

"I want you boys to pick the trees, calculate the angles. It will be the best geometry lesson you could possibly have. I know a stand of hemlock on the property . . . up near the Moose Knoll . . . and we can get the trees out without much work. I think I know where it should go, a flat place up near the Porcupine Creek that comes through. This will be your building. We don't need to put in electricity or plumbing, so you never have to worry about it freezing. We'll put a woodstove in it and you can heat it from what you chop yourself. We'll insulate part of it, I suppose. It will be quiet there because you won't have any roads near it. And if you boys decide someday to go into business . . . like you talk about, the Baker River Film Company, well, this can be your headquarters. How does that sound to you?"

I looked at Ed. His face, unguarded for a moment, revealed that our father had seen into his heart. He was no longer merely a boy with a cockeyed notion of starting a film company, but was instead a young man whose dream had been endorsed by his father. He nodded. I said it would be wicked cool, and my father slipped his arm over my shoulder, his feet tapping the pedals lightly, the nose of the truck pointed away from the setting sun and aimed squarely toward our home.

MY WORLD EXPANDED even a little more when later that spring Sarah's father bought her a secondhand canoe, a fourteen-foot Old Town. We carried it up to Lake Wachaputaka, where she kept it chained to an adolescent beech tree and stored the paddles and life jackets underneath it. It was her boat. She bought a stencil and wrote *Sarah* at the tail end—white print against the Adirondack green—to show her ownership, then she spent the better part of two weeks trying to name the canoe properly. She haunted the library and asked my mother repeatedly for books of poetry that might inspire a name, but she came up empty.

"Naming a thing," she explained whenever she saw me, "is identifying its nature. You can't rush it."

"We should take the canoe out and try it for a while. The right name might just come to you."

"How about *Cloud*? Sometimes if you go against what a thing is, it can work for a name."

I listened as one might listen to a creature from a different land explaining an unusual tribal custom. Neither Ed nor I had a canoe, or any kind of a boat, but if we did, the last thing to trouble us would be its name. But I sensed its importance to Sarah, and I was happy to help. Sometimes we biked to the library together; other times we sat on her screened-in porch, our bodies bending over a book, her colt legs bare and tanned, her hair dangling down and brushing my shoulder. Outside the New Hampshire sun grew stronger in the sky, and the screens glistened with heat and blue jays called with their tin-can voices and the hostas flowered like white bells.

We were on the edge of things, of becoming a young man and a young woman, but we dallied on the childhood side, still able to pretend to be merely friends, unable, or unwilling, to leave our youth for the more dangerous terrain ahead. It was our last season to live in that world, and without speaking we both knew it and visited it often, neither of us brave enough to cross the boundary into that other land, the boundary that cannot be uncrossed once it is breached.

Sarah also stopped wearing shoes whenever possible. She carried a pair of flip-flops on a string around her neck, or in the basket of her bicycle—handy if she wanted to go into a store—but otherwise she vowed to go barefoot until she had to return to school. Though I had no delusions about going barefoot myself, around her I stripped off my sneakers and threw them in her bike basket, both of us pagan and free. Besides, we had decided to become expert canoeists, and so going barefoot was not an impediment to our last savage summer.

Sometimes Ed came with us, but more often we canoed by ourselves, paddling in lazy J-strokes, the water sliding beneath us, the lily pads and turtles skimming past us in the fetid decay of backwaters, the occasional knock of our paddles against the gunwales sweet and resonant. Our early summer gained a rhythm: in the morning I worked with my father and Ed on the barn plans, and in the afternoon I went canoeing with Sarah. I would have gone anywhere with Sarah, but it was pure pleasure to push off the shore—I took the stern because I was heavier—and watch her first strokes, her hair catching the sun, the wake of the boat spreading behind us.

Lake Wachaputaka was a classic north-country lake, cold and tea-colored, and many days we had the water to ourselves, the wood shoreline fragrant, the shallows dotted by dace and smallmouth bass rising to feed. An osprey hunted the northern edge of the lake and we watched it hammer the water, its extraordinary stoop a free fall, its wings tucked back, its neck extended, its mouth finding silver flashes of fish.

We had several destinations, but we particularly liked visiting a tiny, rocky island set off on the east end of the lake. The island had no name so we called it Ghost Island because unless you knew where to look, its outline merged with the shoreline behind it and the island disappeared. In that way it was like Bridgadoon, a magical place that rose out of the fog each morning and retreated into the evening shadows.

"We should bury something here," Sarah said one afternoon when we went ashore, yanking the canoe to a rest on a flat boulder. "Something we could never tell anyone about. And we should make a map and each take half. That way no one but us would know where it was unless they had both parts."

"What would we bury?"

"Something to remind us of this summer."

Were all girls like this? I had no idea. But I would have done anything for her, and to bury something on our secret island, to possess half a map that matched a half she would keep with her, seemed wonderful and an indication of our movement toward each other. And I was not surprised when a week later, shortly before she left for a vacation with her family, she loaded a small spade into the canoe and a green canister, her eye catching mine.

"Is that it?" I asked.

She nodded.

"What's inside?"

"I don't know. I asked your mother to put something inside it and made her promise never to tell us. I was going to ask my mom, but I knew she couldn't keep a secret if I begged her to tell. Your mom can. We can't dig it up unless both of us agree. And I want enough time to go by so that we forget where it is."

"How can we forget?"

"We will in time. We have to save the map. Keep it someplace safe for when we need it."

We paddled across the lake, our strokes by this point well matched. A storm threatened from the west. A thick tailwind stirred the water behind us, but we dug deeper in the water and pushed through it. The island retreated into the shoreline. The dull afternoon light turned everything gray and somber. A kingfisher flicked in the pines beyond the island, its body as bright as a match head on the quiet afternoon.

As we stepped out of the canoe, a warm rain began to fall. The drops fell in thick pellets but fortunately the storm brought no lightning. We propped the canoe upside down between two rocks, our back to a large hummock that blocked the wind, then climbed under. The rocks held the canoe high enough so that we could sit comfortably and watch the storm race across the lake and listen to the drops pound the deck of the boat, the patter drumming and insistent. Sometimes we played casino—it was our favorite game that summer—but this day we merely sat and watched the storm.

"Do you ever think," Sarah asked after a little while, "that you can't get something like this inside you? I mean, you can watch it, and it goes into your memory, but it's never whole and complete. All you can get is the feeling. That's why people take pictures, I think."

"I'll remember today."

She looked at me. She smiled a tender smile. It was like the storm, really. Maybe we couldn't get it inside in one whole piece, but you could feel it and you knew it, and you knew you had been out in it.

"Where should we bury the treasure?" she asked.

"Somewhere where the water won't climb up and get it."

"I want it to be in the ground, not just under some rocks. Someone might find it if it's under rocks, but no one would dig out here."

"We both have to know, right?"

"Yes. We're the pirates, I guess."

"There's a spot near the center. The little pine is growing there. It may be rocky, but we can probably dig enough to bury the canister."

"You promise me you won't tell anyone about this? Not even Ed?"

"I promise."

When the rain let up, we scratched out a hole almost in the center of the island. The small pine had cast its roots everywhere, and digging around them proved difficult. We were barefoot, too, so we could not put our weight on the back end of the blade, and the sun had grown hollow by the time we finished.

"Count out the steps from the northern end," Sarah said. "That way it will be official."

We paced out the distances from the four cardinal points, then, satisfied, we slid the green canister in the hole. At any moment I might have dissolved into humor, but Sarah's seriousness prevented that.

"We'll draw the map when we get home," she said. "Do you remember all the distances?"

"I do."

"Good. Tell no one, Allard. This could grow into something interesting if we let it. If we let it stay and hide and become a faint memory, then it will have power on us. If we expose it right away, it will mean nothing. I know that somehow."

"I won't tell anyone. But what about my mom?"

"She knows what's in it, but not where it is. We'll never mention it to her again, promise?"

"I promise."

She pressed soil around the canister, and when she was satisfied it had been properly buried, she grabbed handfuls of pine needles and spread them evenly over the ground. Finally we stood back and inspected our work. Unless you had an uncanny eye, you would never notice any mark in the surrounding soil.

"You can use the canoe while I'm gone, Allard," she said on our way back to shore. "You and Ed, if you want. Just do me a favor and don't come to the Ghost."

"I won't."

"Do you think it's weird that we buried something out there?" Her back faced me. We paddled in a steady rhythm.

"No, Sarah, not weird."

"I'm not going to name the canoe, I decided. It feels like it doesn't want a name and that's why I can't find one."

"Okay."

"I'll miss you while I'm away," she said.

"Me, too."

ALL THROUGH THAT SUMMER the barn timbers we had cut lay in a long, straight run of Porcupine Creek near the barn site, their massive bodies like slender whales that had miraculously appeared in a New Hampshire stream. The water, our father assured us, cured the wood and gave it, he said, ample drink. At the tail end of July, Sarah, finally back from vacation, arrived with Lester Hawkins on a hot, humid morning, this time driving her own team, which she and Lester had named Early and Late.

Her presence stunned me. She had grown in the short time she had been away. She was wearing blue jean shorts and L.L. Bean muck books, her hair held back by a piece of twine. Her casual beauty made me feel something strange and urgent in my chest. The easy friendliness of our time on the lake suddenly felt scoured away by the curve of her hip, by her breasts, by the cool, languid movement of her clunky boots on the ground. I found it difficult to concentrate; coherent speech was a labor. Sunlight had turned her skin brown and golden, and her white T-shirt advertising the Twig, a local bar and grill, seemed to catch the morning light and steal it from others.

Our father conversed with Lester Hawkins as we secured the first chain over the butt of our largest beam. If either of the older men perceived my interest in Sarah, as they undoubtedly did, they did not tip their hands or embarrass us by commenting. While Ed and I worked, our hands digging under the bole of the tree to string the chain underneath it, Sarah sat in the shade of her team and pulled a paperback from her back pocket. Between flurries of effort, Ed gently guiding me and telling me what to do, I tried to catch a glimpse of Sarah's book cover. It would make a point of conversation, I figured, if I had happened to read the same volume, but the book appeared to be brown pages only, a splinter of a novel shoved into her pocket and forgotten until she needed it. She read with complete absorption, her hand occasionally lifting to wave away the flies and mosquitoes her oxen attracted. I glanced at her every chance I got. I hoped to see her looking at me, but she seemed to think we had a job to do and didn't want to bother us.

"Ready," Ed called eventually, lifting back from the log like a rodeo cowboy successful in tying a calf.

Sarah folded her book casually and stood near the head of her team. Lester Hawkins and my father checked the chain, then gave the go-ahead. I dropped the end of the chain over the team's cargo hook, and Sarah bent near and whispered into Early's ear. Then she walked forward and the oxen followed. The log came easily out of the water, but I sensed the team cared more about staying near Sarah than pulling the load.

"Whoooooaaaaaa," Ed called when the log cleared the stream, breaching and landing with a wet, slithery whap. "Right about there, Sarah."

When the log was secured on land, we rolled it into position, making room for the others. Our next job was to remove the bark, but for the time being the log stayed on the hot forest floor, its sides sending up a tiny cloud of steam where the sun warmed it. Sarah brought the team around and we repeated the process until all the pieces for the bents, and three ridgepoles, lay like pencils ordered and neat on a desktop. My father had done the initial cuts and the beams appeared perfectly matched. The bents formed the rib cage of the barn, and seeing the beams side by side gave me a first glimpse of what the building might become.

"You've got something now, boys," Lester Hawkins told us when we stood at the edge of our raft of wood. "You skin them out and they'll be dandy. You bring Sarah back when it's time to haul them up. We can use gin poles, but I've always liked a pair of oxen on the other end of the line."

I used the break to approach Sarah. She had led the oxen away to a small patch of grass that grew in the shade of a large oak. The oxen slurped at the grass and flicked their tails at the flies that followed them everywhere. She had a rubber bucket in her hand and had started to walk to the creek to fill it. I intercepted her.

"How was your vacation?" I asked, not sure where to start the conversation.

"It was nice," she said, "but too long in the car. My father had to see everything. We went to Yellowstone and Glacier."

"I'm glad you're back."

"I'm glad to be back," she said, not quite catching my meaning. "Did you do anything exciting while I was gone?"

"No, it was pretty dull. We worked on the beams and we got this site ready."

We had reached the creek. I took the bucket from her—I was wet already from splashing around with the logs—and filled it. When I stepped back onshore, she passed me a small piece of paper, carefully folded.

"It's the map," she whispered. "Of Ghost Island. Don't look at it now. Look at it tonight."

"Okay."

"You haven't told anybody, have you?"

"No, I promise."

"Me neither."

"It's a pretty good map," she said as I put it in my pocket. "I had trouble drawing it to scale, but then I figured that didn't really matter. I mean, we're the only ones who will look at it."

I nodded. I wanted to kiss her. I wanted somehow for her to be mine. But I heard Ed shouting something to Lester, then my dad started up the chain saw. Ed began chopping at a maple stump and I saw his ax flash in the light that filtered through the trees. I walked Sarah back and helped her water the oxen. We worked side by side, the map folded and safe in my pocket.

It took us a month to finish the logs and to set the joints in the bents, but on a Saturday in early September we drove to our land—a quarter mile away from the river and from our home—for a barn raising. Leaves had begun to curl and color, but summer still held sway, and the clouds above us moved as they did in June, like white doors to someplace higher. As we drove, my mother outlined the day.

"The fiddle band is coming to join us and they're planning to have a square dance later on for anyone who stays around to celebrate when the barn is up."

Sarah and her folks met us at the pull-off. She had hooked her oxen to a wagon made from two converted pickup beds that Lester Hawkins had outfitted with large, knobby tires that could go over any sort of terrain. Sarah held the team steady while we transferred the picnic supplies to the wagon, then climbed on to a rickety bench that served as seating. During the short drive uphill she told us the 4-H club from nearby Holderness said it might show up to lend a hand, and a Cub Scout den from Hanover had heard about it and made calls of inquiry, too.

At the clearing near Porcupine Creek the bents lay formed on the ground, their mortise and tenon joints fresh and dark. While Sarah went back down with her team to wait to give a ride to anyone who needed it, Ed and I helped unload the food and coolers. Our mother had made my favorite cake—pineapple upside down cake—and Mrs. Patrick, who had become one of my mother's closest friends, had built a barn frame out of breadsticks. In the late morning we laid the food out as the two moms instructed: chicken salad on rolls, and celery stalks and scallions in jam jars, tuna-fish sandwiches on dark rye, and watermelon, plates of sliced tomatoes, summer squash, cherry tomatoes in white bowls, snap peas in cones of newspaper, two apple pies, two pumpkin pies, Toll House cookies, and pitchers of lemonade and cider. We fetched small stones from the creek to keep the corners of the tablecloth anchored, while my father and Lester Hawkins went over, one last time, how they intended to hoist the bents. It was not a terribly complicated business, but they wanted to do it right, and safely, and they enjoyed the contemplation of it as much as anything else. Charlie Patrick stood by and refereed.

Sarah returned with a wagonload of visitors, friends, and neighbors who had volunteered to help, mixed in with members of the 4-H club and a few Cub Scouts. Ed took on the duty of explaining to newcomers the intricacies of the barn raising. His hammer flapping at his side, his tape measure ready as a frog's tongue, he squatted over the bents and explained the geometry behind the angles, the physics of the weight-bearing loads. I assisted him when I could, but eventually I began tagging after Sarah, happy to take the run up and down the short hill with her to bring up more visitors.

Our local fiddle band, who called themselves the Crunchy Boys, arrived on the third trip. They came in playing, as they usually did, their instruments sawing the crisp air as they bobbed behind the oxen team. The music sounded fine in the fresh air, the brook supplying a bass line under their string runs, and as soon as they arrived, everything took on a festive feeling.

"Now isn't this something?" Lester Hawkins repeated to various people who swung into his orbit.

"Feels like we've gone back a century," a scoutmaster said in my hearing. "Feels like something that slipped by without our knowing."

The band had staked out a place on the edge of the clearing where they wouldn't be in the way, and a few Scouts lined up some stumps for seats. A little past noon, when we judged that anyone promising to come had arrived, my father took over. He quieted the fiddle players and climbed on a pine stump to get everyone's attention. Someone whistled. People gradually quieted.

"It has been said," my father began, his voice strong and certain, "that we stand when we build, and that that which is vertical contains the human spirit. I don't know if that's true, but I suspect to build is to believe in the future. I want to thank Lester Hawkins, Charlie Patrick, Sarah Patrick, and my boys, Edward and Allard Keer, for their dedication to this project. I also want to thank my wife, Emily, and Beatrice Patrick for their patience while this building took over most of our waking hours."

The crowd laughed at that.

"And now I want to explain what's going to happen and how we're going to divide into crews to lift the barn."

"Just a moment," Charlie Patrick said, coming to stand beside my father. "Hold on just a second before you do that."

Charlie Patrick nodded at Sarah, who plucked something from the wagon and carried it toward him. It was a large box, wrapped in bright tin-colored paper. The crowd moved aside and she turned once she reached a position beside her dad. Charlie put his arm on his daughter's shoulders.

"The Patrick family owes a great deal to the Keer household,"

Charlie said. "Some of you may know the story and I don't want to go into it here, it's not the time or place, but let's simply say that our lives, my family's life, would be . . . well, profoundly changed if not for these boys."

He choked a little on his phrase and Sarah moved closer to him and hoisted the box into his hands.

"Would Edward and Allard step forward, please?"

I cast a quick glance toward Ed. He did not like public spectacle, but at the same time once asked to do something, he did it without wavering. He stepped forward, and I followed him. Sarah handed us the box. Charlie Patrick smiled a big smile. I looked to see my parents' reactions, but they appeared not to know any more about what Mr. Patrick intended than we did. Both of them looked curious and slightly reserved.

"Open it, boys," Charlie said.

We did. Ed held the box while I tore through the paper. A moment passed when I couldn't see inside because of the Styrofoam popcorn, but then I dug deeper and extracted an elegant plastic case with the word SONY on its side. It was a new, small, handheld state-of-the-art video camera. I lifted the case so the crowd could see, while Ed dropped the gift-wrapped box in his excitement.

"It's a new video camera!" Charlie announced to the crowd. "For the Baker River Film Company! Congratulations, boys! Happy shooting!"

Ed was clearly touched by the gift. I held the package in my hands to let him open the carrying case. He extracted the camera as if lifting an old bottle of brandy from a wooden carafe. He slid his hand in the side grip and looked through the lens. As excited as I might have been about the gift, I understood for Ed it had meaning beyond anything the people around him imagined. We had cameras, but they had always been hand-me-downs or outdated equipment we found at yard sales. This was something different altogether. He turned and looked at the crowd with the camera still to his eyes. People laughed and one of the fiddlers drew his bow across his fiddle strings in a donkey bray.

"Thank you, Mr. Patrick," Ed said, his mouth speaking from below the camera. "Thank you very, very much."

"Use it in good health," Mr. Patrick said. "Here's to a great film company."

We shook hands with him and the crowd clapped. I suspected Mr. Patrick had given us the gift in front of the crowd so that our parents could not refuse it on our behalf. Besides, it was a generous, thoughtful gift that spoke to our interests—a combination our parents would endorse as part of our ongoing education. Sarah made a joke of sticking her hand in front of Ed's viewfinder and he jumped a little. The crowd enjoyed that. Mr. Patrick picked up the empty box and Sarah gathered the wrapping paper. It was time for my father to explain the barn raising.

"I'd like you to assist me, Allard," Dad said. "We're the general contractors on this particular job. Is that okay with you?"

"It's fine, Dad."

"All right, then, let's get busy."

It was a glorious afternoon. After arranging the group under Ed's control, and explaining what would happen as they lifted, my father stepped back and nodded. Ed checked the footing of the bent once more, nodded that it was ready to go up on the stone piers we had built, then shouted to his crew that they could lift away. In one huge shrug, the bent came off the ground and rose, lifted slowly into the air. Everyone cheered. My father hopped everywhere, bracing the bent with boards, jumping and moving quicker than I could anticipate. Gradually the first bent gained its ninety degrees. When Dad finished anchoring it, a center team lifted, bringing the middle bent toward the first. This time the crowd began to see the form and let out a whoop. The fiddlers began to play, and before they had gone through a complete song, the third and final bent rose, lifting to meet the line of the first two.

While others watched the bents and clapped at the shape of the emerging barn, I watched my father. When he saw the last bent take its place, he ran his hand gently on the seam of his blue jeans, a sure sign that the building had met the plan in his head.

"Almost like we knew what we were doing," he said softly to me. "Looks almost like a barn should look."

"True lines," Lester shouted to anyone who bothered to listen. "Raised by hand."

While the teams still held the bents vertically, my father and Lester Hawkins mounted ladders and secured the bents in place. It took two hours to accomplish. The barn gradually became a solid basket of wood, rich and lovely to look at. When my father was finally confident that the frame needed nothing else, he hoisted the tallest ladder up against the king post and handed me a small branch of pine.

"Allard, run up and nail this to the highest point," my father said. "It's traditional to mark a building's first day with a pine bough. It honors the trees."

"Ed should do it," I said.

"You're the one to do it," Ed said as he handed me his hammer and a couple nails. I pinned the branch against the ridgepole and hammered a nail through the meaty part of the twig. Everyone clapped while Ed, experimenting with the new camera, aimed his lens at me, then panned the camera around to capture the crowd. And for just a moment I turned and saw the world as if from heaven. My father and brother stared up at me, smiling. My mother stood by the picnic tables, and I saw Sarah standing beside her ox team, her face turned up at me, her eyes the only eyes that captured mine.

It was the world that I lived in, the world of my youth, and

I knew and trusted it and believed it would always remain with me, carried in my heart like blood or knowing. And I understood for the first time that the great land did not exist in the north, or anywhere distant at all, really. It was here instead, on a hillside in New Hampshire, beside a white river flowing south and carrying the snow away each spring.

5

Fiddle music. A belt-high campfire, with pine smoke rolling down the hillside as the early evening settled over the mountain. A quarter moon rising with a bright, solemn ring around it. Now and then a good breeze that had made its way across Canada, crossing the Great Lakes on its way to find us. The breeze like a broom to dust us off and turn the trees merry. A breeze strong enough to make us stop and look, hold down a paper plate or a napkin, enough to remind us of winter. The band playing and laughing and calling squares. A few people tapping their toes, heel, toe, knowing the movements and guiding the others through the elaborate arm swings, do-si-dos, honor-your-corners, forward and back, allemande left. Sarah, watching. The start of each reel another stab that I hadn't asked her to dance.

It should have been easy, it *was* easy, except that it meant crossing the clearing and standing in front of her and asking plainly what was on my mind. It meant declaring myself in front of my family and friends, risking that she might cross her arms and say,

"No, sorry, I don't dance." At the same time, I could hardly breathe while watching her. Everything about her seemed perfect. Her hair, the way she cocked her hip as she stood and watched, the way her hand reached to rub the hairy muzzle of her oxen. Twice, or maybe a thousand times, I began toward her, took a step, only to hide my motion in some other task. I feared that another boy would ask her to dance or that she would become bored and decide to leave. Then I remembered she would have to ferry some visitors back to the bottom of Porcupine Creek now that it was dark, so she couldn't leave until the end, but she might get so involved with her oxen that she would not have time to dance.

The time to ask her was *now,* exactly now, and the wind pushed at me and shoved me forward, and without really knowing how it happened, I found myself in front of her, my throat tight and choked, my face trying to smile. The music had paused and people called for new squares to form, so I stepped a bit closer and made a motion at the dance floor.

"Sarah, would you like to dance?" I asked, and my voice felt caged and shaky.

"I'd love to," she said simply. "But I probably smell like oxen."

She took my hand and we walked beneath the barn bents onto the area cleared for dancing. I couldn't turn to face her. My entire focus rested on our hands linked together. My face felt hot and red. I was aware of others watching us—our mothers, certainly, probably our fathers—all of them nodding as if something long anticipated had come to pass. Sarah and Allard. Then the music started again.

If I had fallen in love with her before, now she had suddenly, after all the time we had spent together, finally become a real girl, someone who drifted away in the circle, then came back to me. I watched where she went, saw her beautiful hair bobbing as she swung with another person, then released her elbow and came to me. Four times I got to swing her in my arms, and our eyes stayed on each other's, her body resting against mine, her hand on my shoulder above my arm. She looked entirely happy, young and light on her feet.

I promenaded her four times around the square, her hands locked in mine. We danced under the frame of the barn, the moon above us, the pines ringing us. And when the first square ended and the call went up for a Virginia reel, we stayed on the floor and danced, again sashaying up and back as a couple, everyone clapping our progress, the other dancers diving under the arc formed by our arms, my joy at having Sarah with me nearly too much to bear.

"I should get ready to bring the others back down the hill," Sarah said when the Virginia reel finished. "Would you like to come with me?"

"Sure. Right now?"

"It's probably time."

The moon had taken prominence in the sky, and a few stars just awakened stepped out into the darkness when Sarah and I readied for the first trip down on the wagon. Some people passed by and shouted their good-byes, heading off into the darkness. But the older ones appreciated the ride, and Sarah held the team steady while I handed the riders up. In minutes we had a full load and I climbed aboard with Sarah, her shoulder against mine. It felt as though we had become a team, passed an important milestone that we hadn't understood fifteen minutes before.

"Everyone hold on. Ready?" Sarah turned and asked the people behind us.

They nodded or said yes, and we shoved off, descending the trail in a slow, even plod. Once we left the barnyard, the forest swam up and took us. A glimmer of moonlight found the deep pockets of Porcupine Creek, and we listened to the water run in a steady splash to the valley below. The oxen's bells jingled. We passed a few walkers in the dark shadows, who waved quietly, tired from the day outdoors.

I hopped down to unload the passengers, and when I boarded

again, I took Sarah's hand. She got the oxen started back up the hill—we figured to take three runs—and I kissed her as we moved, our mouths tentative at first. We gradually kissed with more assurance and broke apart only when we encountered people coming toward us. The interruptions made the moments of kissing more delicious, and we kissed on the bumpy ride, the curious wagon creaking behind us. At the barn site we loaded a second batch of people, and Lester Hawkins called to the scattered crowd that this would be the last run of the night. He made a joke and said the oxen needed to get to bed. The few remaining people laughed and waved us off, but not before my mom stepped over and asked if I was seeing Sarah home.

"I am," I said, although we hadn't discussed anything of the kind.

"Okay, take a flashlight and don't be too late. Sarah, honey, I'll tell your mom and dad. You two enjoy yourselves. It's a pretty night for a ride. Be careful on the road. Make sure you put the light on the wagon."

In the smallest instant before we left, I saw my mother and Sarah exchange a glance. I knew what it said: that my mother recognized Sarah's claim on me, that she approved of it, and that it made her remember what it was like to be a girl courted on a soft summer night. Sarah nodded and hitched the oxen forward. We rode slowly down the hill and I took Sarah's hand again in the darkness, but we did not kiss.

It took us better than an hour to drop off the wagon and the oxen and put them to bed. Then we set off on foot over Wainright Hill, the most direct trail back to our river. We both knew the way. The night had turned chillier, but we stopped at every opportunity to kiss and that warmed us. I kissed her against a large oak tree, and near a split-rail fence at the southern end of Wainright Hill, and each time Sarah's body filled my arms with greater passion and pleasure. When we struck the Baker River, we stopped and sat for a while and watched the moonlight drift and sizzle on the water's surface. Sarah drew in the dirt with a stick. I did not feel shy any longer, but still speech was difficult because one word threatened to release a thousand. I wanted to tell Sarah everything—everything I had ever thought, or felt, or hoped—and I wanted to know everything about her in turn. It felt almost too huge, too important, to squeeze into a single night, and so I felt locked and awkward, our kisses the only thing that released us.

"I liked dancing with you tonight," Sarah said after a little while. "I liked square dancing."

"Me, too. I was afraid to ask you."

"Why?"

"I thought maybe you wouldn't want to dance. I don't know. It's hard to ask things like that for me."

"Don't ever be afraid to ask me things, Allard."

"Do you think you'll want to live here when you get older? I mean when you're through college and all?"

"I think so," she said, her voice soft and quiet. "I love this place."

"So do I. I don't even know why, exactly, but I love everything about it. I can't really imagine living anywhere else."

"I like the seasons and the way we know people in town, and the river and the mountains. We're lucky to live here."

A little later she said she had to get home. When we reached her house, I kissed her one more time in the darkness beyond the porch light. She kissed me hard, then slid her lips next to my ear and whispered, "I love you, Allard, I do."

Then she ran away. She did not look back. The door opened and she popped in. I began to run slowly, jogging, and then the memory of her whisper, the passion of her kiss, filled me with a wild energy. I ran. I sprinted. I ran as only a teenage boy in love can run across land he knows intimately. I ran and touched tree branches, jumped over a fence, rolled down a hill, and came up onto my feet still sprinting. My lungs filled with glorious air and I listened to the sounds of various dogs, dogs of my childhood, dogs that called to me across the wide river valley. Wind blew the autumn grasses and I ran down the rivers of the windfall light, as my mother had often quoted Dylan Thomas. Everything was green and beautiful, and I ran beneath the straining moonlight onto the fields of praise.

6

EVERYTHING WAS SARAH. I woke each day thinking of her and went to bed with images of her in my mind. I turned fifteen in the end of autumn and in the beginning of winter we crossed from the land where we had lived the past summer, and there was no returning. I haunted her house. She became a figure at our dinner table, eating in our midst as easily as I ate at her home. In captured moments we kissed and found each other's hands. It was our first great love and it was tender and eager and everywhere. In giving, we received more. In taking, we wanted to give. Our parents were patient, though they could not have kept us apart even if they had the will to do so. They laughed at us often; just as often, they watched with joy probably mixed with memory and pity and apprehension at such passion. We were a match strike, a pin, a bird darting to a feeder. In the first snow we gouged a dark trail from one house to the other. The snow did not cover it all winter.

Fortunately, we did not lose ourselves altogether. Ed anchored us. His interest in film exploded with Mr. Patrick's gift of the new video camera. Ed went everywhere with it attached to his hand, and he quickly became adept at filming and framing the casual events of our lives. He took over a corner of the barn, near the woodstove my father had put in, as his office, and that became our regular hangout on afternoons and weekends. We dragged a cranberry-colored couch there from the Patricks' house, then made a desk of planks and sawhorses. My mother found two ancient armchairs at Goodwill and bought them for us. We added things slowly. Ed used an army-green set of shelves to hold his growing supply of equipment. We also brought treasures from the surrounding forests—paper wasps' nests, a jay's skull, a fully shedded snake skin. The Baker River Film Company took shape with each addition, and each day brought something new, something exciting, something we had not anticipated.

That winter we—Sarah, Ed, and I—also developed an interest in pigeons. One of us had read about the role of homing pigeons and their great flights during the World Wars. We researched the American Homing Pigeon Association and ended up joining, and we sent away, half on a lark, for a dozen birds. The website explained how the birds carried tactical messages to troops up and down the trenches during the wars, and how each side engaged falconers to bring down working birds. We also learned that Cher Ami, a pigeon flown in World War I, was awarded the Croix de Guerre, France's chief award for heroism.

They seemed the perfect subject for our first videos, and we became mesmerized by their fly-outs, the crackling clap of pigeon wings as they scattered.

With my father's help, we built a pigeon loft behind the barn and screened it in to keep owls from preying on the young birds. By early spring we had a thriving flock, the pigeon cooing as relentless as the hum of Porcupine Creek running past. My mother approved of our new hobby and said it taught us geography and empathy toward animals. But in truth we thrilled to the dove-colored feathers, the bright flash of the birds as they darted into our coops, the heckling burr of their coos as they settled on their perches.

The late afternoons—through the tail end of winter and the beginning of spring—became pigeon-centered. After school each day, Sarah rode her bike to the barn. With her Lab, Natasha, running along beside her, they made excellent time, zooming in from their house in under twenty minutes. Sarah had a wicker basket on the front of the bike that she filled with pigeons homed to her house. She also brought early wildflowers and grasses for them. Each afternoon I watched her arrive, her leg kicking through the girl's lower center bar, her movements causing my chest to contract. She stood the bike against one of the pines, then took a moment to stretch a rubber band around the cut ends of the flowers. Then, in a gesture that had no equivalent in my boy's world, she gracefully arranged the flowers as they protruded from the basket, even stepping back and leaning away to inspect their proportions. Finally she snatched them out of the basket, told Natasha to stay, and ran to our pigeon roost, shouting, "Ee-aa-kee," a greeting that had somehow become a secret signal among us.

I was in love with her, completely and utterly. Positioned on a ladder against the pigeon loft, I answered back, "Ee-aa-kee," not in the least self-conscious, the three syllables spilling out and calling us together. Ed, too, if he were around, answered, "Ee-aa-kee," and as silly as it may have sounded, it formed the echolocation of our youth and of my early romance with Sarah.

She wore a white man's shirt underneath a sweater, usually, and a pair of jeans and Converse sneakers. She smelled of soap and a light perfume, and as she climbed one of the ladders propped against the loft, our eyes found each other's and our day truly started. Whether Ed was there or not hardly mattered. We looked at each other amid the pigeons strutting and fluffing, our eyes momentarily distracted, then reunited, by the pigeons' bodies.

"Any dead soldiers?" she asked, untying the grasses or flowers and laying them out for the pigeons to pluck.

It was the question we all asked when we arrived at the loft.

"Not that I've seen," Ed reported.

"We've been lucky. A fox cleaned out the Harrisons' henhouse. Decapitated the whole flock just about," she said.

"They do that, don't they?" Ed said from his own perch. "Just take off their heads. I've heard about that."

"Foxes can't climb trees," I said.

"No, but weasels can. Weasels can climb about anything," Ed said. "And the owls are always watching."

When it was finally spring, we scheduled our first training race for an upcoming weekend. Sarah's father—who liked to be involved in these projects—promised to drive us west to Vermont where we intended to release the birds. We each had our favorite. Sarah had named a thin, elegant bird Sky Top, because the top of its pigeon head glimmered blue especially at dawn and dusk. Ed's bird, Foggy, looked gray and indistinct, a ghost bird that seemed to disappear in certain light. Foggy was the largest of our three special birds. My bird, Gray Lord, possessed a strange monocle around its right eye and Sarah had mentioned it looked like a British lord. Although we had other birds—and we discovered they multiplied prolifically if we didn't separate the genders—we determined to start with our three favorites on a so-called century flight of one hundred miles.

We also decided to film it. Our working title was *We Three,* but that changed because it sounded pretentious. After much talk, we changed the title to *Sky Top,* because, we all agreed, Sky Top was the prettiest bird we owned. Once we decided on Sky Top as a film topic, the rest fell rapidly into place. One by one, we filmed hours of video of him roosting, flying, strutting. Ed provided the narration, and Sarah and I wrote the script. Naturally, we couldn't entirely nail down the film until we witnessed the actual flight, but Ed spent a long time talking about motive, the *why* of the film.

"Why should anyone care about a single pigeon making a flight of one hundred miles?" Ed asked repeatedly in the days leading up to the century flight, the conversation circling as we cleaned and fed the pigeons, all of us on different ladders. "That's the question. That's what we need people to feel—that they don't know anything at all about racing pigeons, but, wow, here's an interesting story."

"Character is plot," Sarah said often. "That's what my English teacher always says. She says we're interested in characters, not simple events. If all you need to make a film interesting is a bunch of events, then it would be easy. No, we have to care about the characters and see their predicaments. We have to care about Sky Top."

"Pressure applied to character," Ed agreed. "Exactly."

"Maybe, though," I typically added, because it had somehow become my position to defend, "the story is more about us. Maybe it's about our love of the pigeons and not so much about the pigeons at all."

"So you say we should film ourselves?" Ed asked.

"Maybe," I said.

"He has a point," Sarah agreed. "We can film it and see how it comes out. Film us, I mean."

"If I do the filming, then I should be out of the thing entirely," Ed said.

"Not necessarily," I said. "We can film you. Then we cut it all in."

"But it's mostly about Sky Top," Ed said. "We're animal-film makers."

"We'll know what it's about when we see it," Sarah said.

We had bummed a two-stroke generator from my father, and in the soft spring light, Ed pulled and pulled until the generator kicked into motion. Then we plugged in Ed's Apple computer that he had received at Christmas. It had an early version of Film Maker, but it proved sufficient to load our day's shooting, so that, in time, we had hundreds of hours of pigeon footage. Much of it was gluey and tedious, the camera having difficulty focusing on the constantly moving pigeons. But some of it, in tiny flashes, demonstrated lovely camera work. Precise and poetic, Ed had the best eye and the best technique. We watched over his shoulder as he fanned through the early clips, deleting hunks of film while putting other shots in a TO USE folder.

Sarah, on the other hand, filmed us. She liked watching us tend the birds and she used the camera well, catching us in candid shots we seldom saw her taking.

For my part, I had some ability at sequencing. I saw time in film, if that makes any sense, and knew instinctively what element should follow what in our ongoing attempt to give the images shape.

They were full, splendid days. The air coming in from Porcupine Creek, the misty smell of gasoline from the generator, the occasional flash of the pigeons behind the barn, all three of us intensely involved in the film, we entered a creative world easily and completely. Our project filled us in ways we could not have anticipated or dreamed. The Baker River Film Company was born in those afternoons and it grew each day, forming us as we formed it.

In early evening, I would walk Sarah and Natasha home. We carried pigeons homed to each other's house in the bike basket, so that we simply exchanged pigeon baskets when we reached her place. The distance wasn't great, but we took our time, stopping often to neck and whisper. What cliché can describe those walks? That I loved her? That at times I watched with wonder that this beautiful girl had an interest in me? We kissed constantly, almost as if we needed to kiss to live another minute, and of course it was youthful and indulgent, but we were still young and tender and in our first love. Both of us, I suspect, believed life would always be as it was on those late afternoons. The thrill of her otherness, her femaleness, seemed an endless mystery that I could never stop exploring.

After kissing her good-bye, I rushed home and often saw one of our pigeons flapping overhead. It thrilled me to see one. At home, after saying hello to my mother and father, I rushed upstairs where Ed waited. We had hung a tiny three-bird loft from our attic window, and I usually returned to find one of my birds waiting with a message from Sarah. We might have called one another, but we wanted to demonstrate the utility of the pigeons, so we exchanged three messages every night. Ed, from his bed, nodded at the window.

"You have one from Sarah," he said. "Bluebell, I think."

"It got here fast."

"Bluebell is a strong flier."

I opened the window and knelt so I could put my hand slowly into the chicken-wired loft. The way to catch a pigeon, we had discovered, was to let it come into your hand voluntarily. I held Bluebell in both hands, like a person carrying a warm bowl of soup, and slowly managed to untie the message around the bird's leg. *I'm excited about the race on Saturday,* Sarah wrote in minuscule handwriting. *And the film. My father says we can leave at sunrise to give the birds a full day of flying. Love, S.*

Rather unimaginatively, I wrote back, *I saw Bluebell flying above me on my way home. Love, Allard.*

I attached the note to a mottled bird named Succotash and released her from the bedroom window. Her first wingbeats struck my hand, then she gained air and flew off in the wild, happy pattern that athletic birds use. She could cover the distance to Sarah's house in minutes, we knew. Afterward I stretched out on the bed, imagining Sarah hearing the tinkle of the bird bell that meant a returnee. She would reach in, detach the message, then write one of her own and send it back on a second pigeon. What we wrote, Sarah promised, was not as important as the fact that we wrote. Each pigeon, she said, was a thought.

"So, how did you like the new footage?" Ed asked from his bed, where he read old *Field & Stream* magazines Mom brought home when they were discarded from the library.

"I liked it," I said, lying back. "I can't wait to see them fly on Saturday."

"Sky Top never looked better."

"We're going to leave at first light. Mr. Patrick has a state park picked out one hundred miles away. He can get us there on the dot, so we will have exact measurements."

"They're going to book it back, believe me. Then we can cut to that shot we have of Sky Top coming into the loft. It's kind of cheating to mix in the earlier footage, but unless we want someone to stay here and try to film the homecoming . . ."

"I'm not staying and neither are you. And besides, we only have one camera."

"I talked to Dad about running electricity to the barn. He said it's awfully expensive, but he'll consider it. He'd have to bring it in from the street."

"Even a better generator might do it," I said, touching on a theme we discussed frequently.

"Two thousand bucks for a good one."

On Saturday Mr. Patrick arrived at 5:30 a.m., the agreed-upon hour, and we loaded his Jeep Cherokee with a wicker carrying case for the pigeons, the camera equipment, and a basket of sandwiches. My father came out to say hello to Mr. Patrick.

"Big pigeon day," my dad said, standing a pace or two away from the driver's window. "You should have good weather for it."

"It's hawk migration time," Ed said from the backseat after we had loaded the equipment. "They'll be flying in pretty dangerous territory."

"Great morning," Charlie Patrick said, glancing up at the sky. "You sure you won't come along?"

"I have an instrument to deliver or I would," my dad said. "Have to run to Boston."

"Too bad," Charlie said, sipping a road cup of coffee. "We're going over to Green Mountain National Forest. Do you know it?"

"Driven through it plenty of times," my dad said.

"A hundred miles, pretty much exactly. As the crow flies . . . or as the pigeon flies in this instance."

"Well, spring looks like it's finally here. Travel safe."

Spring had, in fact, finally taken over the north country. We drove with the windows cracked open. It felt festive to be traveling with the birds and to share our excitement over the filming. We dug into the sandwiches before we had traveled ten miles. Then Ed began filming us, catching us from different angles as the Jeep went west toward Vermont. Sarah and I made faces at the camera and filled our cheeks with peanut butter and jelly, and Ed filmed everything, even sliding up beside Mr. Patrick to get him as he drove. Then Sarah took the camera and did a bunch of moving-landscape shots, and by the time we finished with all that, we arrived at the national forest.

"I have a hundred miles exactly right . . . here," Mr. Patrick said, pulling the Jeep over on a small dirt clearing. The park service had chained a dilapidated picnic table to one of the trees. The surface of the table held a score of initialed hearts. We made that our headquarters and Ed began filming in earnest.

"We only have one chance at the release, so let's do it right. Sarah, why don't you be the release person? We want to use the pines and snow as a backdrop."

"What about maybe stepping up on the picnic table and filming that way?" I asked. "You could be above the release and you could film Sky Top as he goes past."

"I like it," Ed said, the camera at his eye, checking the light, checking his framing. "Sarah, how does that sound?"

"It would be dramatic. We should try it."

"You kids are becoming pros," Charlie Patrick said, standing back and watching us. "You've thought this through."

"The Baker River Film Company," Ed said. "This is what we're going to do."

"I sure hope so," Charlie said. "There are worse ways to go through the world than working with friends. Especially on interesting projects."

We ran footage. Sky Top in his wicker basket, Sky Top staring into the camera. Sarah filmed us, too, and she made us speak into the camera, saying what we thought of the birds, why we liked flying them, and what were the perils Sky Top would face on his journey home. Ed answered the questions sincerely, and his presence on film proved compelling. On the other hand, I came across as lighter, more rapid, a different type of pigeon altogether. Together, though, we came across as brothers, the Keer brothers, who worked beside each other and understood implicitly what the other was about.

"Are we ready?" Ed asked finally. "We have plenty of shots. Let's set up the fly-off."

We practiced with Gray Lord and Foggy first. Under Ed's direction, Sarah held the birds unusually close to her face, then lifted them straight up, an Aztec princess making an offering to the sun. It was slightly comic, and more than a little over-the-top, but by the time we had Sky Top ready to go, we had watched the first two send-offs on playback.

"What should my face look like?" Sarah asked, staring at the small flip screen on the side of the camera. "I look goofy."

"You look beautiful," Charlie said.

I nodded. She did.

"Just keep doing what you're doing," Ed said. "Let's get Sky Top ready to go."

I handed her Sky Top, then backed away. Ed leaned over her, staring at her through the camera. He adjusted it one last time, then asked me to hold his legs so he wouldn't move. I clamped him down and he nodded and whispered, "Ready."

Sarah lifted Sky Top. Then, gently, she tossed him up and he flew off. His wings clapped and he rose up, and flew directly into the sun—east, toward home—and we cheered and yelled and Ed said, "It's a wrap." But we kept watching Sky Top, our hands up to shade our eyes, while Ed asked Sarah on camera what she thought about letting Sky Top go.

"He has to fly his heart out," she said simply. "And there are dangers, but he'll make it home. I'm confident."

"Bravo," Charlie said. "You all should be proud of yourselves."

I was still watching the eastern horizon when I spotted the hawks. They were red-tailed hawks, common enough in our area, and they followed the lazy thermals northward in spring. Three of them circled. Our birds would have to fly beneath them.

"Hawks," I said.

"Where?" Ed asked.

I pointed. Ed nodded. Sarah followed the line of my arm and nodded, too.

"Will the hawks get them?" Charlie asked.

"They might," Ed said.

"But pigeons are smart," Sarah said. "They know how to fly close to the trees and stay out of sight. It's hard to know what will happen."

"Be a lousy ending to the film," Charlie said.

On the way home, Sarah and I sat in the back and held hands. Up front, Ed and Charlie talked about filmmaking, and about films they enjoyed. We all kept our eyes to the sky, watching for Foggy or Gray Lord or Sky Top, heading home across the tops of trees.

7

IT TOOK THREE DAYS for the birds to return. We never knew why, although we speculated that the hawks had caused them to lie low several times and wait until they could fly safely. Maybe, Ed suggested, their homing instinct was not as sharp as we thought. And maybe they simply could not fly such long distances with ease. Likely, we told one another, we had started them off on a flight that was too demanding. In any case, when the birds finally made it back—they were in the loft on a Tuesday morning when we checked—they looked tired and thin and slightly unsteady. Ed filmed them immediately, speaking as he did so about the demands on the birds. Then we gave them extra cracked corn and made sure their water dishes were full. We whooped when we climbed down and we each said we couldn't wait to tell Sarah.

Word spread that the pigeons had made it back, and by afternoon, Sarah came over and climbed up to the loft, and brought down Sky Top, the pigeon of the hour. Ed grabbed his camera and filmed Sarah's reunion. Ed said at last that he had enough footage for a documentary on Sky Top's return.

It took a month. Into April and May, we edited the film, working daily in the barn office. Spring advanced and we wanted to be outdoors, but this, we told ourselves, was the pattern of our future life: adventure outdoors, then work indoors. Back and forth Ed ran the images, and Sarah and I watched as his talent developed. His genius turned out not merely to include a natural sense of moviemaking and photography, but an unending willingness to get things right. He was not a perfectionist, exactly, but he was determined to give the world his best possible effort. It was my father's love of craft, in the end, and Ed had absorbed the lesson well.

Charlie Patrick arranged for the local elementary school to show *Sky Top* on a rainy Friday in May. He tipped the regional newspaper, and a *Northcountry News* reporter named Molly Anderson showed up and interviewed us. She wore a heavy camera around her neck and asked good questions and listened when we answered. Then she stayed to watch the film afterward.

The second-grade teacher introduced us and did her best to pique the pupils' interest. She stressed that we were local kids, that we had done the film ourselves, and that we were proof of what people could do if they put their minds to it.

Ed introduced the film, then the lights dimmed in the small auditorium. Sarah sat beside me and slid her hand into mine. What happened next had more to do with the setting than with the film itself. For the first time, I *saw* the film. Obviously, I had seen the film a thousand times, but now, as light broke the darkness and the camera caught a pigeon flying across an open field, Sarah's voice intoning, *Pigeons use their wings to row through the air,* I began to see what we had created. Here was our work, and I followed the camera into the loft, then back to Sarah, then to the small film logo we had created: a babbling brook, the Baker River, which slowly goes downstream until the water gathers and rises into letters that spell out *The Baker River Film Company.*

It was good. Of course it contained inadvertently funny moments, and some of the splices were not as true as they should have been, but the camera work saved us. Sarah stole the show whenever she came on, and I squeezed her hand a dozen times and leaned over twice to tell her she looked beautiful. She shook my hand and shook her head, but even she could see it was true. It's a cliché to say she lit up the screen, but she did, and when the final moments came and Sarah held Sky Top against her cheek, I knew we had produced a pretty fair film—better, truthfully, than what I had anticipated. From the corner of my eye, I watched Ed nod.

"I want to do more films," he whispered to me as the lights came up.

"Me, too," I said.

Sarah nodded.

The kids clapped and some of them hooted, happy to have an outlet on a Friday afternoon. The teacher congratulated us and told us we had made a strong impression on the children. But it was the reporter Molly Anderson who lingered behind and gave us an honest review.

"You all did a nice job, and I'm not just saying that," she said, her voice steady and calm. "You should submit it to some contests. See what happens. It has a certain youthful charm that will be appealing to people."

"What kind of contests?" Sarah asked.

"Film contests. Like Sundance, but smaller. You've heard of Sundance, right? Heck, maybe Sundance, too, what do I know? This is a good first step on your résumé. Better than a good first step. And send it to some people who direct wildlife programs. Look them up and send it with a short note, explaining you're young and just starting out. People sometimes want to help young folks get into the business. They'll like your film."

"Thank you," Ed said.

"Nobody opens a door unless you knock, I guess is what I'm saying," Molly Anderson said. "Send it around. See what happens."

We nodded.

"It's a good film, so believe in yourselves," she said. "The whole world may tell you not to, but you should. Don't listen to the rest. Just follow what you know to be true."

Then she walked away.

8

I BOUGHT AN OLD FORD 150 in the fall on my seventeenth birthday, cashing in every savings bond or birthday check I had ever received. Ed never had an interest in automobiles, and neither did my father much, so engine maintenance and repair became my small niche within the family. I worked on my truck daily, fiddling even when it ran perfectly fine, and I drove Sarah everywhere, her bottom scooted over next to mine, her legs separated by the gearshift, her hand finding my hand whenever it was not engaged driving the truck. I picked her up after school, and together we drove to Rumney, New Hampshire, where Sarah and I had become sport climbers on the sheer faces there.

Rock climbing had hardened Sarah's body; her shoulder muscles flexed when she moved her arms. As the weather turned warm again the following spring, she wore a tight tank top to climb and calf-length climbing pants and climbing shoes—thin ballet slippers with chalk applied liberally on their soles—and her hair hung behind her in a dart-shaped ponytail. Her beauty had sharpened.

While before she had possessed a girl's good looks, now she had matured and broadened in the way a woman must. Her looks had become almost too powerful. Going into a store, or a restaurant, people stopped and stared at her. Her dark brows—inherited from her mother—and her blond hair contrasted to make her model-pretty. Men watched her, of course, but so did other women. Walking beside her meant walking beside a warm fireplace, and other people approached her as they would a fire, expecting it to welcome them simply because they found it attractive.

Rumney Rocks, as it was called, happened to be one of the top sports-climbing destinations in the East. Access was simple: the cliffs rose only a short distance from the parking lots. While I could get up and down the faces well enough, Sarah demonstrated early on an uncanny ability to climb. Like all great climbers, she used her legs principally, and her ratio of strength to body weight gave her the perfect climber build. She had caught the climbing fever from an outdoor-rec class she had taken at the high school, and for the first month or so we had *bouldered* in the Rumney Pound, climbing freestanding rocks that enabled us to practice handholds and crossovers. In time Sarah bought herself a set of climbing ropes, and in weeks we became passionate climbers, nearly to the exclusion of everything else. We did twenty or thirty faces at Rumney, increasing the difficulty of each climb.

Climbing is also a sort of gypsy culture, and we joined it readily on weekends, driving to various climbing destinations around New England. We slept in the back of the truck, under a truck cap, on an old air mattress we pumped up by compressor. Through all that spring and into summer, we followed stone trails up vertical faces.

We also had sex. We had seventeen-year-old sex, which was wild and vigorous and often endless. With the heat of the day on Sarah's skin, the slight sheen of sweat from climbing, or perhaps the chill of a late-evening swim still clinging to us both, we enjoyed for the first time true sexual relations. We kissed over and over and over until our lips grew chapped and raw. Our fingers, cut and scraped from climbing, explored each other's body. Each day on the rock faces we trusted each other with our lives, and at night, in the New Hampshire summer, we made love fiercely and often.

Our life changed, though, on a day in August.

"There's a peregrine falcon nest over at Rumney," I told Ed one night, after someone had pointed it out to me. Ed had been accepted at the University of Washington and would be leaving soon. I knew I would miss him. "You could score some footage if you want to come with us. The chicks are gone, but you could get some nice shots of the nest and the cliff light."

"Do I need a scope?"

"Probably."

Ed and I had been gathering equipment, and we now had a fair-size arsenal stacked on his army-green shelves in the barn office. We had been routinely filming animals whenever we could, figuring we both needed the practice and because spare footage might come in handy someday. Strong footage of a peregrine falcon nest could never hurt.

"I don't want to be a third wheel on one of your excursions," Ed said. "Why don't you film it? Maybe you can get a little closer when you climb."

"Aren't you going to climb with us at least once before you head out?"

"I was built for the ground. You two are the long, lanky ones. I'm not that great with heights."

When I told Sarah the next afternoon that I needed to spend some time filming the nest, she shrugged and said she would find someone else to belay her. No worries. And if not, she'd simply hang with me. It didn't seem like a big deal, and it shouldn't have been, except a green Dartmouth van pulled up in the parking lot fifty yards below us, DARTMOUTH OUTING CLUB stenciled on the side. I had the camera half set up on its tripod. Sarah stood beside me.

A dozen men and women climbed out—Dartmouth students, obviously, all young and fit and in high spirits. It was impossible to miss them, impossible to confuse them with the rock-rats who usually inhabited the Rumney cliffs, and I had a strange moment when I happened to glance over at Sarah and discovered her studying them with unusual interest.

"Dartmouth folks," I said, more to myself than anything else.

"Life looks easier for them somehow," she said, her voice slightly winsome.

She watched them as they pulled out a bunch of climbing ropes, and one of the young men seemed to be in charge. He had his back to us.

"You think so?" I asked, my hands working to get the camera squared away.

"Well, they're economically favored, right? Good dentists, good doctors, good clothes. You don't see the local schools out here in shiny vans. It takes money to do that. Then the kids study hard, they get into Dartmouth, and then they produce more kids who also get into Dartmouth. So, yes, life is easier for them."

"You sound like you envy them."

She shook her head.

"I don't think I do. I'd go to Dartmouth if I get in. You can't say no to an opportunity like that. But my dad put me in a public school on purpose. We believe in public education."

"This is a side of you I hadn't seen before. I never realized you felt at a disadvantage."

"No side, really. Just observing. And I don't feel I'm at a disadvantage. You're bending what I'm saying, Allard. They simply look kind of relaxed and like they belong here. It's their demeanor as much as anything."

"You know, there could be a downside to going to Dartmouth. Maybe the highlight of your life is getting into Dartmouth, but then you don't know what you want to do next. So for the rest of your life, people always say, 'But, gee, she went to Dartmouth.' You still have to do something with your life."

"I was just saying, life seems easier for them. They're more assured. They have resources."

"You have resources," I said, not sure why I felt irritated that she found the Dartmouth Outing gang worth such sharp examination. I finished putting the camera on the tripod.

"Nice remark, Allard. It feels like you're trying to pick a fight."

"It feels to me like you are. I mean, you have resources, too. So do I. And just because they have the stamp from some school, well, it doesn't make them better or worse."

"Being a Dartmouth alumnus is a club most people wouldn't mind joining."

"Bull. A lot of people would find Dartmouth suffocating. Do you feel like you missed out by not going to private school?"

"Don't be ridiculous. Why are you being so defensive about all this stuff?" she asked. "It's not like you."

"Maybe it *is* like me," I said, feeling as though someone else had inhabited my body and I was incapable of making him stop. "Maybe it seems kind of snobby that you would take a greater interest in these people just because they're from Dartmouth."

"What kind of wacky ideas are you talking about? I've never heard you be quite such a jerk before."

She was right, more or less, but my mind felt itchy and unkind. I finished setting up the camera while she went back to the truck. I knew what was going to happen next. It was more than a premonition. Fate felt ready to trap us somehow, and while my mind skittered back and forth, nervous and uneasy, my attention stayed focused on the camera with unusual clarity. Like a soldier asked to field dress his rifle blindfolded, I might have assembled the camera with no thought whatsoever, while my mind—firing on different burners—resisted fruitlessly what tormented it.

I photographed the nest. In all my early work with Ed, with

all the hours I had spent behind the camera, I had never produced such competent work. I deliberately lost myself in the technique, carrying the camera left and right, shooting to get one of the young birds that roosted on a pine bough. Ed, I knew, would be impressed, and I had nearly finished when I calmly swung the camera across the rock faces until I spotted Sarah halfway up Baby's Retreat, a medium-rated climb we had done a hundred times.

On a second belay, climbing slightly below her, I spotted one of the Dartmouth guys. I zoomed in on them both, and for a painful moment I watched Sarah say something and look down, her face radiant with beauty, and he—good-looking, curly haired, broad, and well built—looked up and returned her smile. I watched as they continued to climb, both of them chatting, their bodies smooth and fluid against the rock.

It should have meant nothing. She had climbed with plenty of people on our trips together, often with guys, and none of it had bothered me. But seeing the easy confidence she had on the wall, the remarkable muscular tension of her legs and arms, and beneath her the spidery ascent of the Dartmouth jerk, my heart fell to the ground.

I knew something had begun that would not easily let us go, and that as much as she had participated in the small betrayal, I had given her the opportunity and pushed her into it. Some peculiar, dark element of my personality had invited my own pain.

"This is Jeff," she said when she arrived back at my truck. She looked warm from climbing, but she also evinced a sunny demeanor that seemed false and self-congratulatory, a satisfaction that she had this young man in tow and that it was exactly an answer to our earlier conversation.

"Hi," I said, and shook his hand. "Nice to meet you."

"Sarah said you were filming," Jeff said. "What kind of camera do you have?"

I handed it to him. He was tall and muscular and wore a

Dartmouth fleece over a gray T-shirt. His hair, dirty blond, had begun to recede along the front hairline. He was tan and healthy and had already changed into flip-flops, which meant, I understood, that Sarah had walked him back to the Dartmouth van after their climb. He may have been twenty. He possessed the easy, calm assurance of other Dartmouth people I had met previously. He glanced at the camera, put it to his eye once, and handed it back to me.

"You might think about the new Nikons," he said, apparently finding our camera lacking.

"Well, we do what we can," I said.

"Allard and his brother, Ed, are making films," Sarah said, and I noticed she had not included herself. "Wildlife films. They've made three already."

"Really?" Jeff said. "That's great. And you're local here?"

"From Warren," I said.

"The funny town with the rocket in the village common?"

"Guilty," I said.

"It's so weird. That rocket, it sits right beside that church, and you have a rocket and a steeple side by side."

"We live there, we know," Sarah said.

What were we doing? How quickly things had changed. Jeff was perfectly nice—and would continue to be, I knew—and yet he was a snake slithering into our Garden of Eden. I knew it. I wondered, on the other hand, how Sarah did not see what had happened, how she could stand by and pretend that she did not see Jeff's motive. We made our good-byes and Jeff said we should come over some time and hang out. We agreed. We said we'd definitely see him on the rocks. Then he went back to the Dartmouth van, where other climbers did yoga postures to stretch out their limbs.

"He wants you," I said on the drive back.

"Who? Jeff? Don't be ridiculous. You are so strange today."

"So I'm just being jealous?"

"He said for us to come over and hang out. Us. You and me."

"He means you, Sarah. He could not care less about me."

"I'm being weirded out right now. You've never been like this before, Allard."

"Neither have you. Tell me this. Why did you go climbing with him?"

"Because he was there and he had people to belay and we happened to be at a climbing destination, in case you didn't notice."

"You're not being honest."

"Oh, because I wanted to jump him and ravage him? Is that it?"

"I don't know exactly what it was," I said. "I'm still trying to figure it out. I didn't like seeing you flirting with him."

"I wasn't flirting."

"Yes you were, Sarah. I'm trying to be calm. I am being calm, I think. But if you're honest at all, you need to admit you wanted to flirt with him and you wanted it to hurt me."

"You're nuts."

"Am I really?"

We drove home in silence. I dropped her at her house and she didn't kiss me good-bye. I watched her walk toward the front door, then break into a run. My stomach gave birth to a rat gnawing at my intestines, climbing on the bones of my ribs, my throat closed and choking with the greasy weight of the creature snarling and grinning as it ate.

"That isn't Sarah," Ed said. We had watched the footage of the peregrine falcon I had filmed at Rumney, and Ed had given it two thumbs-up, pronouncing it the best thing I had ever shot. I had told Ed the entire Jeff story and he had taken it in, whistled, then sat on the edge of his bed. I could barely get my stomach to settle.

"I didn't think so, either," I said. "But it was. It was weird."

"So she climbed with this guy?"

"With Jeff."

"But there's no harm in that."

"It was all nuance, Ed," I said. "You know what Sarah's like. She's beautiful and guys are always going to give her attention. I know that."

"Okay, so what?"

"So this is the first time I saw her *use* that. Use her beauty. It scared me and I think it surprised her. It sounds strange, I know, but maybe she doesn't really understand how beautiful she is. I mean, she hears it, I'm sure, but to have it sink in, once and for all . . . it's like having a special superpower."

"So she's Spider Woman?" Ed asked, trying to lighten things.

"You know what I mean."

"I think I do. But it doesn't really fit with Sarah. Are you certain you're not building this up in your head?"

"Maybe. I don't know."

"The good thing is you don't have to do anything about it. It's her call, so to speak."

"It's like the Tree of Knowledge, and we're Adam and Eve, and Jeff is the snake. It sounds crazy, I know, but that's what it feels like," I said, revisiting my earlier image of the situation.

"Mom would give you hell for blaming it on Eve."

"I'm not blaming her. I'm saying we're sort of trapped in a set of circumstances. I mean, if God is all knowing, didn't He know the snake would manage to get Eve to bite the apple? She was set up. Anyway, that's what it feels like . . . like we're playing out a scene that's inevitable."

"Like you're doomed?"

"Sort of, yes."

"Maybe you're both ready to move on. You've been together for a long time. Maybe she's moving on, but doesn't know it yet."

"You think that's it?"

Ed shrugged. As he readied himself for bed, I lay beneath the map of Canada, my soul completely shaken. What I should have done, I knew, was call her, or drive over, but I felt a stubborn resistance. It was not the best part of my character, but it ran deep and wide, like a vein of coal that smolders. I alternated between feeling on the verge of dismissing the entire thing, or claiming my independence. I felt vengeful and hurt, and those were new emotions for me, especially concerning Sarah. Yet, in reality, nothing had happened. It was a wind change, that's all, and I tried to reassure myself.

As I finally started to fall asleep, I heard the pigeon bell go off in the small loft attached to our window. Pigeons no longer meant as much to us, but we still kept a couple around. Sky Top had died; so had Foggy and Lord Gray, all from causes unknown. It was a surprise, then, to hear the bird come into the coop, and I went to the window and gentled her inside. I detached the leg band and put the bird back in the coop.

As soon as I opened the message, I recognized Sarah's writing. The message said simply, *Ee-aa-kee?*

I took the message to bed with me and read it a dozen times. Was she trying to remind me of earlier, better times? Of our long-standing love for each other? I fell asleep with the note in my hand, the pigeon burr familiar and calming at the window.

9

At my father's request, I drove with him to the Berklee College of Music in Boston. He had to deliver two new basses before classes began. It was a few days after the "affair de Jeff" as Ed called it, and I hadn't spoken to Sarah since; she had gone on a college visit with her mother. Neither of us had made the effort to contact the other, which was odd in itself especially with Ed leaving soon, but perhaps, I thought, a little time needed to pass. Sarah, I figured, had felt the same way. In any event, I was glad to have something to do with my father. I hoped that it would take my mind off Sarah.

The Baker River threw stars of light as we passed it heading south, and leaves gathered sunshine and held it. We had the instruments in the back of my mom's Subaru.

"Did you ever count how many instruments you've made over the years?" I asked my dad when we hopped onto I-93 heading south.

"Your mother knows," he said, his eyes tracing the tree line at the side of the highway. "She keeps the addresses and contacts for all the buyers. It's like a big family tree to her. I don't know exactly. I'm more interested in how many I have left in me."

"You have plenty left in you, Dad. How old are you? Fifty-five?"

"Try fifty-seven."

"You can keep working as long as you want, Dad. Don't stop on anyone's account but your own."

"I'm getting older, Allard. Sometimes my hands know what to do and I let them do it," he said, his eyes following the traffic now. "I kind of stand back and watch and they perform like marvelous little creatures. It's rather fun, actually. Like having elves in the house."

"I wish I had something like that."

"You boys have the films. They're awfully good for your age and experience."

"Ed's better at it. I can do it, but Ed's better."

"Don't be so sure, Allard. Ed is terrific in many ways, but so are you. Don't underestimate yourself. You have a thousand talents."

I nodded. A little time went by, then my father brought up what was on his mind. It was why he had asked me to accompany him to Boston.

"I understand you and Sarah are experiencing a little rift," he said, his eyes forward. "It's none of my business, and you can tell me to mind my own knitting, but I figured a dad ought to make himself available at a time like this. First love and all that."

"How'd you find out about it?"

"Oh, it's pretty big kitchen news. Your mother heard from Mrs. P. Then it spread to all corners of the earth, I suppose."

He looked over at me and smiled. It was a joke. I smiled but my face felt heavy.

"It's weird, Dad, that's all. I mean, Sarah is beautiful, but she also has a great heart. She's not mean at all. Think of the way she treats animals . . . I mean, she can't harm a hair on the head of any animal. And then, with this guy Jeff, I saw her take an interest. She knew it would bother me, but she did it anyway."

"Has she made plans to see him? This Jeff?"

"I don't know. I haven't talked to her."

"Why not?"

"Because suddenly there seems like we have a distance between us. It's hard to describe."

"You know we love Sarah."

"I know, Dad."

"There's an old saying that the heart is forever inexperienced. Who knows why really smart people get married and divorced five or six times . . . the heart is forever inexperienced. If it helps any, I always imagined that each of us had a well-kept lawn and a compost pile somewhere inside us. The well-kept lawn is where you spend most of your time. It's the view you show to most people. But all the clippings go back to the compost pile. Sometimes you can take something out of the compost pile to nurture the lawn, but most of the time the compost pile just molders. But it's still part of your personality. So Sarah is ninety-nine percent well-kept lawn, but she still has a compost pile somewhere back there. So do you. So do I. Maybe the compost pile is having its day right now."

"That's a little wacky," I said. "Not to hurt your feelings."

He laughed.

"You're probably right. It's just a way to say you should be tender with her. And she should be tender with you . . . but maybe you can't be right now. It's hard to know. But remember, whatever hurt feelings you have toward Sarah, there are also a million memories of good things you can also tap into. Concentrate on the well-kept lawn and let the compost pile take care of itself."

"I can't imagine things without her."

"She probably can't imagine life without you, either. But life has a way of shaking things up. Just go slowly right now. Don't do anything rash and I bet it will all work out for the best. You know, one other thing. Sometimes we forget to show people that we love them. It's possible Sarah feels a little taken for granted. She's just your old pal, Sarah. Maybe you can figure a way to remind her what you two mean to one another."

He reached over and patted my knee. Afterward we listened to a sports talk show centered on the Red Sox and the Patriots. We arrived at the college in Boston as the radio program ended on the hour. A security guard in a small shelter asked where we were going. My dad told him the office of the head of the music department, and the guard handed us a visitor's tag to put on our rearview mirror. We rolled gently over the speed bumps until we found a parking spot near the right building. I climbed out and carefully took the two bass cases from the backseat and locked the car.

"This way," my dad said. "I usually like to hand off my instruments directly to the musicians who will be playing them, but since classes haven't started yet, I've arranged to leave these two with the department head."

I gave one of the cases to my father and we went inside. The head of the department was a great admirer of my dad's craft and told him several times how wonderful the music always sounded coming from his fine basses. Our meeting took less than half an hour, then we were on the road headed back home again.

10

My dad's words about showing Sarah what she meant to my life haunted me the next day or so while Sarah was still away. We didn't speak, which was strange, but it seemed we both needed to take some time. I talked to my mom, too, and she agreed with my dad: that to accuse and cross-examine Sarah was a bad way to go. She added that any heart that strays is straying from something, not to something. The next person is simply a symptom of what went wrong in the ongoing relationship. Better, she agreed with my father, to show Sarah how much she meant to me. Nevertheless, I lived in agony, trying to forget the way Sarah had looked around Jeff.

Meanwhile, Ed was packing up to leave for college. He was heading out to the University of Washington, where he hoped to work under Morgan Davis, one of the preeminent wildlife documentarians in America. Morgan Davis held a professorship there, but his real work—and his notoriety—came from a remarkable series of films he had made about murder in the animal world. It upset many people who romanticized animals, with critics calling it one-sided and edited for deliberate controversy. On the other side, many behaviorists found in it confirmation of a more factual representation of animals. What many people overlooked, but not Ed, was the exquisite beauty of the films and the incredible patience the footage demonstrated. It was a masterwork, and Ed planned to train under Morgan Davis.

We were both surprised when, the day before he was leaving, a letter came that announced that the Baker River Film Company had won a $3,000 prize from a documentary-film contest in Missoula, Montana. A five-minute short on the impact of the lawn sprinkler on an average suburban lawn—ants getting laced with bombs of water droplets, a spiderweb catching the spray and gleaming in white bars in the evening sun, a robin pecking at the worms the water drove up from the soil—won second prize in the annual Short Documentary Contest sponsored by the University of Montana. It was our best work yet, a painstaking short that had all three of us working ridiculous hours, and had been finished just in time to submit it before the deadline. It had already secured Ed a place at the University of Washington. Now it had won second place. Sarah and I also planned to use it this fall in our application packets to colleges, Sarah to Dartmouth and me to the University of Vermont.

Ed called Charlie Patrick, who took down the prize information for Sarah and congratulated us both effusively. He said he would pass it along to Sarah when she and her mother checked in that evening. They would be home the next day in any case.

"I knew it, I knew it," Charlie said over the phone. "I knew the Baker River Film Company would win one of these contests. It was just a matter of time."

"Second place," Ed reminded him.

"Oh, that doesn't mean a hill of beans. First, second, what the heck? You have talent, that's what this means. You have real talent and you're all still very young. It's a fine film. Sarah is just going to be over the moon."

"Congratulate Sarah for me," Ed said. "And tell her we would not have won it without her. I'm heading out tomorrow so I won't get to see her and tell her myself."

11

On the basis of our prize money, I asked my father for a loan.

"For drugs? Gambling?" my father asked at his workshop bench, reaching into his hip pocket for his wallet. "You come to a loan shark and the loan shark has to wonder why this person needs money. Is he a good risk?"

"I want to do something for Sarah."

"How much?"

I told him $200, I thought. He handed me $75 and said he would get the rest from Mom.

"Enough?" he asked.

I nodded. He patted my shoulder.

I learned from Charlie Patrick what time Sarah was due the following day, and when she arrived at five, I was on the front step, waiting.

"I want to take you to dinner," I said before we could get into any explanations or questions. "Can you be ready in an hour?"

She looked at me. All the tension, all the affair de Jeff, still rested between us. I watched her begin to tell me she was tired, that she had been on the road, but then the old Sarah, my Sarah, softened her eyes.

"What should I wear?"

"Something pretty and warm."

"Pretty and warm don't necessarily go together, Allard. For future reference."

I kissed her and told her I would be back in an hour. I went home, showered, put on a good shirt and a warm sweater, then drove back to pick up Sarah. She came to the door wearing a dress with a sweater over it. It looked funky and beautiful.

I opened the truck door for her. She made a funny face as she slid inside.

"Aren't you the gentleman?" she said when I came around to the driver's side.

"Not enough when it comes to you. I could do better."

She bit her lip and looked at me. I started the truck. I drove her to Cloud Meadow. It was a mountain pasture owned by Lester Hawkins, a high, beautiful parcel of land that overlooked Mt. Carr. Most of the locals knew it. At this time of year, asters and black-eyed Susan grew everywhere, and the clouds, on certain nights, seemed to rest on the grasses. I had arranged with White Mountain caterers, a friend of my mom's named Sally Peterson, to serve us dinner in the meadow. Sally had a small card table, covered by a white tablecloth, set up in the middle of the meadow. Her catering van sat beneath a row of ancient oaks, the back doors open. Sally wore a white kitchen smock over jeans and Birkenstocks. She waved when I pulled up beside her.

"What did you do?" Sarah asked me, suddenly smiling and crazy. I could tell she was delighted. She jumped up to her knees and strained to see the dinner table.

"I thought we could have dinner and talk."

"Oh, Allard." She leaned over and kissed my neck. She kissed me three times.

Then she hopped out. She knew Sally, of course, and they hugged and laughed. Sally escorted us to the table. I held out Sarah's chair. Everywhere, on all sides of us, wildflowers stretched for three acres. A half-moon, just rising, had already climbed above the mountaintop. It was a glorious September evening, with a slight breeze that came over the meadow and combed back the grasses. The wind also played with the candle flames Sally had placed in the center of the table.

"I've been told by the authorities that you are both entitled to one glass each of wine," Sally said, pouring us red wine. "I could be arrested for serving underage minors, but under the circumstances I think we'll chance it. As long as we stick to one glass, we'll be okay."

She waited while I tasted the wine.

"Amusing," I said, sipping, "and a bit provocative, but it should do."

"I'm glad you approve," Sally said, bowing a little. "It's actually a very nice wine. Enjoy it while I get the first course prepared."

Sally walked back to the van. I raised my glass. Sarah raised hers.

"I love you, Sarah," I said, my eyes on hers. "I don't want you to ever think I take you for granted, or don't understand how lucky I am to have you in my life. We go back forever and I hope we go forward forever."

Her eyes filled. She touched my glass.

"I'm sorry," she said. "You didn't have to do all this."

I shook my head.

"I'm sorry. I wanted to do this. I wanted to show you somehow what you already know. That I love you."

"You're a romantic." She cocked her head a little to one side. "I had no idea."

"Sally helped."

"It's beautiful here," Sarah said, looking around. "It's perfect. Is Lester going to show up with some oxen?"

"Not tonight. The meadow is all ours."

"Well, I guess we can't have everything."

Sally served us. She played her role and remained friendly and warm, but she did not linger at the table. She had cooked Cornish game hens stuffed with wild rice, and she served it with a fresh, green salad. It smelled and tasted delicious. Sarah ate with a good appetite. We talked about the Missoula award, what it meant to our film careers, how Ed's departure for college was going to affect us and our filmmaking. General talk. She told me about her college visits. She liked Dartmouth best of all, although she said Williams and Amherst were beautiful. She had talked to a professor at Dartmouth about their environmental programs. She wondered if she couldn't combine her love of writing with environmental studies, especially as it impacted animals.

"Are you two ready for dessert?" Sally asked us when we put down our forks. "I made crème brûlée, which I am quite proud of, given the fact that I just caramelized it in the back of my van."

"I think we are."

"I'm going to clear away some dishes, and then bring back dessert. I also have a thermos of coffee for you. Then I'm taking off. You can pick up the table and chairs and the last few dishes and bring them by tomorrow. Does that sound all right?"

"It was a wonderful dinner," I said.

"It was amazing, Sally," Sarah said.

"I'm glad you enjoyed it."

Sally hugged us both when she came back with the desserts and coffee. Then she popped into her van, eased slowly over the meadow, and left. Meanwhile, the crème brûlée had come out beautifully. We broke through the brown, sweet surface into a bay of custard. I poured Sarah coffee, then served myself. The moon had continued to drop slowly to the horizon, but behind it a few stars had shaken free of the last light.

"About that whole Jeff thing . . . ," Sarah said.

"Jeff who?"

She smiled. "We don't need to discuss it?"

"I don't. I'll discuss it if you need to."

She shook her head. Our eyes stayed on one another's. Then she stood and curled into my lap. I held her. We didn't say anything else for a long time. A white-tailed deer stepped free of the hedgerow and began feeding calmly in the meadow below us. Another deer joined it.

"You see them?" she whispered.

I nodded so she could feel it.

"I want to have your baby," she said softly a little while later. "Not now, so don't panic. But someday. Someday I want to have a big house, not expensive, but a house with a view, and I want a kitchen with a woodstove where people want to sit and talk and laugh. And I want to do good work, important work, work I can be proud about. And I want a lot of dogs. And maybe a cat, too, but the cat has to be aloof and be mostly my friend. I want Ed to live over the hill, or just a little ways away, and I want my parents to survive to an old age. And I want the Baker River Film Company to become synonymous with the best films anyone has ever seen. I want to keep watching animals, like right now, like those deer at the foot of the meadow.

"I want it all to blend, Allard, I want there to be no lines between things. Work as play, and love as play, and getting out and seeing new things, but coming home, too. I don't know if I've ever told you all this before, but I thought about it on the college trip. I thought about what I want, and what I am willing to give, and I am ready to give you everything, Allard. We're young, I know. Everyone says it as if we didn't know that ourselves. Maybe we have a chance at a pretty good life, and we need to be careful, but also we need to take chances and we can't suffocate one another. It's tricky. But you're in it all, Allard. Everything I think about, or dream of, you're the center of it. I hope you know that, and if I haven't shown you that, or made you to understand, then I'm sorry."

I nodded again. I held her closer. We watched the deer work along the meadow, and we watched the stars come out more vividly. Now and then Sarah reached for her coffee and took a sip and held the cup so I could sip, too. She gripped my arm when the deer, sensing something, lifted their heads. Then, in a flash, she jumped up from my lap and ran toward the deer. The deer flashed their white tails and ran across the meadow, their great haunches pushing them to incredible bounds. And when they disappeared, they might have soared into the darkness, jumped so high that they landed on the moon and rode it over the mountains and into the sea. Sarah ran with her arms out, jumping as the deer had jumped, and I ran after her and tumbled her into the grass, and then, for an instant, we breathed heavily, face-to-face, eyes-to-eyes, body-to-body, the world nothing but each other.

12

At Dartmouth, Sarah declared herself an English major with a reading interest in environmental science. I was majoring in film at the University of Vermont. Ed, meanwhile, had already decided to stay in Washington after college to work with Morgan Davis as an apprentice filmmaker.

During her sophomore and junior summers, Sarah worked at Ravine Lodge as a hut girl. It was a source of great pride to her. The lodge, built for Dartmouth students, families, and friends, squatted in the shadow of Mt. Moosilauke, where, many years before, the first alpine ski race in America had taken place. The Lodge, as it was referred to, embodied much of what was selective about Dartmouth: the building, hewed from New Hampshire timber and hucked together with mortise-tenon joints my father would have appreciated, possessed a casual, late-nineteenth-century elegance. The large keeping room—looking out on the west branch of the Baker River, the misty twine of water that had grooved out our valley—was the site of square dances and taffy pulls, events deliberately conjured to enchant alumni by their old-timey coloring.

Nightly the large river-stone fireplace at the center of the keeping room flamed with pine firelight, and the world of modern communications drifted away, replaced by a romantic illusion of roughneck lumberjacks, ax-wielders, brush cutters, tree toppers, and hobnailed-boot men. Men and women known to each other by their year of graduation—so that there were '63s, '02s, and '89s, and so forth—pulled on flannel shirts, L.L. Bean fleeces, and wore expensive hiking boots up the many tributaries that led to the bald, gusty mountaintop. At the start of each academic year, Dartmouth's incoming First Years descended on the Ravine Lodge and spent the weekend hiking the trails and bonding as a class.

It was tempting to be cynical about the place, but it served as an anchor to an extensive stretch of White Mountains forest conservation, and Mt. Moosilauke, with its skirt of swirling waters, proved an inexhaustible host. Each summer weekend, and well into the fall, cars lined the long access road from the Sawyer Highway, and with delight the visitors greeted their hut girl, Sarah Patrick, who met them with her bright energy and green Dartmouth T-shirt. She cooked and cleaned, did trail maintenance, hauled wood, served pancakes, and occasionally, when called upon, sang silly songs and participated in skits and charade games, besting everyone with her joyous laughter and her formidable intellect.

By now I was deeply in love with Sarah. To be near her during the summers I built a sleeping platform in a massive oak not far from Ravine Lodge, and there, like Robin Hood, I courted her. She came to visit whenever she could. No one else visited that part of the forest.

"We should have kept our pigeons," Sarah said one afternoon after we had made love on the air mattress I had lugged up for comfort. We lay together looking up at the treetops, the summer breezes warm and fragrant. Beneath us the Baker River splashed by, its bed littered with large white rocks left behind by glaciers. Sarah needed to be back to the Lodge at four to help with dinner prep.

"That feels like a long time ago."

"Not that long."

I gently tickled her back and played with her hair. She kissed the side of my neck.

"Have you heard about the run? I'm doing it this year," she said. "It's my last summer here."

"The Hanover run?" I asked, feeling sleepy and luxurious. It was a fifty-mile run, completed in legs, to bring a fire from the alma mater to the Lodge.

"I'm doing the last leg. It's about an eight-mile run, but it's up and down hills."

"Really?" I asked, and rolled over to look at her.

"Thinking about it."

"Thinking about it, eh?"

"Only young once," she said.

"We should film it."

"Actually," she said, and her tone made me realize that she had been heading to this from the start, "I have a chance to write it up for the *Alumni Magazine*. One of the women who came to the hut this summer does PR at the college, and she thought it would make a great feature. We got to talking and I sent her some of my writing and she gave me an assignment."

"You've been holding out on me. Why didn't you tell me?"

"I'm scared, that's why. I've always wanted to write and now here's this perfect chance to try something and I'm scared."

"You can do it. I know you can."

"Do you really think so?"

"You were born to do it, Sarah. You've been reading and writing since I met you."

Sarah's voice became excited. "She says it might even be

something the *Globe* would run. She has a contact there, I guess. She said they are always looking for a young perspective, something new. So I could do it in first person and I might be able to include some background about living at the Lodge. You know, summer jobs, that kind of thing. Or maybe it would be a second article. It all depends. But I guess what it means is I'm going to carry a torch down Mt. Moosey."

"I want to be with you, but I don't want to get in your way."

"I want you at the beginning and at the end. I'm afraid if you were next to me, I wouldn't pay as much attention to the things around me. Do you understand?"

"Of course."

"You can see the torch coming over the ridge. It's on a full-moon night. I guess it's beautiful."

We made love again. We took our time and our kisses lingered and connected us. A few clouds passed over the sun and we kept kissing, our eyes on each other, our bodies moving together. I told her I loved her. I told her I believed in her. I told her this article was the start of a whole career for her. And then our bodies kept us from talking and I kissed her over and over while rain began on our rickety roof, and we shivered together at the coolness that found our skin, and when we released each other her warmth stayed with me.

THE FIFTY-MILE RUN took place on the first weekend in October, a night scheduled for a full moon and clear skies. The Mt. Washington weather station called for temperatures in the low forties, a westerly wind, and a soft frost at higher altitudes. Standing behind a torchbearer in the center of Hanover, New Hampshire, Sarah and her fellow group of hikers wore fleeces, rip-away hiking pants, and water camels to keep them hydrated. The start of the hike, for everyone but the torchbearer, was merely ceremonial. Sarah would go part of the way with them tonight, then get a ride to the other end of the trail, where she would hike up and meet the advancing party at dawn. Then she would carry the torch the last eight miles. No matter what, she was heading into a long night of hiking.

I trotted beside Sarah for the first mile. She ran at the back of the pack, but her gait was smooth and untroubled. Drivers honked when they saw the torch; entire households came out and stood on their porches, pumpkins skirted by leaves, and whistled and cheered. For half a century the torch had been carried from Hanover to Mt. Moosilauke, and when I kissed Sarah good-bye at the forest entrance, her eyes shimmered with emotion.

"See you later, gator," she said, and put her hand softly on my cheek.

"You can do it," I said.

She nodded. Then she ran into the forest. I stood with a few well-wishers and watched as the torch began climbing through the forest. It was a spectacular night. At the Ravine Lodge, I knew, the remaining staff rang the climbers' triangle, signaling that human beings had taken to the hilltops, and that we awaited their return.

I slept at home, under the eaves, to catch up with laundry and to visit with my parents, but in first light I drove up to the Lodge and began hiking the trail from the opposite direction, hoping to intercept Sarah. The weather had remained calm and crisp; a few of the river rocks held stiff collars of new ice. Morning mist rose off the stream and cut the trees off at the knees. I startled a doe before I had gone a quarter mile. It looked at me briefly, then ran off, not afraid but cautious, and I watched it climb above me and disappear, its body taken by first shadows and the dead leaves that matched its colors.

I pushed on and a little while later I saw Sarah.

I had never seen her look so exhausted; I had never seen her more joyful. Mud dotted her clothes. Her hair had come undone and looked wild and untamed. A line of sweat had dried on her cheek, leaving her with a dull mark that flowed to her chin. But it was morning and she had made it. Three other hikers were with her. She bore the torch proudly. The other hikers carried unlit torches in case the one Sarah carried faltered.

"You did it," I whispered to Sarah. "You made it."

"What was I thinking?" she asked, her voice happy. "But it was beautiful, Allard. The moon gave us such good light. I could see the torch coming toward us from miles away. It was moving to see it."

"You did it. All your life you'll know you did it."

"If I live. I'm so tired. My feet are killing me. Blisters on blisters."

But I could tell she wouldn't have missed it. The sun grew increasingly bright behind us. More people had come up the hill to cheer them on and we surrounded them as they reached the Lodge. Someone rang the triangle to acknowledge that human beings had returned from the hilltops, and then the hikers—Sarah in the lead—brought the torch into the keeping room.

"We light the first winter fire," Sarah said because it was the ritual. "We bring the light from Mother Dartmouth."

Then she put the torch to the prepared kindling and the fire passed from one spark to the next. It flickered and it climbed and light filled the chimney. Everyone applauded and people stamped their feet and whistled. And Sarah, her eyes locked on me, called, "Ee-aa-kee, ee-aa-kee, ee-aa-kee," until her strength ran out.

"SHE LIKES IT but it needs revisions," Sarah said, her feet in my lap, her hands typing on her laptop. She had just finished reading an e-mail from Janice Ewing, the editor of the *Dartmouth Alumni Magazine*.

I had changed the bandages on her feet once already that morning, and now, in her dorm room with an afternoon rain falling against the window, I changed them again. The blisters had healed and turned red, but one, near her right ankle-bone, had become mildly infected. Sarah had worn only flip-flops for a week despite the falling temperatures.

"There you go," I said, painting her heel with first-aid cream, and trying to get her to stay still. "She likes it."

"I think she's just being nice."

"You'd like it better if she were mean, wouldn't you?"

Sarah ran her feet in quick little kicks against my lap. Her eyes hadn't left the laptop.

"I'm serious!" she said.

"So am I. She likes it, Sarah. She wants to run it in the *Alumni Magazine*. It's your first published piece."

"It's got to be perfect. I will die if it isn't perfect."

"That attitude should make your life easy."

"I misspelled *grammar*," she squealed, reading the e-mail from Janice Ewing. "I put an *e* in it! How could I miss that? That's ridiculous!"

"A typo."

"But I missed it!" She fluttered her feet on my lap again.

"She's probably shown everyone and they probably had a great laugh at your expense, and they probably think less of you as a human being and a writer for a typo."

Her eyes didn't leave the computer screen. I slipped her feet off my lap. I had to go. I had work to do back at UVM. I bent down and kissed her. She put her hand up on the back of my neck.

"You're not going," she said. "Not yet."

"I am."

"I'm sorry I'm obsessing," she said, and finally looked up from the computer screen.

"Oh, is that what you look like."

"I'm sorry, honey, sweetie, smoochie."

"She liked it," I whispered into Sarah's ear. "She liked it fine. A professional editor liked your first feature. She said there was much to admire in it. It's going to run in the magazine. It's your first publication. Be happy."

"I know. I know. I should be happier and I will be. I will be in a little while when it all sinks in. Right now, though, I'm making the changes in my head and I can't help it."

"Ed and I are going to talk this afternoon. He's got some news about films and some possibilities for next summer. I'll tell him you're becoming a published author."

"Tell Ed he's too far away on the West Coast. I'm sick of him being out there."

"I'll tell him you said so."

"I mean it."

She put her laptop on the couch and stood. She kissed me. She walked me into the hallway on her sore feet. She put her weight on her heels like a woman with a new pedicure.

"Okay, say hello to Ed for me."

"I will."

She kissed me one last time. Then she looked me in the eye. "She likes it, right?"

I nodded. She nodded. Then she turned around and heel-walked back into her room.

I called Ed from my cell phone on the ride home. He picked up on the third ring, his voice slightly out of breath. He had been out trying to change a tire on his truck. He had forgotten his phone inside, so he had to run in and grab it when it rang.

"Sarah's getting published," I said, driving through the rainy countryside. When Ed picked up, I looked for a place to pull over. "That piece she wrote for the *Alumni Magazine,* they liked it. It will run next issue probably."

"Good old Sarah. Congratulate her for me."

"I will, but call her sometime. She misses you."

"I miss her. And you. And New Hampshire, but Washington is an awfully pretty state. It's not a bad place to spend time."

"You shooting anything good?"

"I am, but listen. I want to run something by you. Are you on your cell?"

"Yes, but I'm finding a place to pull over. Hold on."

I steered the car off onto a small pull-out. Rain continued to fall. A few sodden leaves fell and adhered to the windshield. I cracked the window to get fresh air. The whole world smelled of wet leaves.

"So Mom called and she was a little spooky about Dad," Ed said. "Can you hear me okay?"

"Yes, fine. What about Dad?"

"She made a couple references . . . I don't know, maybe I'm reading too much into it."

"That he's having an affair?" I asked, my brain having difficulty with the notion.

"Dad? Oh, God no. You imagine? No, she was asking if I had noticed Dad being more forgetful when we talk on the phone. I don't know. It was weird. She didn't come out and say anything, but she kind of circled it. You hearing anything back there?"

"No, not a thing. Like Alzheimer's, you mean?"

"I don't know. That's the weird thing. I didn't want to come right out and ask Mom because that felt like an invasion of privacy. It's probably nothing. Mom worked it into other stuff . . . you know, when I was coming home, was this guy Morgan working me too hard. Basic Mom stuff."

"This is the first I'm hearing about it. Maybe we should ask when we're all together."

"Maybe," Ed said, "and maybe we should mind our own business. Mom and Dad are pretty private about things. We'll notice it if he really begins to change, won't we?"

"I guess so. I've got a sick feeling in my stomach. *Dad?*"

"I know. And maybe I misunderstood what she was asking. You know how Mom can be subtle when she wants to be. Dad's still pretty young. Probably Mom's just being paranoid. I didn't mean to dump this all on you, but I figured, who else am I going to ask? We can't do anything one way or the other, right?"

"Right," I said, although I wasn't entirely sure.

"Listen, let's change the subject. I have a lot of news from Morgan. We've been shooting this thing on tidal pools. Really interesting. There's a John Steinbeck tie-in . . . he was a big tide-pool guy. Anyway, Morgan said he liked how I was handling things and he thought maybe I could do more for his company. It's just a foot-in-the-door kind of thing, but it might build. If it does, he can pass things along to us. I figured you'd be psyched to hear it."

"I am. What kind of things?"

"Oh, scut work. Nothing big at first. But gradually we can be like little remoras and dine on the bits the shark doesn't eat. I'm doing a bunch of starfish shots. They're pretty cool, actually."

Ed made a sucking sound that was supposed to be like a remora fish suckering onto a shark, I guessed.

"You're insane," I said.

He made louder sucking sounds. Then he let it go.

"I've got to run, brother of mine. Keep an eye on Dad, okay? And get out here one of these days and see this place."

"Money."

"I know, I know, but get out here. I'll be home in a couple of months for Christmas anyway. Maybe not, but I think I will. Okay, I love you."

"Love you, too, Ed."

After we hung up I stayed and watched the leaves fall on the windshield. I smiled thinking of Ed's sucker sound. I thought of my dad, the possibility that he was beginning to fail, and that it didn't make sense. But maybe it did. I rolled down the window all the way and breathed a couple deep lungfuls of Vermont air. The late leaves fell softly through the autumn afternoon, their flight to the ground restless and drifting and fated.

A few months later, in the winter edition, Sarah's article appeared in a full, glossy layout. The story appeared nestled between sepia-tone photos from the 1940s and vivid shots of the current hikers.

We sat at Murphy's, a basement restaurant off the main street in Hanover, an advance copy of the magazine spread out between us. She had been paid $250 for the article and she treated us with the money.

"I'm in love with you," I said, because I was.

She smiled. She ate more French fries.

"It's a weird thing," she said, her face serious for a second. "This writing stuff. I've always wanted to do it. But you go off and you do something, and then you write about it, so you taste it twice. I didn't make that up, by the way. A poet said it, I forget who. So you taste it twice, and you experience it twice, but then it comes out and you see it in print. And you like it. I like *this,* believe me. But somehow it has to try and match the image you have in your head and it never can. Have you ever experienced anything like that? With film?"

"I have," I said, thinking of the screening of *Sky Top* years before.

"It's got something to do with the parts, and with the whole," she said.

I reached over and took her hand.

"This is what I want to do," she said, and pointed to the magazine. "This and more. Bigger. Deeper, but like this."

I held on to her hand and she squeezed my fingers. Then she crossed her eyes. I laughed.

The next week she received a call from the editor of *Yankee Magazine,* who had read the piece and asked her what other ideas she had and could she come down for a meeting.

13

"I WANT TO ASK SARAH TO MARRY ME," I said. "And I thought I should tell you first."

It was the night before Christmas, and I sat at the kitchen table with my father and mother. As soon as I spoke, my mother nodded and covered her face in her hands. My father reached over and placed his hand on her forearm.

"I think I speak for your mother when I say nothing would make us happier. We love Sarah, and have loved her from the day we met her," Dad said, the formality of his expression slightly comical. "You know that, Son."

My mom pushed out of her chair and came and put her arms around me. She hugged me. She rocked me a little. Then she kissed my forehead and pushed back my hair in a way she hadn't done in years.

"My baby," she said, and kissed me again on the forehead.

"Does Sarah know?" Dad asked.

"She suspects. We've talked about it in general. It seems like the right time. I haven't told you yet, but I got that internship with Ken Burns in Philadelphia for this last semester. Full course credit. Ed helped me, and Morgan Davis . . . anyway, it seems like the logical next step. I'll pick up some experience before we graduate. At the end of the summer, Ed should be done with the project he's doing with Morgan, and we can finally set up the Baker River Film Company on a full-time basis. That's always been the plan."

"That's wonderful," Dad said. "What will you live on?"

"I guess they have quarters for interns and a small stipend. Real small. The details are a little hazy right now, but it should work out."

"What about Sarah?" Mom asked, sitting again. "She'll finish school here, of course."

"We're ironing out the details, but, yes, she'll be here. We probably won't see each other much. She's writing. She actually has three chapters that built from an article she did. It's good. She might end up with a book out of it."

"Sounds like a plan," Dad said. "We're proud of you, Allard. That's quite an accomplishment to be asked to intern on a Burns project."

"Thanks, but Ed and Morgan Davis put in a good word for me. Anyway, there was a connection."

"Are you planning on using Grandma's ring?" Mom asked, changing the subject slightly.

"If that's okay?"

Mom stood and disappeared for a while. When she came back, she slid the box containing Grandma's engagement ring across the table toward me. I opened it. I knew the ring. It was an empire cut in a platinum setting. I had always planned to give it to Sarah.

"It should be cleaned, and maybe you could consider a new setting . . . to update it," Mom said, looking at the ring with me. "But it's a beautiful ring. Kind of a classic, 1930s look. I think it will be to Sarah's taste."

"When were you thinking about getting married?" Dad asked. "If she says yes, anyway."

"She'll say yes," Mom said, taking the ring for a second and holding it so it refracted light. She put it back on the table, but still kept turning it. "She's been saying yes all her life."

"Late summer," I said. "Ed needs to finish his project and that would give us a little time to plan. Mrs. P is likely to go a little over-the-top. But Sarah hasn't even said yes yet."

"It's as natural as rain," Mom said.

We heard a truck pull into the driveway.

"I think your brother just arrived," Dad said, leaning back and looking out the window. "He brought some cold weather with him, that's for sure."

I ran out to help Ed. He had driven his old Chevy S-10 truck all the way from Glacier National Park where with Morgan Davis he had been filming grizzlies as they prepared dens for the winter. He had a month off now, and he'd headed for home. When he stepped out of his truck, he looked like a mountain wild man—all hair and beard. He wore a University of Washington sweatshirt under a down vest, and a pair of jeans above his Vasque hiking boots. He always wore his Vasque boots.

"Damn it's cold back here," he said, but he smiled. It was a great, warm smile. My brother's smile.

We hugged. Ed didn't believe in perfunctory hugs. He squeezed me hard enough so that I had to squeeze back just to protect myself.

"You're all grown up, Allard," Ed said, letting me go. "That's great news about the internship. Morgan was really pleased."

"It's working out."

"The great plan, right? We will conquer the world," he said, making his voice sound a little like an archvillain's.

"Let's get inside. Mom and Dad are waiting."

He had only three bags, but he surprised me by pointing out a half dozen Christmas presents already wrapped. Ed never managed to get Christmas presents wrapped, certainly not thought out ahead of time, and when he asked me to grab them, I couldn't help asking him what had changed.

"Tanya wrapped them for me," he said, his breath making a white cloud in front of him.

"Tanya?" I asked.

"Part of Morgan's film crew."

"An important part?"

He looked at me. "Maybe."

"Maybe another worker for the Baker River Film Company?"

"Maybe." He laughed.

I led him inside. Mom met him at the door and hugged him, not even giving him enough time to put down his bags. Dad hugged him next. Then followed the usual excited chatter of a homecoming. Ed plunked down his bags, agreed he was hairy, agreed he probably was tired, agreed he needed something to eat, said the place looked great, smelled great, and he was home. As he sat at the kitchen table with us—Dad had pulled out a good bottle of brandy a client had given him and he poured us all small snifters—Ed said he had driven pretty much straight through; no, the weather wasn't bad, although he ran into snow around Chicago, lake-effect snow, he said, which might make a good topic for a documentary; and then he raised his glass of brandy and toasted the old homestead.

"It's good to be home," he said.

"It's good to have you both home," Mom said.

"And what's this?" Ed asked, pointing to the engagement ring. "You two setting a date?"

"If she'll have me," I said.

Where many brothers would have needed to make a joke, Ed simply put his hand softly on my shoulder.

"There's no better girl in the world," he said.

"Aren't you going to tell us we're too young?"

"Everyone's too young to get married. Or too old. That's how

I figure it. But you two? Everyone's waited for this day since you met."

"A late-summer wedding," Mom said. "Can you make it home?"

"I'll have to, won't I?"

"Have you talked to the Patricks?" Dad asked me.

"I talked to Charlie already and he gave his approval. He was very charming about it, actually. He said I was already like a son to him. I tried to talk to Mrs. P but she told me to go have a drink with Charlie and of course I had her blessings."

"Where's Sarah tonight?" Ed asked.

"They've got a house full of people," Mom said. "Last I heard, she was helping Mrs. P with food and things. She may be over later."

She didn't come over until very late, and then she tiptoed up to our bedroom and climbed into bed with me. She had climbed in with me a million times, but this time Ed, from the other bed, wondered why she didn't even say hello.

"I didn't know you were awake!" she said, and laughed.

Sarah hopped out of my bed and jumped on Ed. She gave him a kiss, then squealed that his whiskers rubbed her. She scurried back with me, claiming our bedroom had gotten even colder over the years.

"Ask him about Tanya," I said to Sarah.

"Tanya?" Sarah asked, sitting up and turning on the light. "Edward Keer, you're holding out on us. Who is Tanya? And what an exotic name."

"She's a gal who works with me on the Morgan team. That's all."

"A gal?" Sarah asked, obviously enjoying this. "A little more description, please."

"She's a woman I work with. She does sound work, especially, but she can direct, too. She went to Oregon State, so we have that kind of Northwest connection. She just started a couple weeks ago. I don't know her that well."

"She wrapped his Christmas presents," I said.

"No way!" Sarah said, and fell back on top of me, laughing. "Edward Keer, you're showing up with wrapped presents? Impossible. The world can end now. We've seen everything."

"She worked as a package wrapper in a department store one Christmas. She's good at it."

"I can't see you properly over there, but I bet you're blushing," Sarah said. "What does she look like? You must have pictures."

"I have her on film. I'll show you tomorrow. She's pretty."

"I want to see now!" Sarah said. "I won't be able to sleep if you hold out on me."

"Tomorrow," Ed said. "I'm tired."

Sarah beat him with a pillow.

"It's Christmas Eve," Ed said, holding his arms up for protection, "Santa will know if we're awake too late."

But he grabbed his camera from his backpack and thumbed it around for a while until he finally found the footage he wanted. Then he handed the camera over to Sarah.

"That's Tanya," Ed said.

She was beautiful. Tall and slender, she wore a heavy sweater in the footage and she held a spatula, apparently making pancakes. Ed did a little voice-over in the video, joking that this was Tanya, camp cook, who couldn't really cook, but was trying. Obviously flirting. She waved the spatula at him and told him to get lost. Then she looked directly into the camera. She looked young and happy and perfectly right for Ed.

"I don't even know her and I approve," Sarah said, running it back again. "She's perfect."

"Let's not get kooky," Ed said. "We hardly know each other."

Sarah made her voice deep, mimicking Ed: "I'll never get married. . . . I have my films to make. . . . I'll be outdoors, wrestling porcupines."

"So sue me," Ed said.

"What's her last name?" I asked.

"Poloski," Ed said. "An Irish girl."

"Tanya Poloski," Sarah said. "Tanya Keer. It works."

"You may be rushing things just a little," Ed said. "We didn't pick out china patterns."

"No one picks out china patterns anymore, Ed," Sarah said. "You boys are such dopes sometimes."

"Run a little more of that film," Ed said to Sarah. "And you'll see some raw footage on the Glacier grizzlies."

"Just ahead?" Sarah asked.

Ed nodded.

I watched over Sarah's shoulder. The footage—bears moving slowly along a ridgeline, one coming through the trees, a collection of them at a salmon run—glimmered with beauty. Ed had filmed it. I knew his style. The film had no narration, nothing to distract the eye. That would come later. The bears looked huge and sleepy and they often stood with snow whistling around them, their fur white, their great grizzly humps coated with moisture.

"It's amazing you're working with Morgan," I said. "This footage is beautiful, Ed."

"He's amazing. He is so good, you'd both be blown away. He worked with those grizzlies like they were puppies. He waded into the water with them . . . he had this idea of setting up a camera half in the water and half out. The lens was halved by the surface water, if you know what I mean, so you could see the bear sometimes up above, and sometimes below. Sometimes you even saw a salmon swim by. It was kind of like some of the shots we used to try on the Baker River, remember? Anyway, you could get a sense of the way a bear moves. But eventually one of the cameras tipped over and Morgan went right in while the bears were still there and he just talked to them, calm as anything, and he reestablished the shot, checking it, and the bears fished all around him. Of course, they were interested in the salmon run, not him, but still. He got a shot of a bear's claws hooking onto a salmon . . . the claws went right in and one of them came out through the salmon's mouth. It's going to be in the promo."

"When will it air?"

"Morgan's handed over a rough cut to the editing team. They do the next step. So, I don't know . . . probably a year from now. They usually film a year ahead, if not more. It depends on a ton of things."

"It's beautiful work, Ed," Sarah said, and gave Ed the camera back.

"I've talked to Morgan," Ed said, putting the camera aside. "He says we're in—all three of us. He says we can all work on the next shoot. He's doing eagles up near Anchorage. Next fall, probably. You'll be finished with the Burns thing, and Sarah, you're writing, I know, but you're signed on, too. If we work it right, it could be the first professional credit of the Baker River Film Company. The first paid one, anyway."

"It's happening," Sarah said.

"It'll be our first real joint project. And Morgan said he would recommend us for a few smaller projects he has coming up. An education company wants to do a series on songbirds . . . cardinals, robins, backyard stuff. Morgan has this idea that he can subcontract it out to us, and if we bring the film in, he will help us edit it. It's not big money, but it would be a solid first project. Ideal, really, for what we're trying to establish. We'll work under his supervision, but we'll have full autonomy. Sarah, are you in?"

"Absolutely."

"Then next fall we get it all started," Ed said. "Say, September . . . October at the latest. That will give me a chance to line things up."

"Will Tanya be on our team?" Sarah asked.

"She might be," Ed said. "You never know."

We talked for a while longer, then Ed dropped off. Sarah and I lay close together under the blankets. She had to leave to go back to her house, but it was warm under the covers and cold outside them. She whispered to me about Tanya and Ed, how happy she was, how she had never expected Ed would find a girlfriend. Then she told me about her house, who was visiting, what they planned for Christmas dinner, what presents she had left to wrap, and invited us all to come over. I held her close, promising to wake her in a few minutes. She said Santa was over Canada last she heard. She said if we could just stay awake, we might see him yet.

CHARLIE PATRICK HAD MANY TALENTS, but none better than his ability to build a superb Bloody Mary. He poured me one on Christmas morning as I waited for Sarah to find her skates. His Bloody Mary tasted of pickle juice, celery salt, and pepper. He made them cold and fresh and didn't stint on the vodka.

"That will set your sail for the day," Charlie said from behind his kitchen counter. They had refurbished the kitchen since the days when I first met Sarah, but the large window that looked out on the river was still in place, and so was the dentist chair. The same woodstove pushed heat at us.

"Thanks, Charlie. Where is everyone?"

"Still asleep. We played a massive game of pitch last night. It ran awfully late. It's like euchre, I guess, and a little like bridge. We've always played it. How's that Bloody Mary?"

"Actually, it's fantastic."

"Every man should know how to mix one special drink," Charlie said, pouring himself a Bloody Mary from his pitcher. "That's just a thought I had, but it may be true. I had a friend who made martinis . . . oh, my, what they did. And smooth. He was a purist. He took great pains with every detail."

Sarah skidded into the kitchen on a pair of wool socks. She wore a heavy black sweater under a down vest and ski pants that whistled as she came into the room.

"Corrupting my man, are you, Dad?" she asked.

"Having a Christmas toddy, that's all."

"Pour me a half, if you would, please," she said, going to the kitchen sink and running the faucet for a second. "I have to make it through this day."

"Maybe I should pour you a double, then," Charlie said.

"Mom said to baste the turkey. She'll be down in a half hour or so. She's just getting in the shower."

"She put it in at an unholy hour," Charlie said, sipping his Bloody Mary. "We're having a bonfire later. I have a bunch of brush to burn off, so we figured it would give us something to do and get us out of the house. It will be down by the river."

"Never miss a chance to burn something," Sarah said. "That's our motto."

"That's right," Charlie said. "And I figured we could burn off the wrapping paper. See, I'm smart that way."

After we finished our drinks, we stepped out into bright cold with our skates. The river lay below us and the sun pulled smoky light from it. Everything felt fresh and brittle. I held Sarah's hand as we skidded down the hill toward the river. A blue jay flew ahead of us, scolding and unhappy to see us disturbing the quiet. It finally settled in a dark pine, its blue coloring like a small Christmas bulb on an otherwise naked tree.

"Have you ever had a man put on your skates?" I asked Sarah.

"Put on my skates?"

"Yes, in a courtly way."

"So that I'm so helpless I need a man to put on skates?"

"Or so loved and admired that a man wants to do everything he can for your comfort."

"Better," she said. "Have at it."

She sat on a large rock and pushed her foot into my hands. I knelt in front of her and removed her boots, then slid her skates on. I tied them carefully. Sarah put her skates flat on the ground when I finished. She leaned over and kissed my cheek.

"Kind of corny, you old cornball," she said, "but kind of sweet."

"A man's work is never done."

I put on my skates, then we stepped onto the river. It felt good and solid and bumpy. The air burned with cold. We skated down toward my house, then broke through the cattails onto Turkey Pond. No one came out this way in winter and we skated in a circle, Sarah's hand in mine, the wind spilling into our eyes. She turned once or twice and buried her face on my shoulder. It felt good, though, to be out, to be moving, and Sarah seemed to share the feeling. We skated all the way across Turkey Pond, which was not far, but it brought us to the tree line where we saw three crows pecking at something in the new snow. When we approached, they jumped into the air, bird priests leaving a mass. Their wings caught the early light and reflected it back to us.

"Let's go back," I said. "You look cold."

"I'm okay when we're moving. But it's bitter. It feels good out here."

"Let's go upstream a little. We can skate to Canada, you know?"

"So I've heard."

"The great land."

"You'll get there one day, I bet."

We skated north, skated as Ed and I had skated all those years before. Whether Sarah knew where we were headed, I couldn't say. But when we reached the spot where we had first met, I took both her hands and knelt before her. She slipped one hand away from mine and put it over her eyes. She started to say something, but then stopped. Then she gave me back her hand.

"We met here, Sarah," I said, "and I've loved you from that moment until this one. I tried to think of some fancy way to say it, but the truth is I love you with everything I have. Will you marry me?"

She nodded. Then she nodded harder. Her eyes filled. She bit her lower lip.

I slipped her mitten off and reached into my pocket for the ring. I opened the antique box and took the ring out and tried it on her finger. It fit, but it was slightly large. Sarah held her hand up and looked at it for an instant. Then she hugged me.

"I'll marry you, Allard. I'll be your wife. Will you marry me?"

"Yes. I will."

"And you wanted to ask here, where I fell through the ice? It makes a circle, I guess."

I nodded.

"Did everyone know you were planning to ask me?"

I nodded again.

"And you had the talk with Dad?"

"And your mother, although she waved me off and told me to have a drink with Charlie. Can I stand up now?"

"I think you can."

"What do we do now?" I asked, standing.

"We tell everyone. But you need to know something, Allard."

I took her in my arms. "What?"

"We've always been married," she said. "That's what I believe."

"I believe it, too."

She moved her hand to where she could see the ring. "This is your grandmother's ring, isn't it?"

"Yes."

"Your mom showed it to me a long time ago," she said, still examining it. "She said she wanted me to have it."

"Well, now you do. We can reset it and have it cleaned."

"Cleaned, maybe, but not reset. I want it just as it is."

A strong wind hit us at that moment and Sarah closed her hand and leaned into me. When it passed, she made us write our initials in the ice with the toes of our skates. AK + SP. We kissed afterward. Then something strong and unpredictable entered the kiss. We pulled deeper, kissed harder, and the entire world seemed to be in the kiss. It was childhood and icy wind and snow and hemlocks. The wind released us for a moment, but we stayed together kissing, our initials catching ice flecks sometimes and sometimes letting them go.

IT TOOK A HALF HOUR to climb Sunrise Mountain the next afternoon, the day after Christmas. We followed a snowmobile trail, pulling three Flexible Flyers after us. They were old Flexible Flyers, yard-sale purchases from many years before. Ed's was the longest; mine was red, with red runners; Sarah's sled seemed more nimble and punchier, and the lettering on hers still called the sled a DEMON CATCHER.

"I told you the track would be frozen solid," Ed said. "We're going to have a fast run."

We had debated whether the sledding would be good. We followed a branch off Corridor 5, a major snowmobile byway. Our hill, Sunrise Mountain, belonged to Tom Loftus, a local barber. We had sledded it for years. Now we stood at the top, the Baker River Valley spread out before us. If we strained and looked to the right, we could see Sarah's house. Our house lay directly below us. The river tied everything together like white string.

"Too fast, if you ask me," Sarah said, her breath a cloud in front of her. "It's going to be slick."

"When was the last time we did this?" Ed asked.

"It's got to be a few years," I said. "I don't think we've done it while any of us were in college."

"We should mount a cam to one of the sleds," Ed said. "It would be a mad angle for a shot."

"Remember when Natasha was young?" Sarah asked. "She used to run with us and bark because she couldn't figure out how we managed to go so fast on our bellies. It made her nuts. Now she's so old she just wants to stay by the woodstove."

We turned the sleds to face downhill and then we sat. It felt good to be outside after a day of feasting and family. The weather had softened somewhat, but it was still cold and bright. Now and then during the night we heard Turkey Pond shift in its bed, the small accompanying booms like heat thunder on a summer night.

"So, Sarah," Ed said, putting his hands behind him and squinting up at the sky, "I have a wedding request."

"Don't you start, too," Sarah said. "Did you hear our mothers planning the wedding last night? The whole thing went from zero to one hundred miles an hour in about two minutes. They had coffee together again this morning so they could talk some more."

"This one won't interfere. I want to take Allard on a bachelor hike this summer before the wedding. Show him the best fishing in the world. My treat. Up in the Wind Rivers in Wyoming."

I looked at Ed. He nodded. It was news to me.

"When?" Sarah asked. "And I want to come."

"Sorry, you're not invited," Ed said, and grinned. "This is going to be a bachelor hike. I have to talk to Allard about the facts of life. Birds and bees."

"Not fair."

"You could come," Ed said, "but I figured you'd be at the tail end of wedding craziness."

"I probably will be. Unless we elope. Why don't we elope, Allard?"

"Okay by me."

"They've already figured out the seating will be on hay bales," Sarah said. "The Moms. These sensible women are already going nutty."

"We'll just go three days," Ed said. "A day up, a day at the lake, a day coming down. Maybe four days, tops. I know a place and the fly-fishing is spectacular. It's Double-L Lake up in the Winds, not far from the glacier. What's the name of the glacier?"

"I don't know," I said.

"Anyway, a guy I work with knows it and I have all the topos and everything else. Allard, you can fly out and meet me and we'll drive back together. I'll work it out so we'll leave plenty of time to get back, so don't worry, Sarah-Pants."

"You have to promise me you will be back in time to do what he needs to do."

"So promised," Ed said, raising his hand.

"So you guys get to escape the last-minute pressure while I deal with a runaway wedding?"

"That sounds about right," Ed said.

Sarah looked at me. "Did you put him up to this?"

I shook my head.

"Bloody bastards," she said.

"Afterward, we get the Baker River Company started," Ed said. "It all falls into place. The master plan."

"Don't try to sugarcoat your little getaway," Sarah said. "You're both rats and you know it. But okay. You can have him for a few days. Just be sure to bring him back on time without any noticeable bruises or casts on his legs. And take a lot of pictures, because The Moms are already talking about doing a sort of running slide show of us. Deal?"

"Deal," Ed said.

Then Ed looked at us.

"I hope you both know how much I love you," he said in his simple, plain way. "I am so completely and utterly happy for you both that I can't even put it into words. You two make everyone around you happy and proud to know you."

Sarah leaned off her sled and hugged him.

"You're an old softie," Sarah said, releasing him.

"I mean it."

"Well, we love you, too."

I rubbed Ed's shoulder.

"You stupid mutts!" Ed laughed, suddenly shooting his legs back and pushing forward with his hands like an alligator. It was an old game, a no-holds-barred race down the mountain. His sled began to pick up speed, and Sarah whooped and pushed after him. I went last. After a second or two, it was all speed, all crazy light flashing by, and the sleds evened out. Ed maintained the lead, but I caught Sarah's sled and grabbed the back runner and shot myself forward. She tried to grab my runner in turn, but I veered away, and then we hit the fast part, a slope we called Speedball, and I tried to edge past Ed on his right. He tried to grab my steering yoke, but I fought him off, and Sarah tried to slip by on his other side. Ed lunged and tried to cut her off, which gave me an opening and I shot by, the leader, and the wind made my eyes water and the snow nearly blinded me, but I did not drag my toes to slow down. I took every bump like a soft sock to the gut, and when I crossed the line— past an old, hollowed-out oak—I pushed up my hands, champion of the universe, the sledding champ of Christmas and forever after.

14

O N THE LAST DAY of Christmas break, a week after Ed had headed back to Washington, Sarah drove me to the Amtrak station in White River Junction, Vermont. I was packed and ready to go to Philadelphia. It was a scratchy, bitter day and we had not had snow in a week, so everything was worn-out and dirty and no longer white. Clouds refused to break up or leave and the weather report called for rain turning to ice later in the day.

"I don't want you to go," she said, driving with her hands at two and ten.

"I don't want to go, either, but I've got to do this."

"Ken Burns. It's so amazing. Do you know how amazing that is?"

"I know. I grew up watching him. Mom made us watch the baseball film and the jazz film. But I liked the one on Jack Johnson the best."

"The prizefighter?"

"Yep."

She looked away from the road for just a second and took my hand. Then she returned her attention back to the icy street. We came down the long hill from Route 91 into White River Junction proper. The windshield wipers moaned and flicked water off and the tires sounded like sand spilling.

"Can we talk about the wedding for a second?" Sarah asked.

"Of course. Fire away."

"I don't want to be one of those people who are always talking about their wedding. I don't. You know that, right?"

"I know that."

"Well, it's growing a little bit. Mom wants to invite some relatives from Michigan that I didn't even know we had. So there's that."

"I want to marry you, Sarah, so however that happens is okay with me."

She looked at me. Then she turned back to the road. "Anyway . . . how would you feel about Ed being your best man and my bridesmaid?"

I laughed. "I'm having this image of him dressed down the middle in a tux and a bridesmaid gown. Half and half."

"Besides you, he's my best friend, Allard. I've thought about it. The Moms will take care of anything I need as a bride. You know, gown stuff and flowers. I wouldn't expect Ed to do that. But Ed is the person I want as a witness to our marriage. You know what I mean."

"I do know what you mean. I think it's a wonderful idea. I completely approve."

"Good. I wanted to ask you before I asked him."

"He'll love it. He's going to be a busy man at the wedding. When will you ask him?"

"Maybe I'll call him tonight. Don't say anything until I do, okay?"

"I won't. I think it's a wonderful gesture and he'll be moved by it. Have you noticed what a sentimental guy he's turning into?"

"It's one of the things I like best about him. He's been with us every step of the way . . . even in the first minutes when we met. He belongs beside us when we marry."

"We still get the bachelor hike, though, don't we?"

"You do, you bums."

We got to the train station early. After Sarah turned off the car, she slid across the front seat and climbed on top of me. We kissed for a while. She unbuttoned her coat and spread it around us so that our heat could stay trapped.

"We're the youngest people I know getting married," Sarah said, still kissing me. "Do you think we're too young? No one gets married right out of college."

"We're already married, you said."

"That's true, we are," she said, and kept kissing me.

"So then it's not an issue. It doesn't matter how old we are. We've been married almost ten years."

"You've been skipping anniversaries. Do you know we're being married on a full moon? In August? That has to be lucky. I think it's the hunter's moon. I'm not sure."

"Am I supposed to think and kiss you at the same time?"

"Not if I'm doing it right."

"One or the other. You can't have both."

A little later we broke off and went inside a small, local bar on a road parallel to the station. We had an hour or so to kill. We ordered two Long Trails and a plate of French fries from a woman bartender, then we sat at a tiny table by a large picture window looking out on the street.

"Do you have any change?" Sarah said. "I want to put some music in the jukebox. They have a jukebox."

"Where?" I asked, turning to see.

"Behind you."

I dug in my pocket and gave her what change I had. I drank some of my beer while I waited for her.

"Come on and dance with me," Sarah said, grabbing a fry and dotting it in a pool of ketchup I put beside them.

I stood as "Who Let the Dogs Out?" came on the jukebox.

"Really?" I asked.

She started jumping up and down and dancing spastically. The bartender didn't seem to care one way or the other. So I danced. I did every stupid dance I could think of. Eventually the music changed to "The Lion Sleeps Tonight." We slow-danced and we sang "Owinga way, owinga way" into each other's ears. Now and then we swung past the table and grabbed French fries. And when the lead singer went into his falsetto riff near the end of the song, Sarah kissed me and led me back to the table.

"I like the way you dance," she said, squirting ketchup on the fries. "But they don't say *o-wing-a-way,* they say *wing-away*."

"I don't know what they say, but they don't say *wing-away*."

"Yes, they do. It's about flying away."

"Have you ever listened to that song?"

She looked at me. Then she took two French fries and turned them into gopher teeth at the front of her mouth. She gummed her bottom lip and crinkled her nose.

"What's got into you, Sarah Patrick?" I asked.

"I'm feeling sad and I'm acting goofy so I won't think about it."

"It's not very long, really."

"I know. But it's the farthest we've ever been apart."

"That's not true. You went to Glacier and Yellowstone once."

"I mean as us," she said, and I knew what she meant.

I reached across the table and took her hand. Rain fell and sometimes it looked like snow and sometimes it caught the light from the streetlamps and glistened like silver cobwebs. We watched until it was time to go.

✦ ✦ ✦

Sarah flew to Philadelphia for Easter. We hadn't seen each other for nearly two months, although we talked every day, sometimes more than once. I picked her up at the airport and brought her to Center City, where I had booked a room at the Kite and Lightning, a B&B recommended to me by a local. The B&B was more than I could afford, but it was a holiday and the only time I would see Sarah before graduation. The Ken Burns crew had scattered; the city, too, cleared out, and when I called the B&B hostess, Keysha, she told me only one other couple had booked a room, so she could improve our reservation.

"We have a fireplace," I said, and Sarah lifted herself across the front seat of the Camry I had borrowed from a fellow intern, for the price of dropping him off and picking him up at the airport, and kissed my neck.

"We are not leaving the room for a long time, are we?" she asked.

"No, absolutely not."

"Are you exhausted? It sounds like you've been working like crazy."

"I have, but so have you."

"Dad gave me two hundred bucks to have fun with this weekend," Sarah said. "And don't turn your face into a prune and talk about not using my family's money. We won the lottery, for goodness' sakes."

"I have no pride anymore," I confessed. "All I want is a soft bed and you."

We parked a block away and had to struggle with our bags, but Keysha answered the second time we rang the bell. She was Russian, we guessed when she hustled away from us to turn something off in the kitchen. Eastern Europe, anyway. She was tall and slender and wore her hair pulled back in a severe ballerina's bun.

"You'll love this room," Keysha said when she returned. She had a mild accent that sometimes emphasized the wrong syllable. "I'm glad to see you're young. Many old people use this room because of the price. But it should be used by young people, too."

It turned out to be a lovely room: brick walls, a trim bathroom with a deep tub, a large window looking out at the William Penn statue, a king-size bed with extraordinary pillows and bedclothes, and a small Rumford fireplace with a fire already set and ready to light.

"Fire?" I asked.

"And wine, please."

She disappeared into the bathroom. I lit the fire. It caught immediately and the draft puffed out once, then drew in the smoke smoothly. It was a shallow firebox and heat soon explored the room. I popped the cork on the bottle of wine as Sarah came out. She had brushed her hair and washed her face. She looked like my Sarah.

"Who is this strange man in my room?" she asked, coming to take the glass of wine I handed her. "I feel as though I should recognize him, but I can't be certain. You resemble someone I used to know."

"You look like a complete stranger to me."

"I'm Lady Farnsworth of Philadelphia."

"Nice to meet you, Lady Farnsworth."

Then we stopped playing. I kissed her. The kiss grew and exploded and we put down our wine and we backed toward the bed. The fireplace popped and crackled and we shed our clothes as we went. Then it was all bedding, and Sarah, and the light of the fire catching her limbs, her hair. I told her I loved her, and she kissed me until I couldn't talk any longer. And afterward I slipped out of bed and put another log on the fire and she said she liked seeing a naked man by firelight.

"Come back to bed," she said. "My bridesmaid and I have been going over wedding plans and I need to fill you in."

"How is your bridesmaid?" I asked as I climbed back into bed with our glasses of wine. I handed her one. We propped enough pillows behind us so we could watch the fire. Outside, the afternoon light stretched and quieted against the buildings. It was a spring light; the hard edge of winter had finally withdrawn.

"My bridesmaid has been very thoughtful, although he was in a bit of a tizz when he heard that he was supposed to throw a shower for me."

"I can imagine Ed's panic about a shower."

"Well, I let him off the hook. Mom is going to throw the shower. Ed probably won't be there. It's a little irregular, but what the heck. He asked if he could make one toast to cover both of us, and I said yes. Is that okay with you?"

I nodded.

"You should understand, too, that I have given up any power over the wedding. You know how King Kong comes back in chains, and then he goes after Fay Wray and climbs the Empire State Building? Well, the wedding has just broken its chains in the past few weeks. King Kong is about halfway up the Empire State Building and acting ticked off."

"Are both The Moms King Kong? Or is it the wedding?"

"The wedding. The Moms are just planes circling and shooting at it. I really think this metaphor works."

"And you're Fay Wray?"

"More or less."

"I notice I don't have a part in this movie."

"You're Fay Wray's intrepid love interest. The guy in the pith helmet with a thin upper-lip mustache."

"I see."

"I thought you'd be flattered."

"Hmmmm. I'm not so sure."

"My dad's been pretty terrific about the grounds and the tent and liquor. He's hired about ten kids to work on the yard and he's out there with them, trying to get the place just right. He even hired a backhoe and leveled off some of the land beside the river so the tent could sit just right. It is going to be pretty, sweetie. Lester Hawkins asked if I wanted Early and Late to be bridesmaids."

"How's your ring doing?" I took her hand and held it up to the light.

"Dazzling. No, not *dazzling*. That's the wrong word for it. *Understated beauty*. That's what I've decided it has. I want to look at it in the firelight later."

"Are you hungry?"

"Yes, except I don't want to leave this room."

"What if the man in the pith helmet went out and got you something delicious to eat and brought it back to you? Would Fay Wray like that?"

"Fay Wray would pledge her undying love to her pith-helmeted man."

"And what kind of food would Fay Wray want?"

"Grapes and cheese. Or a cheese steak or a bowl of Fruity Pebbles."

"That's easy."

"I'll come with you, though."

"It's a man's job to bring food back from the wilds."

"I'm glad you understand that."

"I'm a husband in training."

"You certainly are."

But I didn't leave. Not then. We began kissing again and then neither of us could leave. It was only later, when the sun had fallen behind the buildings, that we both ventured into Center City, the wind whipping in a spring rush, Sarah's arm linked under mine. And we played a game of identifying pigeons, wondering if this one or that one shared a family tree with Sky Top or Foggy or Succotash.

15

THE WEDDING WAS LESS THAN two weeks away when Ed, true to his word, met me in his pickup at the small Wyoming airport, then drove us to the trailhead.

"Dries for cutties," he said, then swung his pack off the tailgate and hoisted it onto his back. Then he snapped the waist belt around his hips and yanked it tight. He did it so easily, and with such a sense of familiarity, that I felt a tiny bit intimidated. The backpack looked well traveled, and Ed, underneath it, adjusted the shoulder straps with a casual tug here and there. My brother. He looked more than ever like a mountain wild man, with a great hedge of hair and wide, solid body. His enormous beard that had turned red with the Western sun.

We hadn't spent much time planning this trip since Ed first mentioned it, but here we were up in the remote Wind River Range of Wyoming.

"Come on," he said to me. "We're burning daylight."

"Give me a second," I said, finishing with my pack. I took a deep breath and tried to get the pressure right in my ears.

"You still jet-lagged?"

"No, I'm okay. I feel a little altitude headache, if you want to know the truth."

"Water," he said, and pushed his copper-colored Nalgene bottle at me.

"I'm okay."

"I told Sarah I'd get you back alive," he said, pushing the water at me again. "If you're feeling poorly, we can camp here for the night and see how you feel tomorrow. There's no pressure, Allard."

"I'll be okay."

"This is your last trip as a single man. You don't want to be sick through the whole thing."

I swung the pack onto my back. I looked at him and let him see that I felt fine. He smiled. He jammed the tailgate of his Chevy S-10 closed, then made me wait a minute.

"Sarah said we need pictures for the slide show she's doing at the wedding," Ed said, pulling a small digital camera out of a baggy pocket in his cargo shorts. "If we put it on the corner of the truck and move back, we can get us both in it."

"Let's do it later."

"Sarah said that's the deal, remember? I get to take you away on a bachelor hike and she gets pictures for the reception. Don't fight me on this."

I shrugged. He turned around and looked at the mountain range behind us. In the late-afternoon light the Wind River Range had turned orange and red and gold. A young moon had come up between two of the peaks and hung on the horizon. A string of pines ran off behind us as far as we could see.

"Not a bad shot," Ed said, bending and maneuvering to look through the viewfinder. "Move back so I can line it up. Now move left. I want to get the moon in it. A little more. Okay, now hold it."

He pushed the timer buttons. The camera emitted a few high-pitched beeps. He hustled over beside me, his backpack making a clanking noise as he jogged, and threw his arm around my shoulders above the pack.

"Say *Sarah,*" he said, his face straight ahead at the camera.

"Sarah."

"Not yet. Now."

We both said, "Sarah." The flash fired.

I started to move, but Ed grabbed me and kept me in place. "I set it for three shots. Do something funny."

"I'm all out of funny," I said.

"Make a face."

So I did. I stuck out my tongue and crossed my eyes. The camera beeped, then flashed.

"Squat down," Ed said.

I squatted with difficulty. The pack felt enormous on my back. He stood behind me and put his hands on my shoulders. He leaned down and put his head above mine. A totem pole. Ed and Allard Keer. Two brothers at the start of a hike in the Wind River Mountains, Wyoming.

"Keep the bride happy," Ed said after the camera snapped the last photo.

"The wedding thing has gotten a little crazy," I said afterward, fiddling with the backpack straps to get them comfortable. "You wouldn't believe it. It's just like she predicted. . . . I had to talk Sarah out of coming with me. She wanted to sneak away with us and forget about it all. The Moms have gone loopy with all their plans. I mean around the bend, no joke. We're going to end up with more than two hundred people."

"That sounds like a lot. There's only eight hundred people in the town."

"She's an only daughter and they have family scattered everywhere. It's a one-time thing. Our side is inviting about eighty people, so it just grows."

"You guys should have run off," Ed said, retrieving the camera. "I thought that was the plan. I can't believe we even know eighty people to invite."

"A wedding is like a monster no one can stop. It's like it has its own life and it just keeps feeding and getting bigger. Sarah calls it King Kong. But you're her bridesmaid, so you probably know all this already."

"Yes, I wanted to ask you. Am I a bridesmaid or a best man on this trip?"

"I think this is your best-man hat."

"Okay. How's your head now?"

I shrugged.

He grabbed my shoulders and looked at me. He smiled. I knew it was a moment for one of his ceremonies, and I tried to turn and start up the trail. But he wouldn't let me. Ed believed in moments.

"I love you, Allard," Ed said, his hands strong on my shoulders. "Sarah is the kindest, warmest, smartest woman in the world and you are a lucky man. And she is a lucky woman."

He hugged me. I hugged him back. He nodded when we pushed away.

"Dries for cutties," he whispered, which meant dry flies thrown to cutthroat trout. That's why we were headed into the Winds. We planned to fish Double-L Lake, a legendary trout pond located around twelve thousand feet elevation, not far beneath the Gannett Glacier.

"Dries for cutties," I repeated, and we punched knuckles.

Ed slid the camera back in his pocket. He tightened his waist strap again. I knew he had been out in Alaska shooting footage of the elk rutting season. He looked fit and tan and happy. Maybe thinner.

"You're getting married," he said. "It's hard to believe, and at the same time absolutely obvious."

"I am getting married."

"The whole thing is working out the way we said it would," he said, referring to some earlier conversations we had held about our film company. "Just like that."

"Let's hike. We've got to make some miles if we want to get in-and-out in time. I can't miss my own wedding."

"It's more than a week off."

We headed up the trail. The Wind Rivers rose above us.

THE SOUND OF A TIN CUP hitting in rhythm to my brother's stride. His backpack large and blue, a rectangle on the trail in front of me. His voice, his legs, his Vasque hiking boots. Late-afternoon light. Water splashing in his Nalgene, the liquid wash of springwater down my throat and into my intestines. Gorp. Cashews and M&M's and raisins. The salt of the nuts and the sweetness of the raisins mixing. Straps digging into my shoulders, my feet tired and hot and steady. A cloud lit by mountain sunlight, its shape a boulder rolling down the sky. Magpies in the dusk flying and landing on a branch, six of them, staring at us. Switchbacks. Sweat and the chill of the sun going behind the mountains. Then the relief of the pack slipping off, a ring of stones, a campsite. The weight of the pack still on my back long after the pack had been shucked. The memory of the weight also on me when we turned to gaze at miles of mountains, vistas, the great Rockies stretching up and away. A valley thousands of feet below. My brother moving effortlessly around the fire ring, camping, bringing water to boil, both of us now in fleeces pulled on over our heads. The day cut in half and turning colder. Now and then the thought of Sarah waiting, swarmed by catering requests, hosting details, showers. Sarah, who would have preferred to be with us, to be in the outdoors, the third leg of our milking stool. And then nightfall, darkness, the pine fire the only light besides our headlamps. A nip of brandy from Ed's old flask. Cheers to us, to Sarah. Ed in the prime of his life, smiling, joyous, alive to the world, my brother under the stars.

"I've talked to Morgan," Ed said from his sleeping bag. "He says we're in this fall. He talked to Ken Burns and Burns loves you. It sounds as though you did a great job down there. So now it's all definite. He is giving us three shoots, all songbirds for kids. We'll get the raw footage, then supervise the editing. Meanwhile, he's doing bees next. How they pollinate the grass crops out west. Next spring, probably."

We reclined without a tent, looking up at the stars. It was cold outside our sleeping bags. We used our backpacks as pillows. The fire had dwindled down to red coals.

"I'm proud of you, Ed."

"Well, I'm proud of you. You worked with Ken Burns. I mean, you couldn't get better training."

"I want to do animals, though."

A shooting star traced its way across the sky. Two more followed in rapid succession, then nothing else happened for a while.

"The Baker River Film Company. How long have we been talking about that?"

"A long time," I said. "Forever."

"What about Sarah?"

"She thinks she has a book contract."

"Seriously?" Ed asked, rising up on his elbow to look at me.

"It looks like it. She sent her manuscript to an agent in New York and the agent thinks she can sell it. In fact, there's a chance it might even go big. Animal ethics, you know, her stuff. How do we use animals, is it justifiable? All those themes she's been examining since she was a kid. She writes beautifully. It came out of an article she did for a magazine."

"That's wonderful," Ed said. "That's really perfect."

"She can write anywhere. And the book is already finished, so she's ready to move on to the next project. She'll come with us, no problem. You know how good she is with film."

"I always knew she would write something important. She was always reading."

"And taking care of animals."

Ed pushed back onto his sleeping bag. "You know that saying," he asked, his hands behind his head, "that if you conceive of a thing, it will come into the world? That's how I feel right now. We've been talking about our film company for so long . . . and Sarah has been part of it, too. It's working out, is what I mean. Even when we didn't know how we were going to do it, I knew it would happen. You know Charlie Patrick contacted me and wants to be an investor? He wants to back us. Have you talked to him about it?"

"A little. I think he prefers talking to you because you're not his daughter's boyfriend."

"Husband," Ed said.

"Not yet."

"Anyway, the point is we have a chance to launch this thing. We really do."

"It's all I've ever wanted."

"Me, too," Ed said. "The fact that it might be happening blows me away."

"You said you were still seeing Tanya. Is it getting serious?"

"I guess so," Ed said.

"You want her in on the Baker River stuff?"

"Well, we can all talk about it. She's talented. And I do like her. She's pretty awesome in a lot of ways. She's bummed she can't be at the wedding, but you can meet her in the fall when things get rolling. Actually, that's not very long from now. But she wanted to come East and meet everyone. She's in another wedding . . . a childhood friend, so she had to be there."

"I can't wait. Mom has already married you off to her."

A little later he fell asleep. I stayed awake, looking up at the stars. A wind fell out of the mountains and carried a few sparks from our fire down the trail. I listened to my brother's breathing. I thought of Sarah, always Sarah, and soon she came to me. I felt her spirit, and it was mixed with the pine smells and the bright stars above us. A little later a coyote called. In time others joined it, their cries plaintive and shrill, their strangled voices like door springs old and rusty. I felt for a moment an odd, disquieting sensation. *Something wicked this way comes,* I thought, remembering the old line. What was it from? Was it a title? I tried to dismiss it, but a tinge of foreboding passed through me and would not leave. The coyotes continued to call around us, and it was not until I matched my breathing to Ed's breathing that I began to fall asleep.

THE NEXT MORNING we crossed the peak in a thunderstorm. It wasn't smart, but we were trapped above the timberline and it was either go forward or back. Electricity sizzled everywhere. I tasted it in my mouth. The fine hair along my neck went up and I thought about the metal on our backpacks, how the frames served as perfect conductors. We could be fast fried like fish, complete with grill marks across our hides. We moved as rapidly as we could, our bodies leaning forward in a near jog. Rain fell in broad curtains, soaking everything. It turned the trail wet, too, and so we hurried like guys in street shoes hopping past puddles on their way to work, careful where we placed our feet, but intent on getting under cover.

"This is dumb," Ed yelled to me as we crested the peak. His voice had to cut across the wind. "We could get 220-ed."

It took me a second to realize he meant the size and shape of an electrical current.

"Suggestions?" I yelled.

"Keep going."

"We're supposed to know better," I yelled again, this time with a crazy, giddy feeling rising up in me. "We're supposed to be outdoorsmen."

"There are no outdoorsmen! Just guys running around in the woods."

"My leg hairs are standing up."

"St. Elmo's fire!"

In ten minutes the storm passed. We watched it tumble across the eastern peaks, the sun slicing the last of it away. A soft rainbow arched across the sky a few minutes later. It did not pass all the way to the ground, but faded into quiet colors that in time became white sunlight. The whole world dripped. We slowed. Ed turned back to me and laughed.

"That was a frog choker," Ed said, using a bandanna to wipe water off his face and legs. "We might have timed our traverse better."

"It didn't look like rain this morning. I thought they were calling for clear weather."

"Just a freak storm. No biggie except we were at elevation. Did you taste the electricity?"

"Like licking a battery. A nine-volt."

"We'll dry as we walk. Let's keep going. We're almost there."

A half hour later we began seeing the pond through pine branches as we descended into the bowl that held the water. It appeared blue and soft, like a bird's chest tucked against the green of the trees. A series of small switchbacks led us down the final approach. I smelled water and mud and felt the sun digging into my pack and drying it. Ed let out a big whoop when he saw a fish jump. A dozen other rises puckered the water. "Dries for cutties," Ed chanted, and he wouldn't stop until I joined him.

We set up camp away from the water. Ed advised that bears walked the shoreline looking for fish or other food, and it was better if you didn't block their way with your tent. We arranged our gear next to a large, flat rock that served as a makeshift table for us. We doubted we would need the tent, but we set it up anyway. Then we strung up our fly rods and went fishing.

We tied on Hornbergs and each caught a fish on the first cast. Cutthroats. Ed whooped again and this time I joined him. Ed said his streamer had been hit three times before the final fish managed to take. We released the fish, but we each had another one on in moments. Cutthroats continued to rise all around the pond. The mountains threw their reflections onto the water. The rain had left the day washed and perfect.

"Are you getting as many hits as I am?" I asked Ed after we had fished a quarter hour. He stood on a boulder only a dozen feet from me, his fly line a great, hazy circle of water and color. "It's almost unfair."

"This pond is jammed with fish. Nobody gets in here. There's no fishing pressure at all."

"Every cast I get two or three hits," I said, raising the rod tip and hooking another fish. "Almost takes the fun out of it."

"Almost, but not quite. Does Sarah approve of you fishing?"

"She's not like that. She's not militant about animal rights. She just does the best she can."

"Another fish," Ed said, his rod bending with the weight.

Then a nice thing happened. On the next cast, after Ed released his fish, our shadows joined. I noticed it almost immediately, but when I looked up, I realized Ed saw it, too. Both of our shadows stretched across the water, and as he moved, I moved. Our arms and wrists worked the fly rods in the same rhythm, and our fly lines turned vaporous whirls around our heads. We might have been a coin, or a single dark cutout from the afternoon sun. The angle of the rays had played a trick and thrown Ed's shadow into mine. Perhaps my shadow looked slightly larger as a result, and at times our arms moved in minutely different cadences, but we shared one light. Ed began to laugh, and I did, too, and finally I told him we needed to cast. Our lines zipped out and broke the shadow, and I understood that we had been occupying the same outline of darkness in an otherwise bright world. For an instant, like parallel hands on a sundial, we had told the exact same time, had occupied the same slant of daylight. We did it a second time, just for fun, and Ed matched his arm motion to mine perfectly.

"You believing this?" Ed asked, his eyes trained on our movement across the water.

"Weird, I know," I said, my eyes watching, too.

"Our shadows are lined up exactly."

"That should mean something. Or maybe it happens all the time and we just don't notice it."

"It's because I'm a little higher than you on this rock. It has to be, right? And the angle of the sun has to be perfect."

"But our motions are the same," I said, "that's what's weird."

"We're brothers."

I let my line go. Ed released his after the next back cast. Then the sun moved a degree to the west and my shadow began to pull away from his. My silhouette stretched across the water and a trout went after my fly and broke the calm surface. I landed the fish in the reflection of snow on the mountain. The whiteness rippled and spread and the fish rose from the water as if from heaven.

WE HIKED THE NEXT DAY toward the peak and turned around at three. By the time we made it back to camp the sun had settled behind the mountains. We fished for a while and caught as many fish as the day before. The weather remained perfect, but by early evening the temperature dropped. We pulled on fleeces and made a fire. Ed cooked four filleted trout directly in the wood coals, their bodies wrapped in foil. He made a big voodoo deal of mixing in a spice barrage he called Trail Spice. It had a little of everything, he said, and was presented to him in a small aspirin bottle by a woman he knew in Montana. She was an outfitter and a cook, he explained, who fed the camp during the grizzly photo shoot.

"Oh, she could cook," he said, sprinkling the Trail Spice onto the fish. "I promise you, every man there asked her to marry him, but she refused. She said she had been married twice and that was enough. She was from Colorado originally. She hummed John Denver tunes while she cooked. I've never seen anything like it. Her name was Janice."

"You eat a lot of salmon on the shoot?"

It was our last night in camp and we both had a tin cup of brandy from Ed's flask. Ed moved around the fire and poked things in and out, lifted things clear and put them back in the flames. It was an art and he was good at it. Now and then he stopped to sip his brandy.

"Lots of salmon, of course," he said, his hand up to block some smoke from his eyes, "but they get so beat-up by the time they make it upstream that some of them lose their flesh as soon as you pick them up. Icky, kind of. But she turned them into stews and soups . . . she had a Dutch oven that she wouldn't let anyone touch or clean. She had a whole system, believe me. She turned out pies and tarts . . . best tarts I've ever eaten. *Only* tarts I've ever eaten."

He laughed and stepped sideways to be away from the smoke.

"So, do you really think you and Tanya might have a future?" I asked. "You haven't said exactly."

"I just don't know if I'm cut out for it. I like Tanya a lot, but the thought of settling in and raising kids, I can't see it somehow. And I say that with full comprehension that you're about to go through that process. But you have Sarah and it makes sense. It's always made sense. Me? I don't know. I seem to meet a lot of women who have *Coyote* or *Fireweed* in their names. Hippie chicks, sort of. It's my work and where it takes me, I guess."

He poked at something, then danced back a few steps to escape the smoke. He put his foot up on the rock that served as our table.

"Eat that cheese," I said, nodding my chin toward a wedge of cheddar cheese we had sliced on the rock. "Saves me from carrying it out."

"The thing is," Ed said, diving back at the fire after he had scooped up the cheese, "that women tend to see me as a friendly-bear sort of guy. You know. The guy to help them move a dining room table, but not necessarily to take to bed."

"Come off it. That isn't true. What about Tanya?"

"It's true, she likes me. But I've never been a chick magnet. Women like me. I'm not saying they don't, but they don't get all misty about me. I don't mean to say I'm not serious about Tanya. I am. I'm not counting it out as a possibility. I'd like to be a dad, anyway. I would. I think it's because of our dad. You ever feel that way?"

I nodded.

"Here's to Mom and Dad," he said, and raised his glass.

I toasted him back.

"Dad was just so good with us," Ed said, using two sticks to begin lifting the trout out onto the rock. "Mom, too, but in a different way. Dad helped us be men. It sounds all weird when you talk like this, but it's true. He never made it look hard. He just spent time with us."

"I can smell those spices now. But you're right. Dad was great at being a dad. No easy thing."

"These should be done." Ed motioned toward the trout. "You hungry?"

I nodded.

I helped him set things out. We had fresh trout, cheese, crackers, peanut butter, and trail mix. Ed said he could cook up some soup, but we decided against it. The trout turned out perfectly—fresh and soft and succulent. Our hike had made us hungry. We ate everything we could, and by the time we finished, the sun had gone down sufficiently to throw its last light against the tallest peak across the pond. "Alpine glow," one of us said, and we watched it slowly crawl off the mountainside.

"We have to finish the brandy," Ed said. "Don't want to carry it back."

"It's only good camping etiquette," I said, toasting.

"We should bury all the fish entrails and the bones. I'll take it down the trail a little ways after we finish the brandy. And after we Zorba."

"We're not doing Zorba," I said. "I'm done with Zorba."

"You are doing Zorba, Allard. And we're going to Zorba at your wedding."

I shook my head and sipped at the brandy, but Ed got to his feet and motioned me to join him. I shook my head again. *Zorba* was a movie we had seen as kids at the library under my mother's tutelage, and we had played it over and over, wearing the tape out. The film revolved around Zorba, a Greek played by Anthony Quinn, who loved life in every molecule and danced when his emotions became too full. His English understudy, Alan Bates, was a cautious, bookish man. Zorba taught Bates to stop worrying, to live, to enjoy, to love, and to dance. And to my everlasting shame Ed and I had danced in numerous family videos, our arms across each other's shoulders, our feet moving in a tense, Greek sidestep that eventually built into complete abandon. We had Zorba moments, when life became too good, too rich, to accept without dance.

"Come on, Bubaline," Ed said to me, quoting one of Zorba's pet names for a French courtesan he bedded.

"You're ridiculous, Ed. Give it up."

"Come on, while the sun is still on the mountain. Come on, Allard. Come on, I love you and you're my brother. I have to dance. I'm too full. I feel too much."

He drank off the last of his brandy and chucked his tin cup at me. And he began to move, his arms out, his fingers beginning the slightest snapping. He bent at his knees and clapped and said, "Oofaaaaaa," and moved back the other way. Light from the mountains peeled away and then went nearly dark, but the illumination from our fire caught Ed's figure. He began to hum the *Zorba* theme, a zither composition that traced the slow, steady movement of Ed's footwork, while promising, also, that it would grow and stab his heart. He flexed his fingers toward me. He did it again. I stood and drank the last of the brandy and chucked the cup down hard on the ground. And then I slipped under my brother's arm. I laced my arm in his.

He nodded.

I caught his rhythm. I began to hum with him, the music second nature, every nuance known to both of us. We bent at the knees at the same time, then moved in a different direction and took one step forward onto our right foot. Then we stepped back and clicked our fingers, and we let the humming grow louder. Our movement gained speed and we began stepping more forcefully, and when I looked over, I saw Ed had his head back, his eyes closed. The stars burned above him and the light flickered around us both and he began moving harder and more quickly. I let my head sag back and I felt such utter joy enter me that I began to cry silently, passionately. Ed grabbed my shoulder tighter and we stepped forward again, paused, then we clicked our fingers and the madness, the pleasure of life, slowly took us over. We built the cadence of our humming until our feet could barely follow. Fish rose and leaped in the water before us and the pale moon pushed free from the peaks and we danced like Zorba, wind carrying the scent of pine and earth across our bodies, our feet like hooves asking for entrance to the earth.

✦ ✦ ✦

"Take a look, Allard," Ed said. "We can cut around this knoll and save ourselves a half hour or more."

Ed had the topo map spread out on a rock beside the trail. We each had a peanut-butter-and-jelly roll-up. The sun had come out strong and solid, and we had been hiking for the better part of two hours already. I stood beside Ed and studied the map. I saw what he suggested. By circling around a knoll that obstructed the trail, we would cut off a half hour or more. We would also be traveling at the same elevation we had already attained, which would save us the wear and tear of climbing.

"Might be rocky," I said. "Otherwise, I don't see a problem."

"A little adventure." Ed laughed.

"I've had your kind of adventures before. They don't always work."

"This one's a no-brainer."

"All of them are no-brainers, according to you."

"Dries for cutties," Ed said, which was his way of pumping me up.

We finished the sandwiches. Then we simply sat in the sun for a few minutes. It felt good to have the warmth on our skin.

"Did I tell you I'm trying to be canine?" Ed asked, his face tilted to the sun, his eyes closed.

"How's that?"

"I read that one of the problems we face as humans is that we are essentially apes. Primates. So we can never be still. We're always picking and pecking at things. But canines . . . wolves and dogs and coyotes . . . they can rest and do nothing at all. Next time you're around a dog, watch him. He'll simply sit and blink and stare off into the distance. They're very Zen."

"And so you are becoming a canine?"

"That's the plan."

"Is that what you're doing now?"

"Yes."

"Would you like a biscuit or a chew bone?"

He shook his head.

"How many miles out?" I asked.

He shrugged. "It's eleven total to the trailhead. I figure we're a third of the way, maybe a little less. We'll make better time on the descent. Eight miles to go, maybe."

"I'm heading back to get married."

"You sure are."

"We should have brought a pigeon and released it up here. See what would have happened."

"Are there many left?"

"A few. Dad took down the loft, but they nest around there. He hung a couple baskets for them. It would be a long flight."

"I liked those pigeons. You remember old Sky Top?"

"Our first film."

"It wasn't bad, you know? I watched it with Tanya a couple weeks ago. It held up. At least it wasn't horribly corny. It really wasn't bad at all."

"Your ears are growing and you're starting to look like a wolf," I said.

He smiled. He kept his face toward the sun.

We pushed off again a few minutes later. I followed Ed when he left the trail. It took us only a few minutes to see that the trail went up and not around the knoll. Glacial moraine—a large, heavy field of rock—formed a collar around the top. That was Ed's proposed route.

"This is going to slow us down," I said, looking at the rocks.

"It's shorter, though."

"Maybe not in time."

"Adventure, Allard. Adventure."

"It's not going to be easy jumping from rock to rock with packs on our backs."

"Adventure is never easy," Ed said, pretending to be Teddy Roosevelt, one of our childhood heroes. We knew some of his bully quotes. "Be brave, lads, and true."

"You're an idiot sometimes," I said. "Did you know that?"

"Off we go."

It was not hard going, but it demanded that we mount the rocks and step from one to another. It reminded me of walking on a jetty by the ocean, all big steps, all long stretches. The footing held steady and sure, but the rocks grew bigger. Most of the time I followed Ed's path. He began overgrunting—like a teenaged tennis star—for fun. I grunted back. We both laughed.

We were nearly finished with the moraine field when Ed stepped on a boulder and it slid forward. It had been sitting in a certain position, balanced just so on a single point, for a thousand years. Maybe more. Maybe since the glaciers retreated. I saw him put his weight on a round boulder and suddenly it looked as though he fell. He went down. His body lowered in one big motion like a man dropping through a floor, and I thought he had fallen, except his torso, his pack and everything, remained vertical. Perfectly vertical.

He had rolled the rock somehow. It was balanced and then it rolled forward, as straight and as fluidly as a billiard ball. Ed screamed. But he didn't go over and that's what I couldn't understand. I was maybe twenty feet behind him and it didn't make sense. And I started to laugh a little—a nervous laugh, Ed being clumsy, all the overgrunting—but then his scream went on and I realized it wasn't just a kind of amused thing, a frustration thing, but came from real pain. I hurried up to him and that's when I saw what had happened.

The rock had rolled forward and trapped him. The entire thing was ridiculously improbable. For it to work, he had to come along at a certain place and time. The boulder had to be waiting all those years. Then he had to put his weight on it just right, and then jump down, and before he could raise his legs to go to the next rock, the boulder behind him rolled down into a perfect little slot and cracked his legs from behind but left him vertical. It was like a bear rolling a barrel. And then he was kneeling in stone.

"Are you all right?" I yelled, because I finally saw how serious it was.

"It smashed my legs."

He didn't even lose his pack. He simply stood a few feet shorter than he had been a moment before. It was as if he had taken a step through a rotten floor, only in this case the rocks had rolled behind him and rammed into his legs.

"What happened?" I asked, shucking out of my pack.

"The damn rock rolled forward and it slammed into me from behind."

"Did it break your legs?"

"No, I don't think so. I can feel pressure on my right leg, but my left leg feels fine."

"This is not happening," I said.

"It's happening. We'll figure it out, don't worry."

"Okay, let me look at this."

"Don't put any weight on the stone directly behind me. That's the one holding me. I'm standing on something solid underneath me."

"Let me take off your backpack so we can see what's going on."

"Okay, but go easy."

I lifted his pack to one side and propped it next to mine. Then I did a slow study of his situation. I saw no blood. I figured he was like a kid who put his head through the baluster railings. All we needed to do was to slow down and think carefully and we would be able to extricate him.

"Stop everything," I said. "Don't move at all. Are you in pain?"

"Some. But not as much as you might think."

"What's that mean?"

"It means the rock isn't constantly on me. It's just holding me."

"Assess the situation, then determine action."

"You're such a Boy Scout."

"Well, we don't want the thing to roll forward anymore, do we?"

Although he had already described his situation to me, it took me a few minutes to see it clearly. The rock wasn't pinning him so much as holding his legs solidly against two rocks in front of him. He couldn't turn. He had to stare ahead and he was in a position like a guy kneeling on one of those kneeling chairs people used when they had bad backs. Half of his body, up to his waist, had sunk down into this hole, but the pressure from the rock rested on his calves.

"That boulder finally got Indiana Jones," Ed said. "It's about time."

"Just hold on and let's do a full survey. I'm going to stick my head down and try to see what's going on."

"Be careful."

I slipped forward on my belly and looked down to see as much as I could. I had to repeat the procedure because I discovered I needed my headlamp to see anything. What I saw with the light beam made my heart sink. The boulder had pinned his legs securely to the rocks in front of him. Unless we could budge the boulder, he wouldn't be able to move. As I looked, my mind went over the facts of the situation. We were at eleven thousand feet. It was late afternoon. It was a huge boulder. It could have crushed his legs entirely if it had managed to slam against the rock in front of him, but the way the surrounding rocks were positioned, it merely trapped him. I put my head down near his knees and tried to see things clearly. Ed remained calm. He joked and kept saying, "Dries for cutties," our little mantra. I didn't like the way the rock looked.

It was tilted down, for one thing. It rested on two rocks that slanted toward Ed. It behaved as a barrel might that had rolled down a ramp and stopped a few inches from the end. I couldn't be certain the rock wouldn't roll a little more if we started moving around next to it. It didn't look as if it would, but I couldn't know for sure.

"What do we have?" Ed asked.

"It's okay, I think," I said, pulling back out of the hole, letting him have what we both knew was a meaningless phrase. "We need to see what kind of movement you have."

"Not much."

"Can you turn sideways? Can you lift your legs at all?"

He shook his head.

"This is like a one-in-a-billion kind of deal," I said. "You know that, right?"

"I'm a rarity."

"We'll figure it out. We just need to be careful and go slowly."

"Solid principles of first aid, Allard," he said, still joking, but the jokes had grown tighter.

"Let's see what kind of movement you have. I know you said you can't do much, but do you have anything at all?"

He tried. He shifted his weight slightly and tried to turn one leg, but it wouldn't budge. He couldn't gain an inch. As I sat next to him, I saw his face start to comprehend how difficult this was going to be. He looked at me a couple times as if to say, *Come on, this is a joke, right?* I knew how strong his legs were, but he couldn't do anything. It became clear in no time that the only way he was going to get out was if I could move the rock. Leverage. I understood, just looking at it, that I couldn't simply push it. I tried. I put my feet against the rock behind me and pushed—merely a test at first—but the rock weighed at least a ton, maybe more. And it was canted downward, so it was impossible. Ed tried to help push, but he couldn't turn around or put anything into it. He tried to push back like a mule kicking, but he had no fulcrum. We pushed from various angles for maybe five minutes before it became obvious we needed a plan B. The whole time, too, it was getting later in the afternoon and a breeze picked up. The sun went behind the knoll and it was suddenly a little cooler. I didn't like it. I started to feel panic jumping around inside me. Ed kept asking, "Are we thinking everything through? Are we examining it every way we should?" Things like that. He tried to keep it light, tried to stay upbeat, but it had started to sink in on him that he was in serious peril. A rock is such a dull, immutable thing, I realized, there really wasn't much to figure. A little later Ed said, "Caught like a rat in a trap." He used a Bugs Bunny voice or something. I never knew which character he was impersonating, but he was right. He was caught like a rat in a trap.

"Now what?" Ed said when we finished pushing on the rock for the first go-around.

"Cell phones."

"Mine's in my backpack," Ed said. "But I doubt you'll get reception up here."

"We can try."

I took both phones and climbed to the highest nearby point. I used mine first, moving it around to look for bars. I didn't have any. Neither did Ed's.

"Nothing," I called to Ed.

"You might have to run for it. Run until you get some bars. But let's try some levers first."

I started to disagree, but then I realized I needed to do whatever he said. His mood might determine the outcome. I spent a half hour dragging back long pieces of pine. We didn't have an ax or a saw, so I was forced to go through wood that had come down in a storm. I searched for hardwood, but at that elevation all I came up with was spruce and soft woods.

"Think like an Egyptian," Ed said. "You are a stone mover. You're building the Pyramids."

"You're out of your mind."

"You only need an inch."

I selected the best piece, a fifteen-foot length that felt fairly solid, and wedged it into the slot near Ed's legs. Little by little, I put my weight on it. It didn't give. It didn't move at all and neither did the rock. I made sure not to jiggle it for fear it would somehow cause the rock to roll forward and crush Ed's legs completely. But it was a chance we both had to take.

"No go?" Ed asked.

I shook my head. I put my full weight on it to show him.

"Try a couple more spots," Ed said. "We've got to budge this puppy."

But we both understood it was no use. I moved around him and inserted the pry bar in several different locations, but the result was the same. The rock wouldn't move. Ed tried his best to help by pushing back and using his strength, but it didn't matter a bit. Even when we calculated a reasonably good way for him to use a second lever, the boulder didn't budge.

"You're going to have to go for help," Ed said evenly when we concluded our experiments.

"I'm staying with you."

"Our best chance is if you can go bring help. You can't do anything here."

"It's getting dark."

"So, I'll be in the dark."

"I don't like that."

"What you do," Ed said, ignoring my qualms and figuring things out as he always did, "is leave everything here. You're going to have to force-walk . . . maybe run some of the time. Keep trying your cell phones. If you get reception, you can turn back. Take down the coordinates of the GPS. If you don't carry any kind of pack, you can make great time. And you can't stop and camp anyway, so it doesn't matter. Just drink out of streams. Don't even bother with water bottles. We figured it was about eight miles. You can do that pretty fast, but it's dark, so you have to be careful."

"I don't want to leave you."

"Not much choice. The longer I'm trapped here, the worse off I'll be. You get down the hill and bring help. They probably need some jacks to move this rock."

"I'll set you up first. You sure about this?"

"Collect some wood for me. I'll build a fire here. And bring me the backpacks and everything else. I might as well use anything I need. It's going to get cold as hell. And if it rains, I'm screwed. Up here, it will be snow."

We didn't mention that the blood flow had probably stopped to his legs. That the whole thing might end up in amputation. That the cold would seep down and cover him.

It took an hour to gather enough wood to see him through the night. I made him a half dozen sandwiches and made him promise to eat them. Ed started talking about Sisyphus, the man whose job it was to push a rock up a hill each day. I listened because I wanted to keep his spirits up, but with the other part of my mind I tried to calculate how long it would take to make it to Lander. He wouldn't survive for many hours trapped as he was. The temperature had already dropped down to the high forties. Ed had a thermometer on his jacket, of course. Ed being Ed.

After I had everything ready, we sat for a few minutes and watched the pika scrambling around the rocks. At sunset they began whistling, and I'm sure Ed thought the same thing I did: that these things could get to his legs and there was nothing we could do about it. They live down in the rocks, where the moraine makes a perfect catacomb for them. I didn't like thinking about them.

"Get going," Ed said, pulling his eyes away. "I'll make a fire in a little while. At least I can do that."

"I don't like leaving you. Why don't I leave in the morning?"

"Time is of the essence, and all that, Allard. The longer I'm trapped here, the more my condition will worsen."

"I could leave at dawn. I don't like leaving you in the dark."

"I'll be okay. I have enough wood and I have plenty to eat and drink. You've done all you can, so get going."

"You're a bossy bastard."

"I always have been."

I hugged him. I deliberately didn't make too much of my departure. I didn't want to convey that kind of message. Better, I thought, to keep it light.

"I'll be right back," I said, standing.

"You better be. You have the phones?"

I tapped my pockets and nodded.

"Lassie, get help," he said.

"Love you, Ed."

"Love you, too. Now go."

I checked my watch as I left: six thirty. I fast walked and ran. It was rocky in patches. It was also uphill for the first four miles. My adrenaline pumped like crazy. I didn't even try to calculate how long Ed might last. He had sleeping bags to put over him and he had food and water and he had the prospect of help on the way. Eventually I made it over the ridge, the highest point on the trail, and when I looked up, I saw a meteor shower. Maybe it was the Perseids. Meteors fell and zoomed by, and at that elevation, on a clear night, it was spectacular. I noted the meteors especially because as I headed down, the weather started to deteriorate. I tried the cell phones at the top of the mountain, dialed 911, but I didn't get any bars on either phone so I turned them off right away. I went as fast as I could. My knees killed me because I went so fast, but I had to keep going.

After a while I came to a long series of switchbacks, which I remembered formed part of the trail. I went down the switchbacks, and I tried to think of a baseball player with a number for each turn I took. Number three, Babe Ruth; number four, Lou Gehrig; number five, Brooks Robinson. A little mind game and it was something Ed and I sometimes did when we had a long, repetitive task like moving wood. Eventually, I reached the bottom and entered a pine forest and I had to go a little slower so I didn't inadvertently leave the trail. But it was pretty well marked and around three in the morning I reached Ed's pickup. We had parked in a high pasture near the Shoshone Reservation. For a second I couldn't find the key. We had hidden it back by the rear tire, but I finally dug it up and I drove out of there like a madman. The phones still didn't have any bars, but I plugged mine in and recharged it while I drove down the rest of the mountain. About halfway to Lander I got a couple bars and called, but it faded out and in and I couldn't get a decent signal. When I finally got onto pavement, I hit the accelerator and went about ninety down a straight highway and it was a little dangerous. I felt tired and sleepy, but wired, too, and all I could think about was Ed up in the rocks, in his skirt of stone. I hated thinking of him alone.

I found the police station on a side road. I don't know what I expected. Maybe a kind of a crack rescue squad, ready to leap up and help me the minute I arrived. But it was just one guy, a kind of chubby fellow named Jacob, who looked to be about nineteen or something and was so junior he pulled night duty. He had one of those shaved heads that I hate, kind of stripped bald on the sides. He was half asleep. I told him what had happened and he made me repeat it twice. The whole time a police radio kept squawking and I nearly went nuts every time it interrupted us. Eventually, though, I got across what I had to get across and Jacob began the alert process. That's what he called it. *Alert process*. He called some people and he waited while other people got back to him. It was still dark and people probably weren't awake.

Lander is a big mountaineering place, the home of NOLS, the

National Outdoor Leadership School, so people are familiar with the possibilities of high-mountain rescue. I felt pretty good at that point, pretty confident. Soon Jacob contacted the local airport, where apparently there was a helicopter they could use on missions like these, but they didn't jump right on it. I watched Jacob's face and I started to see that things weren't going to go easily. It was like an official at the driver's license bureau, when she starts to see something wrong with your application, and you just know it's going sour.

"They're not liking the weather report," Jacob said, hanging up the phone. "The heli crew."

"It can't be more than a fifteen-minute flight."

"Can't put it down if you can't see where you're going. Plus, the winds can get pretty wicked up there. Usually right before dawn is the best time to fly, but you never know."

In bits and pieces, I gathered the rest of the situation. If clouds obscured the peak, then there wasn't anything they could do. It would be dangerous to try to lower people onto the ground, and besides, they made about a dozen calls back and forth trying to figure out what kind of device they could use on the rocks. I knew some of them talked about amputating his legs. That was like a little pebble in the shoe of the entire conversation. This whole exchange took about an hour.

Then they talked about horses, would that be faster, then they had to talk to an outfitter who knew the area, and he didn't think the horses could be much help on a rocky trail like that. So now maybe ten or eleven hours had passed since I had left Ed. Light started to soften at the windows, and when I glanced at the clock, I saw it was past six. I told Jacob that I was going to start back up if we didn't get something going immediately. He said he didn't advise it. He said I was tired and wouldn't make good decisions, and he had a team assembling, just hold on, and I felt torn between staying and making sure they sent someone and the fact that Ed was alone. But I also understood I couldn't do anything for Ed alone except to keep him company, so I decided to wait a few minutes longer and get a team heading up to him. The thing that paralyzed them from starting right up was the rock. They didn't want to hike all the way in without a plan or a tool that would work. And they also didn't want to carry something heavy and cumbersome or it would take forever.

They finally decided on two eight-ton jacks. It took them a while to round those up from a construction guy one of them knew. He moved houses with them and built foundations under houses, cribbed them up, then worked under them. His name was Donny. He wasn't around at first, then his wife said she thought she knew where he was, and so on. Eventually we met at the trailhead. Three guys. I was pretty keyed up at that point, but they wouldn't be hurried. Part of me admired the methodical approach they took. They didn't want to put themselves needlessly at risk, so they did checklists and so forth, and finally we started up about eight thirty in the morning. It was raining and foggy. They didn't like the idea that I was coming along because they knew how tired I was. But I gave them my word that I would stop if I felt it was too much, and I meant it. I had hiked twenty miles in a day before, but this climb was at elevation and the weather wasn't cooperating.

One of the guys—he was stocky and wore thick glasses, Glen, his name was—insisted pretty vocally that I not accompany them. But the leader, a kind of racehorse-built guy named Junior, he said he would want to hike in if his brother were in a similar situation, so he figured he would let me try. The third guy went along with whatever the group wanted. He was short and slight. His name was Frank and he was the medical expert. They all wore red parkas that said WIND RIVER RESCUE on the back. They were looking at a sixteen-mile hike up and back, with the possibility of carrying someone out, so I respected them and I didn't want to make waves. It also meant if I went along that I would be hiking a bunch of miles in a twenty-four-hour period, which is just stupid. I understood their reluctance.

"We're bringing one tent for emergency shelter," Junior said to me before we started. "I'll be honest. The weather report isn't good. It's even possible we may have to turn back. I hope you understand. I will not put the lives of these men in jeopardy for your brother. Is that clear?"

"Yes," I said.

"That said, we will make every effort to reach him. We're good at what we do, so rest assured we have a certain amount of grit. And we understand how much your brother means to you."

"Thank you."

We started back up. They carried heavy packs, and of course they carried the jacks and a litter. I knew by the way Frank asked questions that he worried if Ed had made it through the night. The rain complicated everything. It would make things colder, make Ed wet and force his body heat out of him. It might have prevented him from making a fire, and snow was a possibility at that elevation.

"He'll be okay," I said, my muscles slowly warming to another climb. "You don't know him, but he's very determined. He'll use this as a dinner story for the next fifty years."

"I sure hope so," Frank said.

"I left him wood for a fire," I said, more for my benefit than his.

"That should help," Frank said.

As I climbed, I kept thinking of the meteor shower. White lights across a black sky.

They were good hikers, but carrying that much gear, combined with the wet conditions, they didn't make the time they might have under other circumstances. They radioed about the helicopter on a couple of our breaks, but weather had locked it down. We saw that clouds covered the mountaintops. I didn't dare think about Ed being by himself. I couldn't. I stayed in the moment, concentrating on hiking. The first four miles were all uphill, and we gained a bunch of altitude. I wasn't sure I was going to make it. If it had been for any other reason, I would have given up. We reached the summit at about one in the afternoon. We had to go down into a bowl, down where Double-L Lake had been, and the going got a little easier. The pines became shorter and more stunted, pruned by wind and snow. My legs felt like rubber, though. We considered sending Frank ahead and dividing his equipment among us, but they wanted to stick to protocol and that meant we needed to stay together. It had started to snow, a kind of sleety snow that was more water than crystals, but at that elevation we knew it could keep going and fill up the trails in no time. You don't want to get snowed in out in the backcountry unless you're prepared for it. They had a couple conversations away from me, some looks that suggested maybe they should turn back. But they were good guys. Determined. They kept going.

As we drew closer, the conversation tightened. The conditions put a pall over everything. Eventually we came up a small incline, following the GPS right to the moraine field, and we saw Ed. It was a sort of optical illusion. He appeared to be standing, waiting for us beyond a ridge, because his body was still perpendicular. He had pulled the backpacks close to him, trying to use them as pillows, and they had the effect of keeping him upright. So for a second, before we could really see him, we thought he was alive. I called to him, joking that the cavalry had come, some stupid comment like that, but he didn't answer and I thought, okay, he's unconscious. We got a little closer and the guys sort of blocked my sight line to him. They knew right away. Frank went over and checked for vital signs. Junior led me off—I knew by then. He said that I needed to try to rest because we had to walk out one way or the other, and to give Frank a second to check things out. I pushed past him, though, and went to Ed and I saw he was dead. I couldn't quite believe it. It had been less than twenty-four hours. He was young and strong and it didn't make any sense to me. It was the snow and rain that did it,

Frank said later. Hypothermia, loss of core heat, some combination of things. Frank said he had seen people survive impossible things, and he had seen people die from slipping on a trail and knocking their head. You never knew. They didn't even try CPR or anything else, because Ed's body was cold.

He'd written a note. He'd found a pen in one of the backpacks and wrote on the topo map. He said his good-byes to Mom and Dad and to me and Sarah. He tried to write in such a way that he could laugh it off if rescue came in time. It was kind of joking and sort of, well, maybe I'll make it, maybe I won't. Later, though, he wrote a more serious note and this time he said he had watched the meteor shower. He said he felt his body rise up into space and he knew that was partially his body giving out, but it was something that made him less afraid. He looked down on his body, and for a second or two he was up in the meteors, soaring, and he promised that he was all right, that if he was going that we should accept that. After a while, he tried a third note . . . his handwriting was shaky and didn't hang together. He said his body had begun to tremble. Then his writing became indecipherable, but he kept writing. He drew a picture of a daisy. And he drew a horse. Maybe he was simply trying to control his hands. He ate a couple PowerBars and he put the empty wrappers back in the backpacks. Ecological to the end. I could see him finding the humor in that.

16

WE RETURNED WITH ED in a body bag. They had cut off his right leg at the shin to release him from the rock. They were able to retrieve the leg after the pinch on his body had been lessened, thereby gaining greater torque. They put his foot in the body bag with him. I did not watch the procedure. They told my family about it later, after my father arrived, after he had signed releases to cremate Ed, after they gave him Ed's notes and the rest of his personal effects. No one held it against them.

I was glad they retrieved his leg. I did not like thinking about the pika taking it.

We had returned with Ed's body, hiking into the night, and the officials—the police now took an interest after the Wind River Rescue team radioed the outcome—played the role of the waiting village. Everything I did, every word I managed to speak, seemed removed from me, seemed to swing out into the world in a cartoon bubble. I expected at any moment an overwhelming grief to strike me, but instead I grew less responsive to basic questions. I felt as though my grief were frozen within a long, sharp knife made of ice that had been inserted directly into my heart. That to speak would cause it to thaw and fill my whole body with overwhelming pain. By repelling any warmth whatsoever, I gambled that my grief for Ed could be staved off until I could safely remove the blade with a sharp tug. For now, as we handed Ed's remains over to the authorities, as a female police officer draped a blanket over my shoulders, I invited the icy blade to pierce me deeper.

Junior, the leader of the rescue team, set me up in a small room attached to the EMT center for Lander. The room served as a bunkroom for late-night returns, or a place to collapse after a particularly long rescue operation. It had a table and a chair, a metal cot, a shower, gray cinder-block walls, and a window that looked out on the EMT parking lot and the Wind River Range. Someone—I don't remember who, or how the person had my keys—had brought Ed's pickup to the parking lot, left it there, and brought me back the keys.

"Why don't you get some rest?" Junior told me as he put my pack inside the door. "When you're ready, you can call your folks. They'll want to hear from you. We'll get in touch with you again if we need to, but meanwhile you've had a hell of a long day. I know I'm tired, and you did twice the distance."

I nodded.

"If you need anything, let us know. Try to rest. Take a long shower and warm up."

He waited a moment to see if I would speak. When I didn't, he nodded and backed out of the room.

It was late. My mouth tasted like copper.

For a long time, I didn't move. I stayed where Junior had left me, my face toward the door, my legs trembling with fatigue. I understood what was expected of me: take care of the ordinary. Shower, shave, wash behind my ears. Yet the icy blade remained embedded in my chest. It grew stronger and pulsed colder now that I was alone, but I could do nothing about that.

Before I could move or conceive of the tiniest next step, my cell phone rang. I pulled it out of my pocket. It wasn't my phone after all, but Ed's. I crossed the room and put Ed's phone in the medicine cabinet above the sink. Then I thought that was not good enough, not far enough away, so I stepped outside and put the phone in Ed's truck and I went back inside. The weather had turned colder, or I was colder, and sleet made a noise like a small, stealthy rat eating in a dark closet. When I went back in the room I shivered so hard that I feared my ribs would crack.

I wanted to lie down, but I couldn't let myself. So I walked into the bathroom and stepped into the shower. I did not bother to remove my clothes, but turned the hot water on full and waited for it to burn me. It did. I pulled off my clothes to see if the ice knife still protruded from my chest. I let the clothes fall around me and they clogged the drain and caused the water to build at the bottom of the tub. I grabbed at the icy shaft and tried to pull, but it wouldn't yield, and so I stepped farther into the hot, scalding shower spray. That only caused it to melt and re-form, melt and re-form. I turned off the shower quickly and dried myself. Then I stretched out on the bed, covered myself, and closed my eyes.

A famous painting by Pieter Bruegel, a Dutch master, is *The Hunters in the Snow* or *Return of the Hunters*. Like most northern-Renaissance Dutch paintings of that era, it is muted and tinged with gold. Hunters, largely unsuccessful from the appearance of a dead fox held listlessly by one of the men, return out of the mountains to a waiting village. Life has gone on without them, but they are expected, too, and their return means warmth and cheer, fire and light. The scene is quiet; a winter's day in deep cold and flat light.

The image of the hunters' return haunted me.

I knew I should call someone . . . Sarah, my father, my mother, but it was beyond me. My mind could only focus on the line of

Bruegel's men returning through the early-winter snow, to the candled light of the village below, to the stunned fox, tongue lolling, slowly growing frozen in the rigor of its death.

"ED IS DEAD," I said into the phone.

It was very late. I imagined the police had already called them, but I wasn't sure. I heard Sarah draw in her breath. Saying Ed was dead made it true. It burned my mouth to speak it.

"Where are you, Allard?" she asked.

"Did the police already call you?"

"Yes, they called us, sweetheart. Where are you?"

"He was trapped by a rock and I couldn't get him free. I couldn't save him. I did what I could, but it wasn't enough."

"It's okay. It's horrible, it's horrible, I know, but you're still here, Allard. Tell me you understand that? Tell me you know what I'm talking about."

"His leg wouldn't come free. Even with the jacks, they couldn't get it free."

"Allard, is someone with you? Can you make sure you have someone there? We're making plans to get out there as soon as we can. But we want to make sure you are all right. That's the main thing. Is there someone who can come over and sit with you?"

I looked at the linoleum floor of the room. A black ant, drugged with cold, made its way slowly across the tiles. I watched it go and I had trouble bringing my mind back to the phone.

"Ed is dead," I said. "It rhymes, even."

"Allard, I know, I know something of what you're going through. I do. I know you can't process it all right now. No one could. But we love you. I love you. It's tragic beyond words. We all know that. Right? Isn't that right? But you need to stay strong and get someone nearby to sit with you. I know you. I know how you get when something goes wrong like this. Nothing has ever been like this, but I know. We're making airline reservations right now. Tonight. Then we'll be out to be with you. Just hold on, all right? Just take care of yourself right now."

"Will you call Mom and Dad for me? I can't right now."

"Yes, I will. They already know. They're destroyed, but they are thinking about you. They love you. That's what you have to keep in mind. Will you do that for me?"

"I have to go."

"Allard, don't go."

"I have to."

Then nothing for a second. Then I hung up the phone.

Later, my parents' number came up. Then three local numbers, probably police-related, and then nothing else for a time. I drifted back and forth between sleep and wakefulness. Lights from the road outside sometimes swept across the window, and I imagined someone arriving. I wasn't sure whom to expect, but it felt certain that someone would eventually arrive, that I would have to leave my bed and rejoin the world.

I slept. My body twitched frequently from exhaustion and woke me several times. Once I woke believing I had stepped on a rock and it had turned, and I felt my ankle snap and splinter as it rolled under. Then I became a cartoon character, a cutout of myself able to become perfectly flat. A human sent through a typewriter platen. Sometimes when I came out the other end of the platen my body would be Ed's body, my face his face.

Come on, he would say. *Come on.*

Sometimes he had a fox's head and he hung from one of the hunter's hands and we dark Dutch brought him back to the village.

At first light the next morning, I gathered my clothes from the bathroom, wrung them out, then stuffed them in a plastic bag. I dressed in a pair of spare jeans and a University of Vermont sweatshirt. I carried my stuff out to Ed's pickup and piled it in the back. The street was empty.

I told myself not to get in Ed's truck. I told myself not to turn the ignition key. But my hand moved to the door, then I sat behind the wheel, then I turned the key. Up on the hill, in the morning light, I saw the hunters returning. They carried a black bag, soft as a slug, on straight poles across their shoulders. The bag had not been zipped entirely, so that I could see Ed's face in the slit of the opening, the bag like a cotyledon around him. They carried him down toward me, through the glowing smoke of early morning, and I felt terror and shame. I started the truck and let it idle for a few minutes. Then I slipped it into gear and drove away. I could not wait for the hunters anymore. I could not wait for anyone.

PART II:

FIRST LIGHT

17

MORGAN DAVIS came from Scottish ancestry and it showed in his red coloring and his bright, hazel eyes. He blushed more than most men blush; an uncomfortable situation could bring color into his cheeks. It was difficult to be in his presence without wondering how such emotion could be contained and channeled into his documentaries so precisely. I thought of his films as the product of a chemical light, the burning edge of a magnifying beam. I had learned over the past year or so to listen carefully to him. I loved him as Ed had loved him, and I understood why: he lived the life that we had anticipated.

His wife, Gloria, moved calmly through the world, but she adored her fiery husband. They laughed often; their home, furnished casually, had wide windows, sprung couches, flowers, good food, many bottles of wine, hard-used Oriental rugs, camera parts everywhere, three or four dogs in various stages of rescue, an African gray parrot that had been debeaked by its former owner, and two redheaded teen boys—Alex and Finn—who rode motorbikes on the back Washington hills. On his Saturdays Morgan walked the nearby countryside and took black-and-white photos of miniature worlds—pine swirls in their nutty casings, the shell of a locust shed in spring, a spider leg bent and holding a frayed filament of webbing—to document the small world that escaped him in his films. He had enormous energy and suffered from insomnia, so his days shaped themselves like dumbbells— great weight and solidity in the night and the morning, linked by the necessary handle of his everyday life in between.

On this particular day in May when he invited me to his house for lunch, I went without a second thought. As Ed had been before me, I was a frequent visitor. I had worked for Morgan for almost two years now, ever since I had arrived on his doorstep disoriented in my fugue state sometime after the accident. Gloria, with her inevitable kindness, had taken me in, but Morgan had retrieved me from the lethargy I felt in the deepest part of my makeup after Ed's death—and challenged me. Although he never said it aloud, I knew he believed that work would be my cure, and so he kept me busy with every aspect of filmmaking, pushing me to perfect my skills, asking me often if I intended to be a filmmaker or a wedding photographer. He had a stable of young men and women—students, acolytes, workers, technical geeks—whose skills he mixed together in various recipes. We had been talking about an upcoming film project, and I assumed that was why he had invited me to lunch. I would have gone in any case, but I was especially keen to visit him when he told me he planned on making his notorious Russian pie for lunch.

His son Finn let me in when I rang the absurd gong Morgan had hung on the front porch. Finn wore motocross gear and told me he was heading out with his brother, but he informed me his mother and father were in the kitchen. As usual, Morgan did not say hello or acknowledge someone new had come into the mix, but merely roped me into the conversation as deftly as possible.

"Why do we have so many pots if we don't intend to use them?" Morgan asked his wife, and by inclusion, me. He had a fork in hand and he turned a pie slowly before him, crimping the crust. "Cooking isn't cleaning. Cleaning comes afterward. If I have to clean everything as I go along, I might as well order in Chinese food."

"There's probably a middle ground, Morgan," Gloria said from the sink, where she had water running over a mound of pots. "Things are rarely solely one thing or another."

"There's where you're wrong," Morgan said, winking at me. "My Russian pie is not two things, but one. Take a seat here, Allard, and try some of this wine I have going."

"Hello, Allard," Gloria said from the sink, "you're a brave young man to come over on a day he is making Russian pie."

"What goes into Russian pie?" I asked, pouring myself a glass of wine.

Morgan nodded at his own glass and I gave him a knock, too.

"It's a secret," Gloria said, "although I'm not sure it's a secret if no one cares to investigate the recipe. Mostly cabbage, I think. And eggs and cream cheese."

"That's like saying Thanksgiving dinner is mostly turkey," Morgan said. He took a small paring knife and made steam slits in the center of the pie. "She's testy because our long-standing arrangement is the person who cooks does not clean. She's fussing over a few dishes and pots."

"There's such a thing as an orderly process," Gloria said, "and I'd hardly call this catastrophe a few dishes."

"I'm going to take Allard out to see our latest acquisition," Morgan said. "Our charming Billy. But let me put this in the oven first."

He slid the pie in, asked Gloria to turn the temperature down in fifteen minutes, then kissed her on the back of her neck and led me outside. Morgan tipped his glass at me. The air smelled faintly of the ocean and salt.

"Sit here for a second," Morgan said. "I want to talk to you about the arctic project."

"Okay," I said.

We sat on a small breezeway and sipped our wine.

"I want to put you in charge of the narwhal shoot next month," Morgan said. "Directing credit, the whole shebang."

"Thank you. I'm honored."

"You may not be honored when you hear the rest of the terms. How long have you been with me, anyway?"

"Since Ed died."

"Two years?"

"Just shy."

"Well, you've worked hard. This is no easy assignment I'm giving you. You'll have to be on the ice for a couple weeks and there's no guarantee of success. I'm sending Andy Bottom as head photographer. There's no one better than Andy underwater."

"I like Andy. He's a terrific photographer."

"Yes, he is. But I need to talk to you about some other details of the shoot. And I have to be a little personal, if you don't mind."

"I don't mind," I said, curious where he wanted to go.

"It's about Sarah."

I felt my face flush and my breathing become shallow.

"What about her?"

"I just found out she's the writer *National Geographic* is assigning to cover the shoot. How does that fit into your mental chest of drawers?"

"I don't know."

"Sarah Patrick's a fine writer, Allard, with the proper sensibility for the job. Plus, I think it's time you saw her."

"That's not really your business, Morgan."

"Of course it isn't. The film is my business, but I'd also like to think we've become friends in the past two years. And we both hold your brother in high regard. Is that fair to say?"

"Yes," I conceded.

"You said once that you came to me because you felt disassociated from everything. That you didn't know where to go, but that you felt coming here, to me, helped keep Ed as part of your world in some way. We've never talked about it directly, because you were still deeply in shock. Camping up there in the Winds all alone until you couldn't stand it any longer just prolonged your pain."

"Okay, maybe I'd agree with you. But I'm better now."

"Yes, you are. But you still haven't reconciled with Sarah, have you?"

"No."

"You've made inroads with your parents."

"Some."

I sipped my wine. I couldn't clear my head to think about Sarah. I hadn't talked to her since the night of the accident.

"Ed's death is a sad, sad thing, Allard. But you can't bring him back. So there's no point in continuing to blame yourself and staying shut down emotionally. Do you still feel guilty because you couldn't figure a way to pry the rock off his legs?"

"No."

"No recriminations? 'If only I had . . . ? If I could have just managed to move the stone an inch?'"

"Of course I've had second thoughts. But I . . . we . . . did everything we could think of."

"And you exhausted yourself in attempting to save him, running up and down the mountain. You have to accept that."

I looked at him. Then I looked away. My stomach rolled.

"I'm sorry, Allard." Morgan reached across and put his hand on my forearm. "I'm probing. But I've wanted to say these things for a while now and it seems like the moment to say them."

"I never wanted Ed to die." The heat of my response surprised us both.

"Of course not. But he did—and you are still living in self-exile. Your emotions are frozen in time. And by not dealing with Sarah, by not allowing yourself to explore your feelings and how blocked they were . . . are . . . by your powerful grieving, you are keeping yourself stuck in time."

I didn't speak for a while. Neither did Morgan.

"Understand, Allard, that the emotional mind sometimes works in opposition to our conscious, everyday mind. You know how you behaved, but not why. What you did, or didn't do, still troubles you. I believe you love your parents, and I believe you love Sarah. But for reasons you haven't determined, you fled from them at a time when your brother died."

"You think that my guilt is something I could not have faced or shared with my parents or with Sarah? Is that your point?"

He made a small shrug. "You said you felt as if someone else performed the actions . . . starting the truck, driving away. A disassociation, you once said.

"I've watched you these past two years, so forgive me for weighing in. I'm simply suggesting that our mental terrain is more complicated than we might think. Your brother's death was the death of many things. He was, as you both told me, the force behind the Baker River Film Company. Big brothers can run faster, hit harder, jump higher . . . it's natural for a younger sibling to admire and attempt to emulate the older one. So when Ed died, it was more than the simple death—you know what I mean—the loss of someone who was very close to you. In some important ways it was the death of a second self. You identified with him; you revered him. His death caused a tremendous upheaval in your psychic world, for lack of a better term. Does that make sense?"

I nodded.

"Somehow, you have to discover why that loss of a second self swept up your love for Sarah. If you were as powerless as you say in the aftermath of Ed's death, it's likely you associated Sarah's love with Ed. Perhaps in ways you don't quite see yourself, you felt yourself worthy of Sarah's love only *because* you had Ed as your brother. Perhaps the loss of Ed means you are no longer a proper soul mate for her. How does that strike you?"

"It doesn't yet. But I'm listening."

"You were shaken to your foundation, Allard. Arguably the most important person in your life died in front of you. You couldn't save him, despite your efforts. You couldn't see any reason for it, because there wasn't any reason for it. No logic. Just an accident. So you ran away. You probably put yourself in danger, too, camping up in the mountains by yourself afterwards, asking the fates to do what they liked to you. Why? Maybe it helped you exert some control over what you couldn't control. But now you need to forgive yourself. You didn't kill Ed. No one killed him. A stone rolled at precisely the wrong moment, and Ed was trapped."

Morgan drank the rest of his wine. "That's my spiel, Allard, and I apologize if I overstepped. You're a gifted filmmaker and I believe you're going to be a very important documentarian, but you need to resolve your internal struggle with Sarah. Some of that is letting Ed go, I'm sure. If you both end up on this shoot, you and Sarah, so be it. It would be good for both of your careers."

I nodded. I felt strange and shaky.

"Now come and meet Billy. He's Gloria's latest animal rescue. He's out behind the house. Leave your glass here and we'll grab it when we come back. You're probably in need of something stiffer than wine after my amateur psychology."

When we arrived at the barn, Morgan swung the door open. Two pigeons flew away, their wings clapping in the old way I remembered. He asked me to lift down two bales off a stack and bring them with us. I hoisted the bales and carried them out to the corral. The bales smelled of timothy grass and barns. The afternoon light crossed the yard and shot a long triangle across the corral. Morgan raised his hand to shade his eyes.

"That's Billy," Morgan said, indicating the large draft horse that stood in the northern corner of the pen. "Meet our Clydesdale. He's blind. Just break up the hay bale and talk to him. He's afraid to move away from that corner. He stays right there, but he'll smell the hay. Just break up the hay and drop it over the fence. He'll find it."

Billy snorted when I began breaking up the hay. Because he couldn't see, everything was a threat to him. He answered the sound of the hay breaking apart with snorts and pawings and bluffs. His size was intimidating. My head came only to his shoulder and his bulk was astonishing.

"Some little boys blinded him with squirt guns," Morgan said behind me, his cigar fragrant and somehow tied to the scent of the barn. "They loaded the guns with acid and sprayed him when he came over to get a carrot. They thought it was funny. Billy ran into a barbed-wire fence and got hobbled and thrashed and thrashed until his body was cut to ribbons. No one saw him until the next day. The boys were from a good, upper-middle-class family, so they didn't get much of a punishment."

"How long have you had him?" I asked, finishing with the hay.

Billy had stopped bluffing and stood with his ears turned toward us.

"Oh, we just got him last week. Gloria couldn't stand the cruelty in his story. When she heard it, she called the animal rescue people and said she would pay for his vet bills and we'd adopt him if they let us. We're not a horse people, but we love Billy. He has great courage. I built this little corral back here with the boys. He breaks my heart every time I look at him. He's so brave and so vulnerable."

"Does he let you pet him?"

Morgan smiled at me. "We worked out a deal. Here, I'll show you."

He stepped to the corral and put his arms on the top rung. Then, to my surprise, he began to sing the old folk song "Sweet Betsy from Pike."

Billy slowly walked toward him. I had seen animals come to humans a thousand times in my life, but I had never witnessed such gentleness in the exchange. Even now, in Billy's slow walk, you could read the balance of trust and flight, the caution and worry that this horse had learned from cruelty. Morgan continued singing, and Billy came closer, his head ducking a little in recognition. In the last steps Morgan held out his hand and let the horse sniff for it, his hand finally unfolding into a caress that Billy accepted. Then the big horse hung his head over Morgan's shoulder, and for a long moment they did not move. I saw the pale thumbs of eyes left by the acid, and Billy looked at me blindly and saw me anyway.

18

"What's she like?" Andy asked.

He sat on the tailgate of our rented pickup looking up at the Twin Otter that had just popped over the mountains to our south. The small plane made a sound like a hummingbird. It tipped its wings a little to let us know it had seen us. Then it began its approach, its landing skis catching light on their flat bottoms. We sat on the northwest corner of Hudson Bay, where it was spring and cold and windy, and waited for Sarah to arrive.

"I don't really know," I said, my eyes watching, too.

"I thought you knew her."

"A couple years back. A different place. I haven't seen her in a long time."

"She break your heart?"

"Something like that."

"You've read her books, though?"

"I have," I said. "They're good."

"I heard they were rants. Kind of strong."

"No, they're good. They take a position. Pro-ecology, pro-animal, pro-environment. That's Sarah Patrick."

"I just met her once and briefly at that," Andy said. "It was at one of those talks for National Geographic members. She's a knockout, but I guess you know that."

"Her book-jacket photo looks good."

"Allard Keer, you're blushing! The intrepid Allard Keer!"

Sammy, our guide, sat near us on an upturned milk crate and seemed to follow the progress of the plane by its shadow. He smoked a cigarette, his entire hand curled around it. He wore a jacket that said NATIONAL GEOGRAPHIC down its right sleeve. He had short, blunt hair, northern hair, and the wide body of a porcupine, with most of his weight centered in his legs and butt. He didn't speak much, but when he did, we listened.

Andy Bottom, tech supervisor and head photographer, kept his eyes on the plane. He was thirty-two. He loved machines and it would have been unthinkable to him to not watch a plane landing. He called his production company More Equipment Than Talent. He was superb at his job and we had worked together a dozen times over the past couple of years.

The Twin Otter glided closer, its sound growing in the arctic light. I stood. I didn't particularly look forward to my reunion with Sarah taking place in front of Andy and Sammy, but I could do nothing about it now. I began to feel nervous in a way that I hadn't in years. The plane did a small up and down, bobbing on the wind, and then it descended in earnest. Sammy glanced at the plane and threw his cigarette away. Andy clicked a few shots on a 35mm. He turned and took a shot of me. I shook my head, but he didn't stop. His assignment was to take photos and I knew it was useless to shy away from them. He turned back and shot a bolt of snaps as the plane touched the lake ice.

Sammy hopped into the truck and drove it slowly to meet the plane. We followed on foot. The front prop switched off as the plane did a short pirouette. Without the plane engine revving, the only sound we heard was wind and the gentle idle of the pickup. I pushed up the hood of my parka. The temperature stood at about twelve degrees Celsius.

"Wow," Andy said when he spotted Sarah.

"Wow," I agreed.

Sarah Patrick. My Sarah. She was stunning.

"Hello, boys," she called.

She turned to face us quickly. She had already begun to unload gear from the body of the plane. Andy yelled a greeting. I raised my hand. Sammy slid the pickup close enough so that she could load the gear directly onto the truck. He said something to her through the passenger window. She nodded. The pilot had stepped out on the wing of his plane and lit a cigarette. Obviously, he had no plans to stay.

We walked around the truck. Andy held out his hand and introduced himself, reminded her that they had met before. Sarah shook his hand, said she remembered, then reached through the truck window to say hello to Sammy. She said something that got Sammy laughing. That wasn't easy.

"Well, who is this?" she asked when she turned to look at me.

I stepped forward. I wanted to hug her, but I wasn't sure if that was welcome. We stood for a moment at an awkward distance. Then she reached up and put her arms around my neck.

"Oh, God," she said, "if you aren't a sight for sore eyes."

"Hi, Sarah," I whispered.

"Oh, Allard, you stupid, stupid son of a bitch."

We didn't let go of each other for a long time.

"THESE," SARAH SAID in the back of the pickup, her hands passing me a box wrapped in brown paper, "are from your mom.

Turtles, I think. She said they were your favorite. I stopped in New Hampshire to see my dad on the way up from Washington."

"D.C.?" I asked.

"Yes. That's where I'm living these days."

We rode on top of Sarah's equipment, our backs against the cab. Andy had climbed in with Sammy. It was only a mile to the village. We both had our hoods up to block the wind. We stared behind us.

"You saw my parents?" I asked.

"Of course. My folks are neighbors. Or maybe you forgot."

"How is everyone?"

"Everyone's fine. They send their love. Everything looks about the way it did for the past thousand years. No major changes."

The truck banged over something and Sammy cursed a little. Andy let out a little whoop.

"Your dad seems to have slowed down a little," Sarah said when we made it past the small obstacle, "but he's still working. He has a bass ready to go and has two more orders. Your mom is fine, still spending a lot of her time as the town librarian. She hangs out with my mom a lot. They're fierce Scrabble players. "

"I've heard a little about that."

"Now where are we headed? Fill me in."

"Just a Quonset hut. It's warm, though."

"Any other people?"

"About two thousand in the village, everyone counted in from a couple miles around. A few families living the old way, but not many. We're actually in Fi, a small village."

"It took me three days to get here."

"Hudson Bay is a long way from New Hampshire," I said.

"You thought you could skate here once upon a time. The great land, you called it."

"It would take a lot of skating."

We drove awhile in silence.

"I've missed you," she said. "That's something I probably shouldn't say."

"It's been a long time," I said. "I missed you, too. I missed you a lot."

"Part of me hates your guts. You know that, right? You just dropped out of the world. After all that time, you disappeared."

"And the other part?"

"I can't hate you completely, Allard. We go back too far. I loved you too long. And I know you. I know you better than you know yourself. "

"Well, maybe you'll explain things to me."

"I could, you know? I could explain more than you think. But you didn't give me that chance, did you? You're like a junk drawer in my belly. I can't ever straighten it out. Every time I think I've cleaned it up, someone comes by and dumps something in it or needs something at the bottom and tips everything upside down. I hear from your mom, or my mom, and they tell me things about you . . . they don't know whether they should or not, so it would be comical if it didn't get my belly turning. But here we are, right? We're heading back on the ice. Nothing like a full circle, is there?"

She turned and looked at me. Before I could answer, Sammy pulled into Kangiqsliniq, the Inuit name for Rankin Inlet. We drove down the single road until we reached the Quonset hut. Smoke came out of the chimney pipe at the rear of the building.

I knew one thing for certain: I was still in love with Sarah Patrick, and probably always would be.

19

SAMMY DUNKED A TURTLE in his coffee and pronounced it excellent. Whether he meant the coffee or the turtle, I couldn't say. Andy ate one in about two bites and then demanded another. I ate one slowly, savoring the taste. My mother had always made turtles for me, brownies for Ed. They tasted of home.

As we ate, we watched Sarah.

We didn't stare, but she did not make a move that we did not see. She was beautiful, drop-dead beautiful, with dirty-blond hair that she wore up on the back of her head. Small tendrils fell down and brushed her neck. She smelled good, too, and after my living with two men in a Quonset hut for a week, that was welcome. The only thing new about her that I spotted was a pair of large, black glasses that she slipped on from time to time if she needed to see something up close. Otherwise, she was the Sarah I knew, the Sarah who had searched for my hand under the ice all those years ago.

She came over to us after she finished making her cot, which consisted of tossing a good sleeping bag across it and arranging her luggage in a half circle at the foot. She grabbed a turtle as she sat down. She appeared tired but happy. She had the glasses in her shirt pocket.

"So when do we start?" she asked.

"Tomorrow," I said. "We're waiting for Sammy's cousin Peter."

"So we're what? Five people?"

"On this initial run, yes. Once we locate the narwhal, then we back off and leave the rest to the helicopter crew. They'll film from that point. Aerial shots."

"It's called *Melting*," Andy said. "That's the working title of the production."

"I guess," I said, "we don't need a formal meeting, but we should go through some of it. You probably know all this, but this segment is part of a series on natural events. BBC and *National Geographic* are collaborating. Our program is focused on the retreat of the sea ice and what that means to the animals. Right now, in late June, we're in the process of losing six million square miles of sea ice. We have footage on the polar bears out on the ice during the winter, and that will be mixed with what we film here as the ice recedes. Once the melt gets under way, the bears retreat from the ice to land. As the ice cracks, it produces long, thin leads that eventually run all the way back to the shoreline. A *lead* is just a fancy word for a crack or fissure in the ice that gets wider as spring advances. It can close up, too, if the ice shifts. Meantime, the narwhal cluster in the open sea and wait. They want to go up the leads so they can get to the fresh fishing grounds that are located close to shore. The narwhal are small-toothed whales, so they eat capelin and flatfish. They also need to get close to the shore to confuse the orcas. The orcas hunt them, and the shallow water messes with the orcas' echolocation."

"Biggest seasonal climatic change in the world," Andy said, a dot of crumb above his lip. "The retraction of the sea ice. That's the tagline."

"Narwhal are secretive," I continued. "They are the mythological unicorns of the sea. As I'm sure everyone knows, their most notable characteristic is a long, thin spike that looks like a horn. It's actually an incisor tooth that can grow to three meters long. Scientists speculate that it's a secondary sexual characteristic. Males sometimes hit each other's tusks, or rub them, probably to determine dominance."

"And their horns," Sarah said, her voice tired and quiet, "used to be sold for double the price of gold. In medieval times scholars claimed that a narwhal horn could heal the sick of melancholia and that a cup made from a horn could protect you against poisoning. Kings and queens preferred to drink from narwhal-horn cups for obvious reasons."

Andy reached for another turtle. Sammy stood and opened the potbellied stove, shoved a few chunks of wood inside, then turned his back to pick up heat. He already knew most of what I was saying.

"Sammy knows ice," I said, nodding in his direction. "And his cousin Peter, who will be joining us, has a dog to bring along. Dogs can alert us about bears. Polar bears are willing to hunt us. Forget what you know about grizzlies or black bears. Polar bears follow the ice to shore and they look for food the whole way. In fact, the loss of ice means the bears have less to eat. They'll be hungry. So we need to stay together and we need to be alert. Polar bears are stealthy."

"What else about the ice?" Andy asked. "I know most of it, but just for Sarah it might bear repeating. No pun intended about bear."

"The ice will be getting thinner and weaker," I said. "We'll travel out on it by snowmobile. We have a long sled, or pulk, to pull behind and that's where we'll ride, with our equipment. The sun is up twenty-four hours a day. The ice is already beginning to get soft and break, so we have a three-week window at best to get to the outer edge . . . maybe as little as a couple days. The narwhal try to get up the leads early on, but they need to breathe air, so if the ice closes back over them, or traps them, then they have to halt for a while. We know which bays they come to traditionally. We'll put sound sensors down in the water so we can hear them. Peter lives here year-round and he knows this terrain better than the rest of us. He should be here this evening. Sammy is from farther south, but he knows this kind of work. Once we spot the narwhal advancing up the leads, we want to photograph what we can, then clear out. We have the helicopter on call and we will be in radio contact. Andy, do you want to talk about the gear?"

"We have a lot of gear," Andy said.

"Anything else?"

"A whole lot of gear."

"Are the Native people here permitted to hunt the narwhal?" Sarah asked.

"Yes," I said. "In small quantities for sustenance."

"*Mattak,*" Sammy said, his voice containing a smoker's gravel. "Skin and blubber. It's a delicacy."

"If the ice thins too quickly, then we're out of luck," I continued. "Our best chance is to go to the edge of the ice where the narwhal will school and wait for the leads to form."

"I'm curious what they told you," Andy asked Sarah. "What's your assignment?"

"Factual reporting, mostly, on exactly how bad the melt actually is," she said. "And on how you're filming it. They may give me a sidebar or a short section for opinion, too. Two thousand seven had the greatest ice melt in history, so that colors things. I've researched it to provide context. People hear about the polar bears being in trouble, but they don't really know what it means."

"I think that's everything," I said when she paused. "Sammy, you want to add anything?"

He shook his head.

"Last report on the weather," Andy said, "is cold and dry. It's good weather for shooting. We're above freezing now and then."

"And with the sun all day we can work as late as we need to," I said. "We'll put in pretty long days, I'd imagine."

"Is there a bar anywhere in town here? If so, I'm buying the first round," Sarah said.

"Not exactly a bar," Andy said, "but a place you can get a beer. It's called the Oil Change."

Sammy didn't come with us, but Andy and Sarah and I walked to the Oil Change after we spent an hour going over the equipment. Andy said he needed help packing the sled tomorrow, but otherwise everything was set. Sammy made us take a rifle for bears. He said bears sometimes came into Fi and slipped away with a child. He said bears took men off oil derricks out at sea. He said only a foolish man underestimates a polar bear, and he usually only does it once.

We walked. I carried the rifle. Andy and I had been to the Oil Change nearly every night since we came, if you could still call full sunlight "night." It had a jukebox and a half dozen tables made of boards set across oil barrels. It was run by Spud, a wiry Native who had a tattoo of a bowhead whale on his back. He stripped off his shirt and showed it to us the first night we arrived. He said a bowhead had prevented his family from starving when it had become trapped on a sandbar and gave up its life. Since then, his family has not touched a bowhead or the blubber from a bowhead. When the bowheads arrived, along with the narwhal and belugas, his family members sometimes put to sea and ran beside them, singing songs of welcome.

"He's probably making it all up," Andy said as we walked, "but it's a handsome tattoo just the same."

We pushed through the door to the Oil Change a few minutes later and found it nearly empty. An old Cree man sat near the makeshift bar sipping a drink. He looked up slowly when we stepped inside. Spud, the owner, stood behind the bar and held a plastic machine gun in one hand, evidently trying to fix it. A small boy, maybe eight, stood beside him, his hands halfway up to reach for the machine gun.

"Hello," Spud said, handing the gun back to the boy. "What will you have?"

"Three beers," Andy said. "Is that what we're having?"

"That's what we're having," Sarah said.

Spud nodded. He bent back behind the bar and dug around in a cooler while we sat at one of the tables. The boy with the machine gun halfheartedly pointed it at us, then continued an arc of imaginary fire across the doorway. Andy pretended to draw a gun out of a holster and shoot back at the boy. Either the boy didn't see Andy's gesture or he decided to ignore it. He sidled over and obscured himself by standing behind the old man. To keep our rifle out of reach from a boy who obviously possessed an interest in firearms, I balanced it on a hat rack a few feet from the door.

Spud delivered the beers. He waited around after setting out the drinks, hoping, I imagined, to be introduced. So I introduced Sarah. Spud made a big deal of shaking her hand.

"Welcome to the land of the polar bears," he said to Sarah in a canned voice he had learned from somewhere. "Land of the midnight sun."

"Any word from Peter?" I asked, because everyone knew everyone in Kangiqsliniq.

"Not yet. He was hunting caribou last I heard. He'll show up. He's dependable. You can count on him." Spud went back to the bar.

Andy raised his glass. "To a successful shoot."

"A successful shoot," Sarah said, and clinked both of our glasses.

We drank. Someone flicked on a boom box and it came in fuzzy for a moment before we got a country-western station. I listened and tried to concentrate on my beer. I still couldn't believe I was sitting across a table from Sarah.

"So, Sarah, you're a writer," Andy said. "Full-time? You make your living from it?"

"I do," she said, then drank from her beer.

"I admit I haven't read your work, but I've heard about it."

"What did you hear?"

"That your books were strong, I guess. Is that a good word for them?"

"Some would say so. It's hard to comment on my own work. I let other people take care of that."

"Allard's read them," Andy said.

She looked at me. I nodded.

"And?" she said.

"I thought they were brilliant."

"Why?" she said, looking at me closely.

"For one, because you write well. For two, you make your arguments count for something. You bring something new to the discussion, I think."

She pursed her lips. She seemed to think something over, then nodded. "Thanks. It gives me a strange feeling to know you read them. I've always wondered."

"What's the new thing she brought to the discussion?" Andy asked.

"Animal consciousness," I said, looking at Sarah. "In her new book that just came out she makes the case that we use animals for food out of species prejudice. A pig is as bright as a three-year-old, more or less, and it's only by ignoring that fact that we permit ourselves to eat it. We don't impute any rights to it. Then she goes on to ask by what right do we claim land for development? Why are our needs more important than those of the other species that share it with us? That's the general line."

"It's not an original thought with me," Sarah said, her eyes going wider in an old expression of interest I recognized. "An Australian philosopher named Peter Singer first popularized it. He poses the question as a moral decision. He says in fifty years we will look at our treatment of animals as a grave failing."

"I'm going to need more beer if we're going to talk like this," Andy said.

He called over to Spud for another round. Before Spud brought the beer over, the door opened and Sammy came in with a young man wearing sealskin pants and a large Native parka. It had to be Peter. A large dog came in with them, its tail curved over its back. A malamute, I guessed, or some mix of Siberian. It looked around placidly until Peter spoke to it, then it curled into a ball in a corner near the door. Peter flicked back his hood. He looked to be about eighteen, but hard and drawn through his cheeks. He appeared broad and flat, like a flounder, and his eyes were oil. His head turned slowly, maybe indicating he was drunk, maybe because the heat of the barroom stunned him. It could be strange, I knew, suddenly to find yourself inside after a long stretch outdoors.

Sammy said something to him and together they walked to our table.

"Peter," Sammy said simply.

I stood and shook hands. So did Andy and Sarah.

"Can I get you two a beer?" I asked Sammy. "Have a seat."

He nodded. Peter pulled out a chair and sat. I went to the bar and ordered two more. Spud brought all of the beers together and handed them around.

"Well, we're all here," Andy said. He raised his glass.

Peter and Sammy joined us in a toast. Peter took a small sip of beer.

"What kind of dog is that?" Sarah asked. "A beautiful animal."

"Mixed," Peter said.

"Sled dog?" Andy asked, and Peter nodded.

"You've been out hunting?" I asked.

"Caribou."

"Successful?" Andy asked.

"We shot three," Peter said.

Andy glanced at Sarah to see her reaction, but she didn't exhibit any surprise or judgment. Hunting for sustenance had a different meaning for her, I imagined. Peter drank his beer. The boy with the machine gun turned up the music. The old man who had been sitting at the bar got up and went outside. The dog watched him go, then put its head back on its paws.

"What's your dog's name?" Sarah asked.

"Rope," Peter said.

"Why Rope?" Sarah asked, her smile at the name sincere and dazzling.

"He chewed through a rope when he was a puppy," Peter said.

"Rope, then," Sarah said. "And he'll alert us if a bear comes by?"

"He better," Peter said, which was probably a joke.

"Have you been out on the ice recently?" I asked.

Peter shook his head no.

"What do people in the village think about the ice going away?" Andy asked Peter.

Peter shrugged. Sammy sipped his beer. It wasn't the kind of question you could answer over a quick beer. Not to strangers.

"How do you two know each other anyway?" Andy asked Sarah and me, his face puzzled as if he had just added things up but wasn't sure of the answer.

"We knew each other as kids," Sarah said. "Didn't we, Allard?"

"You knew each other as kids?" Andy asked. "Does someone want to fill us in?"

"We grew up together," I said. "That's all."

"And?" Andy asked, obviously curious.

"And?" Sarah asked, looking at me. She smiled. She enjoyed this.

"And we were engaged, I guess," I said.

"He left me at the altar two years ago," Sarah said, her voice level. Her eyes looked at mine. "There. How's that for a little twist to the story?"

Andy whistled. Sammy and Peter quietly sipped their beers.

"Have you seen each other since?" Andy asked.

"Not until today," Sarah said, her eyes touching mine for a moment. "It wasn't at the altar exactly. It was a little before the actual ceremony. Maybe like a week, to be accurate. There were some extenuating circumstances, so he wasn't a complete jerk, only a partial jerk."

"Okay," Andy said, trying to lighten his voice and our mood, his tone broadly cautious, "I'll leave it right there. I guess I know what I need to know."

Sammy and Peter didn't react. Sarah drank her beer, her eyes on mine over the glass.

CLOUDS AND COLD as we walked. Wind coming from the north, from the pole, sweeping down over miles and miles of clotted soil. Sarah beside me. Andy ahead with Sammy and Peter, talking, turning to see us, talking. Rope trotting on the cold path, his paws throwing up small scatters of ice and snow. Now and then the creak and warp from the lake, the ice contracting with the brilliant cold, the sound doubled and tripled in the frigid air. Sarah's perfume near me, gone, back again. Sarah the girl on the ice. The moon a small sliver on the horizon, a crescent, a coat hook, meaningless with so much sunlight. Rope stopping once, the hair up on his neck and shoulders rising. A fox, not a bear, its eyes two darts of light. The crunch of our boots on the snow, the snow as fine as sugar. Cold frisking us and searching for a way under our parkas, through our trousers.

"Are you angry I signed on for this?" Sarah asked me, her voice quiet. "I thought you might be."

"No, but I'm curious why you did."

"I signed up because I happen to care about the plight of the polar bears. And I am interested in the ice up here. I intend to use it for my next book. And *National Geographic* pays well and it is a credential worth having. That's why."

"You knew I was on this crew."

"Whatever you think, Allard, I don't hate you. If you think that, you've built all it up in your own head. I wasn't going to let your presence stop me from doing something I wanted to do."

"I didn't build anything in my head."

"The thing in your head that kept us apart. That makes you want to punish me, even though I didn't do anything wrong, except maybe love you. And that prevents you from going home. Your parents miss you, Allard."

"I never intended to punish you, Sarah. I was punishing myself."

Then the wind again. And cold. At the door to the Quonset hut, with Sammy and Peter and Andy already inside, Sarah said one last thing.

"And I loved Ed, too," she whispered so fiercely it took me back. "We all loved him. You don't own a goddamn monopoly on his memory, you stupid, vain jackass."

20

WE LEFT LAND ONTO THE SEA ICE early the next morning. Sammy drove the snowmobile at an even twenty miles per hour over the first leg of ice. It was an odd sensation to leave land behind and to head eastward onto the surface of Hudson Bay. Peter sat directly behind Sammy on the snowmobile. Andy, Sarah, and I rode on the pulk that carried our equipment. Rope rode near Sarah and appeared already to be attached to her. The sled was made deliberately long—perhaps twenty feet long—so that it could ford the bumps and chasms the ice threw in our direction. Twice in the first half hour of driving we were forced to climb off the sled and push while Peter wrenched a long pole under the back edge. Hoisting on a three count, we pushed the sled forward while Sammy goosed the engine gently to add its force to the movement. The sled found a center of balance, teetered, then rocked forward. Sammy expertly kept it moving until it slid free of whatever obstacle had stopped it. Then we mounted again, rode sideways to the wind, and continued.

About midmorning, Sammy slowed the snowmobile and had

Peter climb out and walk ahead of our small caravan. Peter carried a ten-foot-long metal pole and probed the ice as he went. He called his report back to Sammy. Then Peter returned and slid the pole back onto the side of the sled.

"The ice is spoiled up ahead," Sammy told me. "We need to belly back toward land and find a different route."

"Is it safe?" I asked.

Sammy nodded.

"Okay," I said.

We stopped for a meal a little later. The sun rolled across the horizon. Peter and I cooked oatmeal. We all ate a lot of it. We sat against the sled to be out of the wind. Now and then we heard the ice boom and shift. Rope went off some distance and did his business. He came back and Peter gave him a slice of jerky from his pocket. Rope lay down and gnawed it between his paws. While we ate, Andy asked Sammy when we would find a lead. Andy wanted to drop a sensor down through the ice so that he could try to pick up the narwhal calling.

"When does the ice actually go out completely?" Sarah asked, a small notebook on her lap.

"July first, most years," I said. "Earlier on the rivers and lakes. In about a week it should really begin to fracture."

Peter said something in Cree—or some form of Native language—to Sammy. Sammy nodded.

"The wind," Sammy said. "A southern wind blows the ice off the land. Without the wind, it's landfast."

"And the ice goes into the Hudson Bay?" she asked, still jotting notes, her bowl of oatmeal half eaten.

"Yes," I said. "Broken up and melting."

We packed up quickly after eating. Because of the jagged shape of the bay, we needed to strike north to move closer to land. Sammy took the ice ridges carefully, ladling the snowmobile over first, then the sled. Once, pointing north, we were forced to unhitch the sled from the snowmobile for fear the coupling between them would spring as it passed over a particularly sharp ice sheer. We tied a rope to the snowmobile once it cleared the sheer, then used it to pull the sled after it. Everyone except Sammy pushed. The sled teetered over it and the rear end came up like the back of a seesaw suddenly released of a child's weight.

"Rough ice," Peter said. "It's thawing and freezing. All these puddles."

"It could get wet out here as it continues to thaw," Andy said. "It will get soupy."

It was midafternoon before we saw the auks. At first the sight of them made no sense. One perceived the movement—like bright bees on an abandoned picnic—but not the source. We spotted them as we approached a tall headland, a great stony finger of rock that extended a half mile into the bay. A hundred thousand birds. A quarter million birds. Shorebirds, auks, and guillemots. They had jammed into the crevices and nicks of stone, their nests nothing but rock, their presence loud and raucous. The adults hovered near the cliff, riding the upward air currents, their bodies suspended, their feathers flaming upward the only sign of animation.

Sammy cut the engine when we got within a couple hundred meters.

"It's showtime," Andy said as soon as the snowmobile halted.

"How's the light?" I asked.

"It will be good," he said.

"They fly out to the ocean," Sarah said, her eyes scanning the cliffs. "They're pursuit swimmers. I've heard about them."

"And by the time the young are fledged, the sea thaws and arrives right beneath them," Andy said. "Almost like someone had a plan."

Peter, Andy, and Sammy began pulling off the camera equipment. Sarah climbed down and stretched her back. Rope trotted off toward the escarpment. I felt the vibration of the snowmobile locked into my legs.

"Do we make camp here?" Sarah asked me. "Or do we push on?"

"We might as well camp," I said. "Andy will be at this awhile. It's as good a place as any."

"It's hard to believe we're on top of an ocean. Do you need a hand?" she asked.

"I do," I said.

Sarah helped me. We erected three tents. In the largest tent we stowed the equipment: extra group clothing, PLBs (personal locator beacons), an Argos (satellite communication backup system), stoves, two pots (one for snow melting, one for cooking), a billycan for hot drinks, food, a second Winchester rifle, a snow saw, a first-aid kit. We left room for Andy's camera equipment. Next we erected two sleeping tents, both specially designed with holes in the roofs—like tepees—to permit the inevitable moisture from our bodies and breath to escape. Moisture, almost more than cold, was the enemy. We laid out air mattresses to keep us off the ice. Finally, we rolled out a trip wire to go around the entire compound. The trip wire connected to an alarm. If a bear tried to approach the camp, we hoped it would nudge the wire and set off the alarm. Failing that, we depended on Rope.

Sarah told me she expected to sleep in the tent I was in.

"I don't know those other men," she said when we finished. "I'm sorry if me being in there makes you uncomfortable, but that's how it has to be."

"I don't mind."

She looked at me. Then she nodded.

I put on water to boil.

"TIRED?" SARAH ASKED in the tent a little later. She had removed her jacket and used it as a pillow.

"Yes," I said. "A little."

"The birds are still making noise. They don't stop, do they? It's like a bad Hitchcock movie."

"The sun doesn't set, so they can keep feeding. They have fifty days to lay their eggs and get out of here. They're busy."

We lay side by side, a dull silver circle above us where the tent gave way to the light. We lay parallel, our shoulders perhaps six inches apart, the spare Winchester between us. It felt familiar to be near her, and yet I wasn't sure how I felt about that. I wondered, too, how she felt. Before I could frame my thoughts, one of the guys laughed at something in the other tent. Someone replied. Then we heard Rope stretch and move on his tie-out. He was tethered beyond the tents, far enough away so that a stalking bear could not use our tents as a means to hide his approach.

"So you're the director of this shoot?" Sarah asked. "Congratulations."

"That's what they tell me."

"This is a much bigger project than I thought, Allard."

"Well, Morgan will help us tie it all together. I'm in charge of getting enough footage of the narwhal and of the general conditions before the melt ends. They have a ton of footage already on the bears and winter."

"Does Andy work for Morgan?"

"He's a freelancer, but, yes, he does a lot of work for Morgan. He's very good."

"He seems to know what he's doing."

"He's better at the underwater stuff than I am. He's probably the best in the business."

A wind passed over the camp and shoved the side of the tent. A spray of ice followed. Then it became still again. We heard the corner of a snore, a beginning, then it was joined by another snore. Then something in the colony startled the birds and we listened for a time as they squawked and clamored slowly back to relative calm.

Then, far away, we heard ice shelving. One layer pushed under or over another layer and the ice squeaked forward, grinding and shaving itself. Everything was in motion, while also being still—the strange contradiction of early summer on the ice.

"Right after . . . ," Sarah whispered, her voice carrying emotion, her breathing short.

She stopped for a moment and gathered herself. Then she began again.

"Right after, I couldn't sleep."

"Shhhh," I whispered to her. "It's okay. Let's not do this, Sarah."

I felt her shake her head and pull air into her lungs.

"Right after we spoke, when I couldn't get through to you by phone again, I thought, naturally, you would come for me. And I understood, I did, if we wouldn't go through with the wedding. It was okay, I didn't care. And it wasn't like we were people who stood on a bunch of formalities. I mean, we weren't like that, so what did it matter if we canceled the ceremony a couple days before? So what? Our friends and family would understand. So I thought you would come for me as you always did. I thought, even this, even this huge, gigantic thing, even this couldn't prevent us from being together."

"Sarah," I whispered, and I knew her eyes were full. "I'm so sorry. Let's not do this now."

"For about two weeks, I don't know, something like that, I couldn't sleep at all, and I would take long walks in the dark. I know it sounds insane, but I couldn't stand the idea of you being alone and not being able to comfort you. I thought, if Allard is awake and alone, then I will be, too, and we would be united that way. It's silly to remember, but I actually think I had gone around the bend a little. Even when they said you had disappeared after the first day or two, when you couldn't be found at first, when you didn't answer my calls, I didn't worry because I knew you were under the same stars as I saw above me. And I knew the closeness we shared, our love, would comfort us and give us strength. I even thought, okay, Wyoming's mountains are higher than New Hampshire's, and I pictured you like the Petit Prince standing on a mountaintop and watching down on us all. It was funny because Dad, of all people, seemed to be the only one who understood. He would wait outside for me to come back each night. No prying, no questions, no judgments. He did that for me."

I started to say something, anything, but her hand quickly came across the space between us and softly covered my mouth. She kept it there for a long moment, then she brought her hand back to her side.

"I have to say these things, Allard," she said, her voice tight with emotion, "and you have to listen. You owe me that much. I'm sorry, but you do. You see, when those weeks were over and you hadn't been found, some people thought . . . they thought you were gone, too. They thought maybe you would kill yourself. But I knew you and I knew what you would do. When Ed's body came back . . ."

She reached and put her hand over my mouth again.

"Oh, Allard, people talk about broken hearts and I always thought that was just a manner of speech, but when I saw his remains in that small, metal container . . . my heart broke for you. I loved Ed. You know that. I loved him like a brother and I looked forward to a long life with you both, toward hikes and adventures and children, and Ed's remains . . . your father, Allard, he knelt on the ground and committed that small metal container to the earth. He put his arm all the way inside the hole. I'm sorry, you have to hear this, Allard, you do. He put his arm all the way down to put Ed to rest so gently, so sweetly . . ."

She stopped for a moment, then continued, hardly able to speak.

". . . in the land your father had bought all those years ago. I knew as surely as I have ever known anything that he buried a dream there, too. Oh, it's all cliché, of course. Funerals are rotten with clichés. Your mother recited a poem, and then Ed was gone and you were gone and I was alone. I didn't hate you, Allard. I never hated you. I knew you were struggling with your own demons. But I thought you would come back for me. I thought you needed me, because I sure needed you. . . .

"Your mother and I, we fell into the habit of walking along the Baker River together. We met halfway between our houses and we walked. By then it was autumn and cold and we had to wear sweaters, so we had all that damn poignancy of New England fall . . . you know, pumpkins and leaves and all that emotional turbulence. We were like old widows in the whaling days waiting for the ships to return. Something crazy like that. And she said she knew you were alive, she didn't worry about that, but she worried you would become haunted. That was her word. Haunted by Ed's death and unable to go forward. And then when you reappeared at Morgan's, I understood that, too. I felt hurt, horribly hurt, that you didn't want to speak with me, come to me, but I accepted it finally. And then time passed and our lives carried us apart, didn't they? No one's fault, Allard. I've forgiven you, if anyone has the right to forgive another person. I knew whatever pain you had caused me, it was a thousand times worse for you. I knew that. So that's my side of things. That's what I went through. I missed you, Allard, and I miss Ed."

"I couldn't," I said.

"Couldn't come home? Couldn't come to me? I know. I don't understand it, but I believe you now. At first I felt punished. But then it occurred to me maybe you needed to punish yourself. I don't know that I understood that part of your personality until I saw it. It was like one of those puzzles, you know, for color blindness. You look and you think you see it, and then eventually the number steps away from the background. That's how I finally saw you. Oh, I thought, that's Allard, too. That's another part of him. Guilt drove you away. Guilt and profound sadness."

"I'm not sure what it was. I know I'm sorry. I know I didn't want to hurt you, but I did anyway."

Neither one of us said anything else for a long time. Then she quietly put her hand over my eyes. She held her hand there and it felt cool and calm and heavy. She left it there as if to block away the world. As if to bring me peace.

21

A BEAR," SAMMY SAID. He pointed.

Rope growled.

It seemed surreal for a moment. We had just finished photographing the birds and the nests again after resting. It took me a moment to see the polar bear. It shuffled a half mile away from us, to the north and west, its body striped by the shimmering waves of evaporation coming off the ice. It had already seen us. As it moved, it swung its large head to gather our scent from the air. I doubted it knew quite what to make of us. We stood upright, not like seals, but in such a fierce environment everything that might be food held interest. Besides, it was the apex predator and it feared nothing.

I walked over and grabbed the binoculars from the sled. It took me another moment to zero in on the bear. It had shuffled on the diagonal toward us, still maintaining a safe distance. It was not stalking, but neither was it fleeing. It seemed curious more than anything else.

"May I see?" Sarah asked.

I handed her the binoculars.

"Wow," she said, the glasses at her eyes. "I've never seen a polar bear in the wild. Formidable."

Sammy looked next. "Male."

Peter looked and agreed.

"So," Sarah asked, "now what happens?"

"Now we stay very vigilant," I said. "Now we watch our backs."

"They do blend in," she said. "I mean, they *really* blend in."

"They can smell a seal from a mile," I said. "They're well equipped."

Andy grabbed his camera and took a battery of shots. The bear continued to move diagonally past us, as if it wanted to go to land.

"We should keep the rifles handy," Andy said, his eye on his camera viewfinder. "You never know. But it looks like he's eaten something recently. His chest fur is tinged with blood."

"He won't forget us," Peter said. "Bears don't forget."

"He'll hunt us?" Sarah asked.

Peter didn't reply. Sammy said something in Cree.

"'A bear brings its own weather,'" Peter translated. "It's a phrase."

"Meaning it is a force of providence?" Sarah asked.

Sammy nodded.

"We should probably move off," I said. "We can put some distance between us."

The wind picked up as we packed Andy's equipment back into the sled. Clouds moved in, too, and Sammy said he didn't like the look of the storm. We didn't have many options, though. I decided to cover a few miles to the north and east, the direction where the narwhal traditionally entered the leads bringing them to the bays. The storm, I imagined, would not permit us to go far. Rope had, at least, stopped growling. We could no longer see the bear.

We made three miles, maybe less, before the storm covered us.

It came in a short, violent burst and attacked the sled and tried to rip things free. It took all of us helping to erect the tents one by one, and even then the wind almost tore them from our hands. When we finished, we mounded snow around the bottoms of the tents to anchor them and to prevent the wind from seeping inside. Snow fell sideways through the air and tried to push us toward the open sea.

"Sometimes you get the bear," Andy shouted over the wind, "and sometimes the bear gets you."

"Let's take a break and see what the weather does," I shouted back. "Maybe sleep a little. This might clear off."

I climbed in with Sarah. She sat on top of her sleeping bag writing notes in a small book. It was a relief to be out of the wind. I knelt on my sleeping bag and rubbed my face, then slowly slipped out of my parka. My fingers and toes felt cold and I worried that my underlayers had become damp.

"I thought the birds were called murres," she said, not looking up.

"The seabirds?"

"The ones on the cliffs."

"Little auks and guillemots," I said. "In Europe the little auks are called dovekies. In Canada they call the guillemots, murres. It's a little confusing, but I think that's right. I've never been able to get it straight."

She glanced up at me. "Cold?"

"A little for some reason. The snow that blows in, it's called spindrift. It seeps into places."

"It's getting wet on the ice. All the melting. I think you're getting splashed more than Andy or I."

I shrugged. I did feel cold. "I'm going to get out of my underlayers."

"You want me to close my eyes?"

"Maybe." I smiled.

"Have you become shy in your old age, Allard?"

"Just around you."

"No one except your mother and Ed has seen you naked more than I have, Allard. At least that used to be true."

"Still true." I waited a moment, then smiled. "Yes. You should. Close your eyes, I mean."

I stripped out of my fleece and pulled off my wick underlayer. Then I turned my back and pulled my pants off. Everything I wore was wet. I grabbed new clothes out of my backpack and climbed into them. While I thrashed around, trying to bend my limbs in the cramped space, Sarah suddenly began laughing.

"That's quite a show," she said. "I'd slip a dollar bill into your long johns if I thought you'd stand for it."

"Nothing like a tent to get to know one another."

"We've shared tents before," she said, her voice still amused. "Even tree houses."

I didn't answer. The wind began to sing and push. Every now and then, almost unconsciously, I felt the surge of water underneath us. If the ice did not remain landfast, we would begin to drift, just as the polar bears did in winter. It reminded me of a children's story, one I couldn't quite call to mind. An image of a bear, forlorn, drifting on the open sea and looking at a full moon, lingered in my brain.

"Better?" Sarah asked when I finished dressing.

"Warmer. I may climb into my bag for a little."

"You should. I'm just writing up a few notes."

"How do you like the shoot so far?"

"I like our team. I've never been entirely comfortable on ice after our little adventure on the Baker River."

"Long time ago," I said, unzipping my bag.

"Not so long ago that I can't remember it."

"Was that the coldest you've ever been?"

"Top ten, anyway."

"It was cold, for sure." I climbed in my bag. I still felt chilled and a bit hungry.

"Are you worried about the bear?" Sarah asked.

"We have rifles, if it comes to that."

"Would it move around in a storm like this?"

I shrugged.

"Was that a shrug?" she asked.

"Yes. A bear might move around in a storm like this."

"How lucky for us," Sarah said. "How long do you think this storm will last?"

"No way of knowing. Our last report was for clear weather, but things change pretty fast up here. You've got all kinds of thermal action with the heating and the sunlight warming places that haven't been above freezing since October. If you take one of those time-lapsed shots, it looks like someone is pulling back a tablecloth across the top third of the globe."

"That was poetic, Allard!" Sarah laughed.

"Just doing my job, ma'am."

She put her notebook down and climbed into her bag. She propped her head on her hand and looked at me.

"It's good to see you, Allard. I'd almost forgotten how sweet you could be when you're not being a complete jerk."

"Not so sweet."

"Are you falling asleep on me?"

"Going to my inner lake."

"What's it like at your inner lake?"

"Quiet," I said. "Serene."

"With no one asking you questions?"

I nodded.

"Sounds boring to me," she said. "Really boring."

"Maybe if you found your inner lake you'd understand."

"I have an inner campfire. It's different from your lake, but it's nice there. People talk and roast marshmallows."

"Can you see a lake from your campfire? Because I'm over there, being quiet."

She didn't say anything, but she didn't stop looking at me, either. I closed my eyes. Suddenly I felt warm and sleepy and the storm didn't matter. If I had any talent for work in the outdoors, it was my ability to go to sleep under any conditions. Once I went horizontal, I slept. Sarah knew that and she wasn't about to let me get away with it.

"You really liked my books?" she asked, her voice quiet.

"Did. And do. They're terrific, Sarah. Sincerely."

"I'm glad you think so. Your mom wrote me a wonderful note about them. She read the new one as soon as it came out. She's probably my most devoted reader."

"She always admired you. But she wouldn't say she liked your books if she didn't. She has standards about things like that."

"You're right, she wouldn't. Not your mom."

"I'm asleep," I said. "You're talking to my subconscious."

"No, you're not."

"The storm could lock us down for a couple days," I said. "You should rest."

"I feel the water moving under us. When the wind blows, it feels like everything is moving."

"It's safe, don't worry."

"What if the water decided to split right here, right under us?"

"We'd be in a pickle."

"Did you say pickle?"

I nodded. My stomach growled. "Everything is always moving. It's the world as we know it. The earth is spinning and flying around the sun, and the sun is moving, and the moon is moving, and wind is moving, and we are moving even when we're asleep. We are traveling all the time whether we know it or not."

"Is that supposed to make me feel safer?"

"Does it?"

"Not at all," she said.

"Tell me about the narwhal. I know you. I know you researched them until you went cross-eyed."

"I did."

"Tell me the mythology."

"Unicorns," she said. "Mostly that. It's likely that the Vikings got a glimpse of them and brought the story back to Europe. Over time it got mixed together with tales of zebras and horses and deer. Unicorns symbolized purity and probably a sense of a creature too good for the world. Stags represented the Christ, so it got mixed together in that wonderful way that myths build on themselves and cross-pollinate. Eventually it evolves and morphs until you need a virgin to trap a unicorn. The unicorn will lay its head in a virgin's lap. It's a stewpot myth, like most of them."

"But you like it?"

"I do, because I'm a virgin." Then she laughed.

I had forgotten how funny Sarah could be, how she liked to tease and have fun. I smiled. I heard her voice get light and happy when she spoke next.

"We own each other's virginity, you know. We are each other's unicorn."

"That doesn't quite fit the myth," I said. "It's a little off."

"So sue me."

"Some people reclaim their virginity. It's called secondary virginity. Some Christian groups, I think. They advocate it."

"Isn't a second virginity something of an oxymoron?"

"It is," I said. "But it's good work if you can get it."

"Okay, so I am a virgin again and I can trap a unicorn."

"Let's hope so."

She rolled onto her belly. She took a deep breath. She opened her notebook again. I heard her write something. The wind scattered snow against our tent and I heard a tarp come loose on the sled. It made a sputtering sound like a kid putting a baseball card in his bicycle spokes.

"Remember how Ed said he used to think about animals waking up in the spring? He pictured the animals slowly unwinding from their hibernation. Remember? Then he would pretend to be a bear, you know, and he would come out of his den and he would look groggy, and he wondered if the world wasn't new to the bear each year. And he always wondered how a turtle knew it was time to wake up. You know, they're down in the pond muck, nearly turned to ice, and then the stars turn and the water warms and I guess their blood begins to flow again."

I didn't say anything.

"Allard?"

"Hmmmm."

"I need to hear about Ed," she said, her voice a quiet whisper. "If not now, then sometime. I need to hear the story from you. We had the reports, you know, the official things, but you never said . . ."

"Leave it, Sarah. Let it go."

"I can't. I won't."

"He died in Wyoming on a mountain. In the Wind Rivers. You read the accident report."

"I know that. But you were with him."

"Yes."

"To the end."

"Not to the end," I said, feeling my stomach flutter. "I went for help. Ed died by himself."

"And he was trapped?"

"Yes, he was trapped. Just an accident. No rhyme or reason to it. It just happened."

"You took a different route coming down, though. That's what your dad said."

"Ed thought we could save time. He said it would be an adventure. We just looped around part of the trail. No big deal."

"Was he scared? Did he seem frightened by it all?"

"Not that I could see. He was in some pain, but it wasn't so bad. Not intolerable for him. It started to snow and that got him. He had a fire going for a little while, but he couldn't keep it going in the snow."

"The report said you walked twenty miles to save him."

"It didn't do much good, I'm afraid."

"Yes, you did. You did all you could. Do you know I collect Ed stories? Every once in a while when I'm home, I bump into someone who remembers him and wants to talk about him. It's always the same. He was always kind to people. No one ever says anything bad, but I guess they wouldn't. I write down the stories in a notebook with his name on it. I thought it would help me remember."

"He was a good guy."

"He was a great guy. You were pretty great, too, you know? Those things you liked in Ed, you had them, too."

"Maybe," I said. "I'd like to think I did."

We didn't speak again for a long time. The wind keened and moved across the ice, lifting snow as if searching for something below it. A pressure ridge, mounting and forming a half mile to our south, boomed with the ice crumpling and pushing up, two plates of frozen seawater meeting and clapping. We listened to the rip of the tarp snapping on the sled. We heard the yawn of five million miles of sea ice retreating. Birds, murres and dovekies, yanked by the wind and chucked out to the open ocean, their offspring waiting, teetering on their rocky perches, foxes circling below. Eggshells. Lichen. The sun rolling like a fat dime across the horizon, muted now by the storm. Far away, the narwhal ribboning the ocean with their wide bodies, their tusks popping up to keep the skim ice from forming. The leads so many black cracks in a white world. Deep down the halibut and char, the capelin, the vibrating blood of small, cold fish.

And Ed a million miles away, Ed, my brother, now soil, now vapor, now plant and root.

22

Tracks," Peter said ten hours later.

The storm had passed. The sun burned brightly on the horizon and the ice had begun to sag and droop. The temperature shot up to a few degrees above freezing. The air felt rinsed. We all wore thick glacier glasses. Peter had been out to use the latrine, and when he came back, he reported the tracks.

"How far?" Andy asked, his hands moving over the sled to stow his gear.

Peter pointed out to a spot a hundred, maybe two hundred meters away. "A big bear. Not long ago."

Sammy said something in Cree. Peter nodded.

"What?" I asked.

"Hunting," Peter said.

"How can you tell?" Sarah asked.

Sammy said something quickly in Cree and Peter translated it.

"Sometimes in spring ice a bear will flatten out to spread its weight to keep from going through the ice. But if they do that, they don't stay in one place. A bear only stays in one place to hide or sleep. He was . . ." Peter completed the sentence in Cree to Sammy.

"Stalking," Sammy said, supplying the word.

"Probably came up at the tail of the storm," Andy said. "Not much we can do about it. Hate to shoot it."

Fifteen minutes after Peter alerted us to the bear tracks, we climbed back on the sled and headed southeast. It was wet going. The snowmobile churned snow and ice back at us, and when we snapped down into the large, expanding melt pools, water flew up and over us. Sammy did his best to avoid the pools, but they spread everywhere now, and the showers from the snowmobile were inescapable. Rope did the only sensible thing. He curled into a ball and kept his back to the showers, but we couldn't manage as well.

After an hour and a half of slogging, we found the lead.

I smelled it before I saw it. The salty scent of open seawater lingered over the ice, rolling toward us as we approached. Sammy ran the snowmobile parallel to the lead, following it as it widened in a seaward direction. When he had gone as far as he dared, he turned the snowmobile around so it faced land and then cut the engine. Immediately the sense of the sea grew and gained strength around us. The water below appeared black and opaque, a vein of the ocean pumping slowly toward land.

"This is our best shot so far," Andy said as we dismounted, all of us trying to frisk water off ourselves. "How far out to open water would you guess?"

"Not more than a mile at this point," I said. "It's receding fast."

I asked Sammy and Peter for their estimates and they agreed.

"Let's do it then," Andy said. "Let's photograph some ice."

"I'm coming in with you," I said.

"I was hoping you would say that," Andy said. "Two's company."

It took time to arrange the dive. We hooked safety lines to ice screws and laid out our dry suits. Peter boiled water in a billycan for our gloves. Andy dropped a thermometer in the water before we started stripping off our clothes. Thirty-four degrees Fahrenheit. He pulled it back up and took a picture of the reading.

"Ready?" he asked afterward.

"As much as I'm going to be."

Sarah helped us dress. We had to strip out of our parkas and underlayers and exchange them for hooded Gore-Tex jumpsuits. The dry suits fit snugly, but not impossibly so, their designs leaving a thin skin of space between us and the frigid water. Before we entered the water, we would inflate the suits with the cartridges of argon—about the size of a flashlight—on our chests. Even with the advanced technology, we would not be able to stay in the water long. In addition to the cold, we also needed to monitor the second-stage breathing regulators that would be warmed by our exhalations, but could still freeze and begin to cut off our air. The cold complicated everything. Sarah handed us the equipment as we needed it, helping especially with the aluminum 80s, our tanks, and adjusting them on our backs. At the end she poured a thin stream of near-boiling water into our gloves. It felt strange standing out on the ice, dressed as a seal, our flippers somehow more absurd on the ice shelf than they would have been inland.

Andy went first. He stood on the edge of the lead, and then, without any hesitation, he jumped into the water, holding his mask securely to his face. He bobbed up a moment later, the suit sufficiently buoyant to require forty pounds on our belts to help us dive. Peter shoved the underwater camera—a Sony digital camera enclosed in an Ikelite casing—to him, and Andy floated on the surface for a second, then turtled and disappeared.

I followed. I scissored my legs slightly and jumped in, my hand to my mask. Immediately the world disappeared in a confusion of bubbles, only to be replaced by absolute silence and the underside of an entirely new topography.

The narwhal live here, I thought as the water cleared.

I looked around slowly. Imagine the sea covered with a translucent shelf, a ceiling of dull ice, the illumination diffuse and as quiet as church light. All sound seemed to disappear for a moment, until I adjusted and began to pick up an undercurrent of ice rubbing and chafing, the restless sea trying to reach toward the sun. The melting ice carved itself into fantastical shapes. Beyond Andy, on either side of the lead, the ice had pulled back as if dented by a can opener.

I thought of Ed for just an instant, my brother, and how he would have loved being under the ice, would have loved knowing the narwhal followed this stream of life to the rich bays behind us. For a count or two he did not seem so far away. Perhaps because of the ceiling of ice, I remembered our beds in the upstairs attic, the sounds of storms hitting on the metal roof, the map of the great land spread forever above us.

We did not have long. An hour was the theoretical limit on our tanks because the cold water made us consume air faster, but to be on the safe side I had called for a thirty-minute dive. We might have made it a little longer, but I wanted a safe margin.

I checked my watch and after ten minutes signaled to Andy that twenty remained. He nodded. He swam closer to the surface and spent some time photographing the division between air and sea. He tried, I knew, to replicate the narwhal's swimming pattern. They would stay near the surface, swimming in single file down the leads, their eyes occasionally rising high enough to peer over the flat plain of ice. Seen from above, they resembled so many needles stitching the ice.

We swam toward the open sea, the safety ropes dangling in bell curves back to the ice above us. I stayed behind and to the side, leaving Andy a full view toward the ice and depths below us. He maneuvered the camera easily, pushing it ahead of him as smoothly as a shopping cart, and the camera lights shot funnels of illumination in any direction he pointed.

We were nearly back to our starting point when we saw Peter plummet into the water.

It happened so suddenly, and looked so peculiar, that it took me a moment to comprehend what had happened. The confusion of the bubbles, the oddity of seeing a person suddenly in the water, did not add up. To make it worse, Peter flailed at the water, falling slowly downward, his legs and arms beating wildly to try to keep him afloat. Clearly, he didn't know how to swim, and the additional weight from his parka and leggings made him a dull dart thrown carelessly toward the bottom. A surge of adrenaline passed through me, part of it mixed with annoyance that someone could be so careless as to fall in the water, but there was no time to parse what had happened. I swam past Andy, moving quickly, my hand extended toward Peter. But before I reached him, I saw his panic and I put two hands up, signaling for him to remain calm, but that was impossible now. He continued to go deeper and I had to move at a slant to grab his hand. As soon as his hand touched mine, he panicked and began trying to climb me, pulling me deeper. I tried to make him understand, but he was freezing and drowning, and he wanted to be up, higher, and I was the only offer he had.

I reached behind me and handed him the safety rope.

He saw it and immediately grabbed it. He had that much reason left. He began hoisting himself along the line and I saw the line itself move over the ice, assisting him, and in the next instant he broke the surface. His free arm still slapped at the water and his feet kicked erratically. I saw Andy near him, apparently sliding his camera onto the ice shelf, then I saw Peter lift and fold halfway onto the ice. I went below him and helped push him up, and in two quick movements—some help from above, some shoves from me— he slid out of the water and onto the ice. His feet left the water last and left a ring on the surface.

Blood. I saw it as soon as I surfaced, the dull crimson gleam of it out of place in the bright sunlight. I stripped off my weight belt and threw it onto the ice. Gradually my ears unclogged from the water and pressure of my diving hood, and I heard Sarah yelling something. Not Sarah, I thought, my heart stopping for a moment. But she moved quickly and competently, pulling Peter more securely onto the ice. She yanked hard. He skidded slowly across the ice.

". . . damn bear," she said.

But I only heard shattered portions of it.

Andy rested on his knees, hurriedly stripping out of his mask and tank harness. His face looked red and cold. Peter, meanwhile, coughed up seawater, his parka coated with an icy sheen. From my vantage point in the water, I could not see the cause of the blood. But when Sammy came over and helped me hoist myself out of the water, I nearly fell on top of the bear.

It lay stretched out on the ice, its mouth snarled open with a second tongue consisting of bright blood oozing into a pool near its nose. A bullet hole below its right ear also leaked blood. It had fallen not more than ten yards from the lead opening. It was dead. It was impossible to mistake its stillness.

"We were distracted and it knew it, damn it," Sarah said, her voice tight with emotion, her face flushed and frustrated. She pulled and tugged and tried to assist Peter with his clothes.

"It waited," Sammy said, the bear's blood on his hands, "and picked its time."

"Rope's hurt," Sarah said. "If Rope hadn't warned us, one of us would have died."

"Peter jumped," Sammy said. "It went after him. I got off a shot and took him."

I realized in listening I had to let the details go until later. Right now, Peter risked hypothermia. To complicate matters, Andy and I needed to get warm, too. The natural decision would have been to set up a tent and get a gas heater going, but our position near the lead was too tenuous. The lead could continue to open; the ice could fracture and submerge in one huge chunk. We needed to be warm, and we needed to move, and those two necessities worked against one another.

"We need to set up a tent here," I decided. "Just one and we need heat. We'll stay as long as we need to in order to get Peter warm, then we move toward land."

"What about the bear?" Sarah asked, still assisting Peter.

"We'll see to it later."

Rope lay near the sled, obviously injured. I couldn't afford the time to inspect him, but it appeared something had smashed his shoulder. A hazy dusting of blood covered his fur.

Andy and I did not bother to strip out of our diving suits before helping Sammy set up the largest of our three tents. By the time we managed to erect the tent, Sarah had Peter down to his long underwear. We moved him quickly into the tent and started an alcohol stove. We put him in a sleeping bag on top of an air mattress. It was as much as we could do for him.

Sarah came in carrying Rope.

"His shoulder is smashed," she said, kneeling and putting the dog softly on the sleeping pad next to Peter. "And he's probably got a couple broken ribs."

"Did he attack the bear?"

She nodded.

"It was so stealthy," she said. "Suddenly it was there. Our attention was on the water and then the bear rose up right in our midst. I've never experienced anything like it. If Rope hadn't barked, it would have taken Peter."

"We should radio our position," Andy said, at last pulling off his diving suit. "In case we need to be evacuated."

I nodded.

"Let's get Peter warm," I said, "and get our equipment stowed. Where's Sammy?"

"He's still outside," Sarah said. "He shot the bear right through the head."

"It's a big bear," Andy said.

"A male," Sarah said. "I hate that we killed it."

In the cramped tent, it took Andy and me a half hour to undress and get into our regular clothes. Sarah boiled water in the billycan. We all needed hot tea. Sammy came in and sat on the sleeping pad next to Peter. He held his hands out to the small stove. He appeared tired and shaky. Peter, at last, turned over and faced the stove. He still shivered in profound shakes and tremors, but that, I knew, was a good sign. His body was returning from the cold.

"What do you want to do with the bear?" I asked Sammy when Andy ducked out to start loading his equipment.

"Too warm, probably," Sammy said. "The meat will spoil."

I nodded. A little later, Andy returned to say he could not establish radio contact. He also said he had stowed all of our gear. Meanwhile, Sarah ministered to Rope. She used some of the tea water to bathe the dog and examine its shoulder. Apparently the bear had cuffed the dog aside in its lunge for Peter. She patted the dog quietly. The tent grew warmer. We drank tea.

"What do you think of the ice?" I asked Sammy a little later. "Can we stay here?"

He shook his head.

"We should move?" I asked.

He nodded.

"We can try the radio again in a little while," Andy said. "Before we move on. Did you hear anything on the sound sensor?"

Sarah shook her head.

"You think the bear was healthy?" Andy asked. "I mean, coming into camp like that."

"They hunt," Sammy said. "They always hunt."

"No reason for it to fear humans, really," I said. "It's the top predator. No way it can understand guns. We may be the first humans it ever saw."

"The bear has followed Peter before," Sammy said. "When

Peter was a boy, a bear almost killed him. Peter was with his father, skinning out a caribou they had shot, and the bear appeared much as it did today. Peter's father pointed his *savik*—his knife—and the red blood dripped down and formed a circle around them both. The bear could not cross it, but it promised to come back for him one day when his father was not beside him."

"The bear spoke to him?" Sarah asked.

"In dreams," Sammy said. "That's why we didn't see him until he was on us. He was not there, and then he was."

"He passed through time?" Andy asked, his voice thin and curious.

"It's not time exactly," Sammy said. "Through dreams."

"But it was the same bear?" Sarah asked.

Sammy nodded.

Just then the ice gave out a long, shrieking yawn, and something in the near distance broke. The ice flexed like a trampoline, which was not unusual on seawater—seawater did not freeze into the rigid plate one found on freshwater lakes—but it still made my stomach roll. I moved over next to Peter and asked him how he felt. He still shivered, but not as badly as before.

"We need to move," I told Peter. "Can you endure a little travel?"

He nodded.

"We should do it sooner than later," I said. "We'll give you new clothes and we'll only travel as far as we need to reach better ice. But we shouldn't stay here."

He nodded again.

Sarah and I dressed him in backup clothing. He helped but he seemed sluggish and quiet, most likely still in shock. It's one thing to have an accident; it was something else to have an animal attempt to devour you. When both things combined, it was not an easy thing to let go. Eventually he wore new clothing and sat steadily on the sleeping bag; he appeared drawn and shaken. The tent, I knew, would be difficult for him to leave. It was warm and quiet. I couldn't quite know what the bear meant to him, or even if it meant anything at all.

Sammy slipped out. I heard him speaking to Andy.

"Well," Sarah said, her voice searching for a normal tone, "this has been an eventful day."

"Just a little," I said.

"Did you get good footage?"

"We did," I said.

"Will you photograph the bear?"

"Just in passing. We need to get off this ice." I turned to Peter. "Are you ready, Peter?"

"Yes," he said.

It was the first time he had spoken since the incident.

We led him outside. He did not look at the bear. I carried Rope and put him on the sled in his usual position. He whimpered when I set him down. I couldn't hazard a guess if he would make it. For the moment, that was not a top concern. My top concern was the lead, which had grown wider since we dove. I did not like the way the ice felt underfoot. The springy, trampoline quality had increased. It felt like walking on a mattress.

Andy and I dismantled the tent and packed it away. Sammy checked the snowmobile and put Peter on the machine. Sarah retrieved the sound sensor and packed it beside us. Sammy, meanwhile, moved close to the bear. He knelt beside it and expertly cut its claws free. He moved clockwise around the carcass. When he finished, he said something in Cree. Peter, from his place on the snowmobile, nodded. Chanting quietly, Sammy threw the toes into the open lead. The claws made a quiet plunk, no louder than pebbles going into a stream.

23

"WHAT DID YOU DO with the dress?" I asked.

Sarah looked up from her notes. She sat on her sleeping pad, her legs crossed. The tent interior felt warm and slightly stuffy. We had set up a temporary camp a mile and a half away from the open lead. Slowly things had come back to normal.

"My wedding dress?" she asked, her voice puzzled.

I nodded.

"That's a funny thing to ask about."

"I remember when you bought it. How happy you were."

"I loved that dress."

"What did you do with it?"

She looked at me. Underneath us the ice shifted and we heard something crack. The crack came from far away, but still Sarah placed both hands on either side of her, as if she could catch herself if the ice fractured.

"I made a scarecrow out of it," she said. "And it worked."

"Seriously?"

She looked at me for a three count, then shook her head. "It's upstairs in the back of Mom's closet. Covered in plastic. It looks like a big, white bell."

"I'm sorry I never saw you in it."

She nodded. She adjusted her notebook on her lap. "It's probably not fair to say that. Not at this point."

It was my turn to nod. "Fair enough."

"Where did you go afterward?" she asked after a little while. "That's something I always wondered. I mean, if we're talking. I never had a clear idea."

"Into the Wind Rivers. Way up. To feel close to Ed. I lived on fish, mostly. Then after a few weeks I made my way to Washington and eventually Morgan. It's hard to explain my mental state at the time."

She looked at me. I couldn't read her expression. She looked down at the notebook on her lap, then back up into my eyes.

"I wanted to come see you, you know?" she said. "But then when you isolated yourself from me and I didn't know where you were or what you were doing, my feelings started to change and shift a little. Deep down I was hurt and my compassion toward you turned into anger. Little by little, water working on rock. I felt abandoned. I kept asking myself what had I done? I kept thinking there was some sort of answer, but eventually I realized there wasn't. I had done nothing, except love you—and Ed. It made no sense. Eventually I became frustrated and felt stuck waiting for you, wondering why you turned against me."

"I don't blame you."

"You should have come home," she said, her voice no longer careful. "I needed you. We all needed you."

"I couldn't. I wish I could explain it better, but I can't. I'm not proud of it. I hope you don't think I was ever proud of it."

She didn't say anything. We listened to the ice again as

it boomed and moved. A flight of auks went overhead, their wingbeats creating a whoosh like leaves skidding on pavement.

"I dressed up one time, you know?" she said. "In the wedding dress. Since you asked, I'll tell you. I don't know why I did it. I was looking for something in my mother's closet, and I was pushing through her things when I found the dress. I took off my clothes right there, and I stripped to my underwear and I climbed into the dress. I wasn't gentle . . . don't think that . . . it wasn't some holy moment where I was thinking of you, believe me . . . but I put it on and I stepped out to my mom's mirror and I looked at myself. And I thought, Allard does not want me. He does not want *this*. And you were so deep inside me, so part of my every day, that I couldn't quite comprehend it.

"Part of me wanted to rip the dress apart, but I thought, at least give it to Goodwill, and that's what saved it. I stepped out of it and hung it back up and I put the plastic over it. Then I closed the closet door and had the sensation that I was done with you. Closing the door to our life together. And I felt as though I could never open it again because you would spring out and come back into my life. Just like that."

I reached over and tried to touch her hand but she twisted it away and shook her head no.

"So I hid, too, you know?" she said, her voice angry. "I went into my work. I spent solid days on research and writing. Days and days and days. I had a special table at the Baker Library over at Dartmouth. After my first book came out, they gave me a study carrel. Just a little desk, but I could leave my books there. It gave me a place to be, if you know what I mean."

"I do."

"When my first book came out, I thought you'd see it and return. You'd read most of it already in manuscript, but I figured seeing it would change you. I had a hard time accepting that you had turned on me. I mean, I loved the book, the writing and the research . . . and it was exciting that it did pretty well. It made some end-of-the-year lists, some nominations for science writing . . . and I was solid enough. I was. It wasn't like you had to come back, that I wrote this book to get you back, but it was part of you, too. Part of our lives together . . . with Ed. I thought it might give you a pretext to contact me, I guess. But you didn't. The second book . . . it was harder to write, and maybe better, more disciplined. But it was an enormous amount of work. I didn't socialize much. I lived a monastic life. I drank ink, as the old scholars used to say. And I cursed you. I wrote that book with the anger I had for you. I'm not angry now, but I was then."

"It's very good, Sarah."

She shrugged. She put her head down. Then she put her hands over her face. She didn't cry. When she looked up, our eyes met in an old, familiar way.

"I don't want to know about your life without me," she said. "About other women, or about how you went on. I thought I did. I thought, if I could just know everything about him, know every detail, then I could forgive him. *Tout comprendre, tout pardonner.* That old thing. Then I gradually realized it wasn't up to me to forgive you. I didn't have that right . . . or even that responsibility. I had this entire conversation in my head for a long time. Things I wanted to say. Stinging things. I figured you would cringe under it like a whip coming down on you. I don't know. I'm not being clear. It's not what I thought it would be like, seeing you. I don't feel any of that old anger. I just feel sad and sorry that we drifted apart. It feels like we were on different icebergs and we couldn't jump across to one another."

"I wasn't healthy, Sarah. You need to know that. I thought about you every day. And maybe I wasn't courageous enough. . . . I couldn't put Ed behind me. For a while I thought that if I left Wyoming, if I left where he died, that it would be a disservice to his memory. That if I began to forget him, then I would forget myself. We would both be erased. It's not something I can really explain."

She took a deep breath. She rubbed her face with her hands and pulled her hat more tightly onto her head. She looked at me evenly.

"I moved to D.C. and took a lover to try and forget you," she said, her tone deliberately matter-of-fact. "Does it hurt you to know that?"

I nodded.

"I'm sorry, but you deserve it. I didn't mean it to come out like that, but that's the way it felt. I was trying to hurt you at the time. The whole thing was about hurting you at first, but then it changed. I realized there were other people in the world. Other men, other good people. I'm sorry now if knowing that hurts you."

"It does, but I understand."

"It's been two years, Allard."

"I know."

"I didn't want you to think I shrink-wrapped myself and sat on a shelf somewhere. I don't want those kinds of lies to linger. I don't want that to be our legacy."

"I didn't think that."

"And I know you're attractive to women. You're handsome as hell. I know women would be interested. I'm sure they fell all over you."

She took another deep breath. Her chest sounded the tiniest bit shuddery. She looked down for a moment, then straightened her notebook on her lap. She squared her shoulders. Then she took another breath and sat quietly for a moment and looked at me.

"What happened up on that mountain, Allard? You have to tell me. I've never known exactly."

"Ed got trapped by a rock."

"It rolled on him?"

"He stepped on a rock and jumped to the next one, but before he could move, the rock behind him rolled and trapped his legs. It was a freak accident."

"I knew the outline, of course. Everyone did. But I hate you for not coming home and explaining it to me. I deserved better."

I nodded.

"Was he in pain? Were you telling the truth when you told me before it wasn't bad?"

"Not terrible pain. I can't know for sure, but he was brave. He was Ed."

"And the cold killed him?"

I nodded again.

"Part of me understands why you didn't come home. That's the weird thing, isn't it? I could understand why you wouldn't want to come home and go through the wedding or try to pretend everything was like it was before. I *know* what Ed meant in your life, Allard. I saw it. I watched it for years. But I thought I meant as much. That's what kills me to realize. I thought . . . even merely as a friend . . . you would come home and console me. I thought we could console each other . . . that's what a couple does, it seems to me. I understood that you had a place in your heart that I couldn't reach. I don't know. It's all confusing to me now. Every once in a while I thought I understood it, but then it would slip away . . . the understanding would become anger or self-pity and I would curse you."

"I didn't do it to be cruel. I just didn't know how to come home without Ed. How to pick up our lives and move on. It seemed impossible."

"But it was cruel anyway."

"Yes."

"Did Ed talk about me at all? At the end?"

"He wanted to make sure to get me back in time. He loved you, Sarah. He said you were the best and he took a lot of pictures for the wedding slide show. He wanted to make that special for you. And then he left the note saying good-bye to you, to all of us. I left all his belongings for Dad to have. "

"Lovely old Ed."

"We had a charmed life, Sarah. That's what it felt like. And then, in an instant, it wasn't charmed any longer and I couldn't cope. I don't know if that explains anything, but that's how it felt. I should have come home. I know that now, but I couldn't do it then."

"You were a coward."

"Yes."

"I hate that part of you. I hate knowing it exists in you."

"So do I."

"Your mother said when you were little you believed a sandman lived in the playground beside the library. Do you remember that?"

"I guess so."

"They had put sand down to make the ground softer for kids, and you had this image of the sand collecting itself and rising up in the shape of a man. Sometimes you said you saw a hand at the bottom of the slide. Other times it was a face with an open mouth under the swings. Your mother said it made her nervous to hear you describe it because the imagery was so complete."

"I remember."

"I guess you finally met the sandman, didn't you?"

I nodded.

"My girlfriends think you are poisonous for me," Sarah said. "They think I am a fool to take this assignment, but I admit I was curious. Self-punishing behavior, they call it. They know some part of me is still connected to you. I guess it always will be."

"I didn't set out to hurt you."

"That makes it worse, doesn't it? To be hurtful in an offhand way? To be destructive without knowing it? Is that supposed to be better?"

"I'm sorry."

She looked at me. "You could have come to me," she said softly, "but you didn't. I forgive you, but I can't forget it. 'All the king's horses and all the king's men couldn't put Humpty Dumpty back together again.'"

She looked at me a little longer, then began writing in her notebook. I listened to the scratching and the wind hitting against the tent canvas. I thought I felt that blade of ice once more, the one that I had after Ed's death, turn slowly deep down in my heart.

24

A NDY RAISED A FINGER, then nodded. He had the sensor in a large lead, his headphones clamped over his ears. He heard them. Open water rested due south of us, perhaps a half mile away. The whales had to be there, waiting for the moment to advance up the lead. Once they began their journey, they wouldn't turn back. No one knew how they determined the moment to head into the ice. It was a perilous journey, the master trick of the narwhal.

"We've got them," Andy said. "There's more than one. They are calling and clicking. It's a pod."

Sarah took the headphones when Andy offered them. Almost immediately she began to nod. She looked down at her feet and concentrated.

"How beautiful," she whispered when she looked up again. "You can almost feel their impatience to start."

She handed me the headphones, then went off to nurse Rope. She had spent a good deal of her time encouraging Rope, and he seemed slightly better for it. He would never run in harness again, but I suspected Peter would keep him alive because the dog had saved him. Rope might recover his strength in time.

The whale chatter came through the headset loud and distinct. I had heard similar calls before, of course, but not in such a remote location, balanced on the retreating ice. And never from a narwhal. I passed the earphones to Sammy, who in turn passed them to Peter.

"Any guess what the ice is like out that way?" I asked Sammy as Andy stowed the sensors back on the sled.

"Hard to know," Sammy said. "This time of year, it's hard to say."

"Should we hike out?" I asked, thinking to reduce our weight.

"We might get separated from the sled if we do," Sammy said. "The ice might shear off any which way. Stay with the sled is my advice. Peter will walk in front of it."

"The bay and the river inlet are behind us," Peter said. "This is where they want to travel."

We followed the lead southward. Sammy allowed Peter to ride awhile, then he stopped and let him dismount. Peter took the long metal pole with him and walked ahead of the sled, testing the ice as he went. Pressure ridges had built out toward the sea, the ice resembling a bomb field. One way or the other, the snowmobile could not go much farther. Peter poked at the ice and led us forward.

A smart wind picked up and blew straight out to sea. It was a straight, steady wind, cold and biting. One by one we put up our hoods. I sensed that we needed to find the whales soon; fatigue had become a factor. All of us kept our eyes out to sea, straining to see some sign of the narwhal. Peter jumped softly from dry snow to dry snow. He jabbed the pole into the ice as many as four times before he trusted it.

Finally, Sammy turned the snowmobile back to shore and shut off the engine. He caught my eye and made a cutting signal, one hand chopping against the other. I understood. We had come as far as we dared on the snowmobile. Travel from now on would be on foot, at least as we advanced seaward.

"I'm going to climb that pressure ridge," I said, pointing to a small explosion of ice about a hundred yards toward the sea. "If we can't see them from there, then we'll have to regroup. Meanwhile, we all need to put on our personal locator beacons. If this ice breaks apart, you'll want people to know where you are."

"I'm coming with you," Sarah said.

Peter gave us his pole after we put on our beacons. I had a fair amount of experience on the ice, but I was by no means an expert. The wind shoving at our backs made concentration on the surface beneath us more difficult. I took a deep breath and told myself to take it slowly. Sarah followed my footsteps precisely, putting her feet where mine had been. The ice, meanwhile, continued to waver under our feet. It felt untrustworthy.

"Gnarly," Sarah said when we reached the base of the pressure ridge.

"It's never easy."

"You feel the ice moving under us?"

"Yes," I said.

"It feels like when you think you're on something solid, like the bedroom floor, and then you step on a sweater or a pillow or something and your stomach gets queasy."

I nodded.

"Why don't you stay down here and let me take a crack at it alone?" I asked. "I'll call you up if I see anything."

"No way. I'm coming with you. I don't want to be the guy in the *Star Trek* movie who gets killed waiting for Captain Kirk to return."

"Do you think I'm like Captain Kirk?"

"He wore tighter trousers," she said.

She started up the pressure ridge without me. It was like climbing sugar cubes, only outsize ones, cubes as big as bread trucks. With crampons it might have been moderately difficult, but without them we were forced into gymnastics, twisting and making bridges out of our bodies to get from one cube to the next. The wind continued shoving at us, frisking to find a way under our clothing. Sarah climbed better than I did. She was lighter and more nimble and had always been good at climbing. I remembered that.

It took ten minutes to reach the top. I arrived after she did. I looked quickly out to sea and was disappointed to observe nothing except the gray-blue open water. It was a pretty sight, with the moon coming up and the sun already in the sky. The moon resembled a cup lifting out of the water, its contents nearly spilling out and returning to the sea. I kicked myself that I had forgotten binoculars. I looked back at the sled and wondered if I could somehow get a pair delivered, but that made no sense. I was still looking, trying to remember where I had left the binoculars, when Sarah's hand touched mine.

"There," she whispered.

She pointed south by southeast. I had to squint and follow the direction of her arm to see the whales. For an instant I thought she was mistaken. Just swirls, I thought. Just waves. Then something extended from the water, something not round and fluid like everything else, but erect and pointed, a finger of bone pointed at the sky. I squinted more and began to see them, one, five, ten narwhal. They paced at the edge of the ice, rising and diving, their blowholes sending teapots of steam into the air.

"They're beautiful," Sarah said. "They're so beautiful."

"They're waiting."

"What do we do now?"

"We wait as long as we can. If the ice gets too unsafe, then we leave. They're ready to come up this lead as soon as it cracks wide enough."

"Their backs are mottled. Can you see?" she asked, her hand up to shade her eyes.

"Spotted, almost."

"I can hear them. When they exhale, I can hear them."

"Are you sure?"

"Shhhh. Listen."

We stood beside each other without making any movement. Wind flapped at our back and pushed us to join the whales. I thought I heard them, but I couldn't be certain. I whispered as much to Sarah.

"This is the great land," Sarah said softly, her eyes on the whales. "We're here, Allard. You've been aiming to get here all your life. Ed would have loved this so. I'm sorry he died."

"So am I."

"When you were boys and looked at the map, it was here, this was what you looked for."

I nodded.

"Life has a way of happening no matter what we do, doesn't it?"

"Yes."

"You broke my heart, Allard. It's still broken. I could lie and say it isn't, but that wouldn't be the truth."

Then she turned and waved to the guys back by the sled. She whooped. They waved back. The whales blew vapor into the air and the vapor turned to white mist that blew out to sea and rejoined the water.

25

So what's next for you, Allard?" Sarah asked.

We sat in the Oil Change, two beers in front of us. Sammy and Peter had already departed. I was flying back with Andy early the next morning. He had stayed at the Quonset hut to put the final touches on our packing, then he was going to join us. Sarah and I had decided to come out for a drink. Spud, the bartender, worked outside on an outboard motor hung in an ash can. Now and then we heard it try to start, fail, then try again. He had told us to help ourselves.

"More filming, I guess," I said. "Morgan's doing something on foxes. I don't know exactly what it's going to involve, but I'll probably be on the shoot. How about you?"

"Well, I'll write this up and see what it looks like. I want to get going on another book, but I'm not sure of the topic. Maybe something about the melt and the animals here."

"Back to D.C.?"

"It's where I live now," she said, then looked down quickly at her hands. "And I'm involved with somebody there, Allard. You should probably know that, I guess, although it isn't your business any longer. I figured . . . I don't know what I figured."

I took a sip of beer. I had a hard time breathing.

"Well, good," I said.

Her eyes glistened a little. She sipped her own beer.

"I didn't know when to drop it into the conversation, Allard. I'm sorry. If I told you right off the bat, that would have been strange. And then it started to slip away, if you know what I mean. The opportunity to bring it up . . . and we were living in such close quarters. I didn't know how to fit it into what we were doing. It felt awkward. It feels awkward now."

"No problem. It's not a problem, Sarah. It's good."

She looked at me. She seemed to study me, then nodded and confirmed something in her mind. She stood and went to the bar and brought us back two more beers. She slid one in front of me. She lifted her tone when she spoke again.

"Do you remember that summer we threw knives at everything? Dad bought the throwing knives for us and my mom went crazy, swearing we would put out each other's eyes. Then Ed bought a ninja star from somewhere. And we put that round of wood up on a sawhorse and threw our knives at it? Remember?"

"Sure, I remember."

"I like thinking about that time. I was really good at that. You and Ed tried, but I was the best. We had a great childhood, Allard."

"Yes, we did."

I couldn't quite look at her. I tried to think of a reason to go back to the Quonset hut, but nothing waited for us there. I took a drink of beer. I felt like drinking a lot of beer. She took a small sip, then put her hand on my arm.

"I'm sorry, Allard. I didn't mean to drop that on you. If it means anything, I didn't do it to hurt you this time. It was just something you need to know."

"You don't have to be sorry. You shouldn't be. I'm the one who should be sorry."

"Can we agree to let it go? I can't blame you anymore. I have such warm, fond memories of you, Allard. That's what I had to remind myself to remember. I know you. I know you wouldn't deliberately hurt me or anyone else for that matter. That's been the best thing about seeing you up here. I saw who you were again. So let's put it behind us and go forward. Can we do that? But you have to do me a favor first."

"What's that?"

"Go home, Allard," she said with surprising force. "Whatever it is that kept you away, or that made it impossible for you to go, it doesn't matter anymore. Go home. Spend some time at home with your parents. They love you so much that they can't even tell you. Will you do that for me?"

I nodded.

"You promise?"

"I promise." I met her eyes.

"Good. That would make me very happy. We can call things square if you do that."

I went and got two more beers. Sarah turned and smiled at me as I came back. But the smile wasn't for me, not really, but was instead for the person she knew once, a fellow worker, an old friend, a chum, a buddy, not for the boy whose hand she found under the ice all those years before.

PART III:

HOMECOMING

26

I SAW THE HUNTERS TWICE on the hillside as I drove across Vermont and entered New Hampshire, the Connecticut River rich and placid beneath the Bradford Bridge. I had not expected to see them, but they appeared in the pale November sunlight, Bruegel's hunters, slowly descending the hillside, the forlorn fox held by one of the men, the village smoky and quiet beneath them. I slowed my truck and pulled to one side. In the horse trailer behind me, I heard Billy shift his weight. When I climbed out, I saw his enormous bulk between the slats of the horse trailer. He turned to see me, his senseless eyes immune to the dull afternoon we had entered. "Shhhhhh," I said, "shhhh. It's all right, boy." He made a deep, contented nickering sound, and I could not imagine why. We had been driving for days.

"Shhhhh, almost there, boy," I said through the slats. "We're in New Hampshire. You'll be okay here. You'll like it fine."

Then for a moment the blade of ice stabbed softly into my

breastbone. I felt it go in and I reached through the slats of the horse trailer and I laid my hand on Billy. His warmth spread up my arm and into my shoulder, and I felt the ice melting, felt it turn to a pool of water and drain away. I patted him slowly and softly, then put my head to the side of the trailer and sang into it as Morgan had sung. Morgan had taken his family on an assignment to Thailand, and he had asked if I would look after Billy until they returned. He said I was the only person he knew who owned a barn.

When I finished I breathed deeply, looking out at the Connecticut River. Thanksgiving. I was coming home.

I climbed back in the truck and drove slowly down Route 25C, up past Lake Tarleton, past Lake Catherine, past the old foundation of the Tarleton House, a grand hotel burned to the ground sixty years before. I looked out the window at the creek passing from the tail of Lake Catherine, and for a moment the past and present mixed. Here was my brother, Ed, jumping in a cannonball from Two Bob Jump; there was the deer meadow, where we could count on seeing deer most evenings, their tracks like two half-moons halved by a blade of grass; on the corner, near the deepest swimming hole—Pollywog Hole—a puckerbush lot where two moose, years ago, fought a bout during the rut. Ed and I had examined the swatch of beaten brush, picking off the moose hair, trying to reconstruct the battle like two Sherlock Holmeses of animals.

At last I came down the hill into the Flats, a fertile plain of river bottom, Mt. Carr stretching upward before me. Billy shifted in the trailer and I felt us swing, his weight enough to throw us off, and I slowed a little and wound down my window. Cold air cut into the cab of the truck, but it felt good, smelled like everything familiar, and I looked up the sides of the hills for the hunters. Maybe they had turned back because I did not see them. I saw only the funny village of Warren and Cates Dairy Farm, a dilapidated sign advertising shorthorn cows dangling from one piece of rusted wire. I drove on, feeling restless and unsure, my back aching from the long days behind the wheel.

I struck the Baker River and followed it north toward my house. Everything, each tree and bend in the road, seemed to pass me forward. I slowed and took my time, glad to have the last bit of sun to guide me. As I gained elevation, the trees became more naked. It was deer-hunting season, I knew. In flashes here and there I spotted the Baker River, its surface congealed with muddy leaves, its season finished, its turn toward ice and stillness inevitable. Finally our house appeared through the quiet treetops. I slowed and turned into our driveway.

I saw my mother first.

She had her foot on a garden spade, apparently separating a clot of daylilies for the front garden. She glanced up at the car, tilted her head slightly to understand the unfamiliar Washington license plate, then nodded. She dropped the handle of the spade and turned to the house, calling something I couldn't make out. Then she walked toward my truck. I climbed out to meet her. The sun threw its last shadows across the dooryard.

She did not speak. When I moved a step away from the car, she gathered me in her arms.

"My baby," she whispered as she held me. "My sweet, sweet boy."

Over her shoulder I watched my father come down the front stairs.

As he moved across the front yard, I was astonished to see him crying. I felt my own face cloud, and when my mother moved away, he put his arms around me. He shocked me by his strength. He pulled me tightly against him, forbidding me to move. Twice when I began to ease away, he fastened me tighter. He shook his head no and clung to me. He did not release me until I held him as tightly as he held me.

Then my mother put her arms around us both. We stood for a long time without moving. Leaves blew slowly across the yard.

"I'm sorry," I said, my voice too tight to speak clearly. "I'm sorry about Ed, about everything."

And I wept.

BILLY STOOD IN THE PALE LIGHT of the headlights, his hindquarters pushed back into the stall my father had built for him. Because of Billy's blindness, he did not register the bright light. I stood near him, moving my hand over his skin, feeling it flex and twitch in exhaustion. He had already consumed three rubber buckets of springwater. He was tired and thirsty and on unfamiliar ground.

"I slapped together the stall when you said you were bringing him," my father said, leaning on the top railing of the stall. "We can do better, but this should be okay for the time being."

"Thank you, Dad."

"Well, it's a horrible story about the poor thing. Your mother would have him in the house if she could. You think he'll be okay here? Lester Hawkins came by and took a look and he said it should be all right for a horse."

"He's still sedated. I don't know. It was a lot of work to load him. He didn't want to leave his spot. Really, he just stands in one place."

"This is Morgan's horse?"

"More his wife Gloria's," I said. "They are good friends to me and to Ed. I am happy to do a favor for them."

"He's welcome here, anyway. Your mother will dote on him. I just hope he settles in all right."

"I think he will."

My father nodded. The temperature had dropped and white

stars had come out along the tree line. Dinner waited back at the house, but we had to tend to Billy first. I continued to rub Billy, trying to gauge his state of mind. Maybe, I thought, it was better to keep him mildly sedated until he became familiar with his surroundings. For the time being, he had an ample dose working through his system.

"I'll swing back up and check him later," I said. "Mom's waiting for us. We should go."

"Cold weather makes you hungry."

I nodded and Dad looked around. Then he leaned back against the stall.

"I suppose we should finally run electricity up here. I don't know why I've always resisted it. I talked to a fellow about solar, but we don't have a good south-facing exposure. Not close, anyway. They call it solar south."

"I could help you with that. Bringing up electricity. I'd like to do that."

I saw my father study me. The light gave shadow to his profile.

"Are you staying, Allard?" he asked, and the hopefulness in his voice—the fact that he had tried to control the hopefulness—went into my heart.

I nodded.

"I'm home. I told Morgan it was time to come home. We left on good terms and he'll continue to give me work. I'd like to open the Baker River Film Company here in the barn, the way Ed and I envisioned it."

"You're serious? Do you mean it?"

"If you'll allow it."

"This is your land, Son. It always has been. Take what you need. Take any portion of it."

"I'd like to build a simple cabin here. With you, Dad. I don't have a lot of money, but I have enough, I think, to start the company. Andy Bottom, a friend I worked with on the arctic shoot, he's interested in coming aboard and he has some backing, too. We would travel a good deal, but we'd be located here. And I'll look after Billy."

Dad nodded slowly, as if getting used to the idea.

"You're home to stay," he said finally. "It's hard to get my mind around it. Your mother will be over the moon."

"If you'll have me."

"What do they say? Home is a place when you go there, they have to take you in."

"I want to come home, Dad."

He reached up and held me in his arms. We didn't move for a long time. When we broke apart, he cleared his throat and ran his fingers down the seam of his pants in the way I remembered him doing it.

"We could build a fine cabin here," he said, his voice gaining strength as he considered it. "Nothing to it. We could take the wood right from the land. We could lay up a chimney, too, with the river stone. Of course, river stone tends to crack with heat so maybe we can do better. We'll figure it out. You want to get started right away?"

"As soon as possible."

"Temperature might work against us, but if we hustle, we can probably keep you out of the weather. If you wanted a big house, I'd say we should wait until spring. But a cabin's another matter. Let's draw some plans up and see how they look."

I patted Billy one more time, whispered to him that I'd be back, then followed my dad to the truck. Our headlights passed over Billy as we left. He did not follow us with his eyes. He had turned to a statue, a mammoth horse on a fall night, the light of the moon and stars occasionally passing across his wide rump.

When we passed by the Patricks' house, my father made a simple statement.

"Sarah will be home for Thanksgiving," he said, his eyes deliberately straight ahead. "I guess she's engaged. That's what we've heard, anyway."

"Really?" I said, disguising the jab at my heart.

He nodded. "Time keeps moving whether we want it to or not. It's funny that way. A fellow she met down in Washington."

"Good for her," I said.

He glanced at me. He seemed to weigh speaking again before he decided against it. He told me what was for dinner instead. Roast, he said. And garlic mashed potatoes.

27

THE MAP OF THE GREAT LAND looked small and faded on the rafters above our beds. I did not look at it right away, but kept it for study until I climbed under the covers, my bags arranged on Ed's bed. My mother had not touched our room to any significant degree. She had removed the pigeon cage outside our window, put in a new rug, and changed the bedspreads to a sedate blue. She had also acquired a better light for the table between the beds, but the room remained essentially the same, and heat still had difficulty climbing to warm it. It felt familiar to be in my childhood bed.

I turned off the light and waited for my eyes to adjust. Then I reached into the drawer of the table between the beds and searched until I found our old flashlight. At first it did not come on, but I unscrewed the top and shook the batteries into different positions, and finally it sent a pale light toward the map. I passed the beam over the wall, scanning the remembered names, verifying that the Baker River, if one followed it properly, would lead to the great land. I saw the approximate position of Fi, and of the ice shelf, and the spot where the narwhal ran up through the leads to chase springtime into the low country.

When I went to return the flashlight to the drawer, I saw Ed in his bed.

It was not Ed, of course, but something in the arrangement of my bags on his bed suggested his shape. I felt my breath shorten, my heart stall. My eyes watered a little and I glanced back at the map and I could imagine him here in the New Hampshire land he had known and loved.

"Oh, Ed," I whispered, and I felt his kindness, his gentleness, surround me. "Dries for cutties," I said. And if it is possible, I felt him pass through my body, and I experienced old joy. Ed of the Baker River Film Company. Ed, who drew a daisy with his last strength. Ed, who led me through my childhood and approached every day as if it promised adventure. I felt him leaving and I knew it was wrong to hold him any longer. He passed into the map, going north, rising up into the geese currents above the house.

I had made that same journey, too, riding with Sarah in the western wind that carried everything to the sea. But we had returned and Ed could not. I listened to him, his keening voice carrying him away, his salute to the woods and streams, to the small animals of our acres contained in the sharp break of wind over our eaves. He waited for his company, for our old homing pigeons, Sky Top and Foggy and Gray Lord, cooing and calling him, taking him north to the land where my father promised us the white bears rode plates of ice into the darkness and where the turtles tracked the turn of the stars on their carapaces. He did not say good-bye. He would be frost, I knew. He would be pond ice. He would be a fish rising, the dimple on a summer pond, the shudder of a doe shrugging a fawn into the world.

28

MY FATHER AND I drove to the cabin site first thing Thanksgiving morning. He brought along an old cracker tin filled with crumbs for the birds. I went to check on Billy, who seemed comfortable in his new location. I broke up hay for him and spent some time mucking out the stable. When I finished, I found my father sitting on a white-pine stump, feeding the birds. They flocked around him and pecked at the ground in front of him.

He smiled and raised his hand when he saw me. "How's Billy doing?"

I sat down on the stump beside him. Morning light chopped at the top of the trees. It was cold, but not bitter. The weather report promised a chance of snow.

"He's doing okay. Doesn't look any the worse for wear. I'll keep him on the sedatives a little while longer."

"Probably a good idea. He'll have to get his winter coat on pretty soon."

"He'll be okay."

Dad scattered some crumbs out for the birds. A few titmice darted in and grabbed a crumb, then furiously flew away.

"We picked a pretty spot for this barn, you know that?" he asked. "Almost like we had good sense."

"It's a beautiful spot, Dad."

He tossed some more crumbs out. Then he made me turn over my hand and poured some crumbs in my palm. I tossed some out for the birds.

"Over the years, I've walked most of our property, but I never found a spot I liked better. I know it sounds crazy, but this spot spoke to me. It always did. Your mom collects scraps and pieces of bread in this cracker tin and then sends me off to feed the birds. She wants me out of her hair sometimes, I suppose. She'll just drop it into the conversation that the cracker tin is full, and that's my clue to head up here and spend a few hours."

"Pretty subtle." I held out my hand and he poured more cracker dust in my palm. I tossed it over to a few grackles that had landed several feet away.

"Your mother calls this stump the philosopher's stone. Her tongue hasn't lost its edge over the years. What do they say? A woman's tongue is the one tool that doesn't become dull with use?"

"You taught her to take good care of her tools."

He smiled and tossed another handful of crumbs on the ground. "You can see Sentinel Mountain if you walk up a little ways. Mostly you see our land, which is what I like. Look at that, a robin." He pointed to a bird that had landed at the edge of the clearing.

"It's getting a little late for him."

"They'll be on their way soon. I miss the birds when they're gone. The real songbirds, I mean. I miss the hermit thrush most of all. If I could hear one sound on the last moment of my life, that would be it."

"Not Mom correcting you?" I asked.

He laughed and softly slapped my knee. "Well, maybe both sounds together."

We didn't say anything for a while after that. The birds came and landed and went away with their treasures. My father didn't play favorites. He let the birds earn their rewards and distributed the crumbs evenly. At last he turned the tin upside down and shook out the final crumbs. He knocked it twice to make sure it was empty.

"At the end," he asked quietly, gazing at the birds, his hand slowly coming over to rest on my leg, "did Ed look as though he suffered?"

"No, Dad, he didn't. He looked okay."

"The cold then, right?"

"I guess, Dad."

"I'm sorry to bring it up, Son, but I needed to ask that one thing. The rest of it I've put to bed for the most part. Of course, you never do that completely, but I've made my peace. You know, I've felt him beside me a few times. You probably think I'm crazy, but I have. He liked this place. This creek and the barn, of course. I can't go past a river without thinking of him."

"Me neither, Dad."

"Your mom will sometimes unearth something of his . . . an old scarf or a reading assignment or some crazy thing . . . and that will set her off. But for me, he was always here in the outdoors."

"Me, too, Dad."

"I just can't bring myself to imagine him suffering. That's why I needed to ask. I didn't want to ask before. A little time had to go by. Any of us could die at any time, but I can't believe in my heart that we deserve to suffer."

"He didn't suffer, Dad, I promise you. The cold took him away, that's all. It's not the worst way to die, I don't think."

He danced the cracker tin gently on his knee for a moment, his thoughts far away. He finally removed his hand from my knee.

"Want to lay out the cabin footprint tomorrow?" he asked.

"I'd love to, Dad."

"I always wanted to try my hand at a building. We did the barn, of course, but this will be a little finer. It's different from constructing an instrument, but similar in some ways, too. It's wood trying to be a tree again, that's what I think."

He started to rise, but then put his hand back on my knee. Sunlight broke free and scattered up against the barn. Porcupine Creek began to steam with coolness and heat trading places.

"You know I'm getting a little wifty, don't you?" he asked. "Or maybe you don't know. We're just finding out about it ourselves. We've done some tests, that's all. We have to do some more before we know anything for certain."

"Alzheimer's?"

"They're not calling it that yet. But I've gotten a little forgetful. That's the truth. I might as well admit it."

"How do you feel?"

"Pretty good most days. I'm more of a problem to your mother than I am to myself. I can't remember a damn thing. A crazy jumble, believe me. If you've ever seen a windfall where a hurricane or a big wind took down a lot of pines, it's like that in my head. Jackstraws. Not every day and not all the time, but you have to bushwhack a good deal to go forward."

"I'm sorry, Dad. Does everyone know?"

"No, oh, Lord no. Just your mom and now you. I'm telling you more so you can keep an eye on me a little. I didn't want you thinking your dad had gone crazy."

"I'd never think that, Dad."

He shrugged. "It comes and goes. Sometimes it feels like I'm riding above myself, watching the world through a pair of antennae. It's hard to describe. Other days it all comes right in through the window and I can't remember if I am remembering correctly, or if it all is a shadow of a shadow."

"She'll be apples, though."

He smiled. "She'll be apples," he agreed. It was an old phrase he used to express that things would work out.

"What can I do for you, Dad? Name anything."

He danced the tin a little more on his knee. He smiled. He turned and looked at me. "Who are you again?"

"Dad . . ."

"A joke, Allard. Don't take things so seriously."

He stood slowly and let his back straighten. I stood with him.

"Not a bad little barn," he said, inspecting it on his way back to the truck. "We got a couple things right when we built it. Who would have guessed?"

"It's a fine barn."

"I won't be driving much longer. Your mother has already made me promise to stay local, though how a man who forgets things is supposed to remember a promise is beyond my powers of reasoning."

"I guess she means you should stick to your usual routines."

"You might as well take the truck." He tossed me the keys. "Probably a little dangerous to have me on the roads. It's a good truck. It has less than sixty thousand miles on it."

"We'll see what happens. No need to make a lot of decisions right away."

We looked at each other over the top of the truck. He smiled. The sunlight wedged up along the side of the barn.

"So Sarah's engaged?" he asked. "Did I hear that correctly? I know I said so the other night, but has that been confirmed by the kitchen staff?"

"Seems to be. Mom says so."

He shook his head. He started to speak, stopped, then started again.

"You two belong together, you know? People say a lot of romantic claptrap about childhood sweethearts, but Sarah set her cap for you a long time ago. And you for her. Can you win her back?"

"I don't want to interfere with her life any more than I already have."

My father laughed. He smacked his palm on the hood of the truck. The sound shocked us both.

"Allard, your fatal flaw is you never understood that life is messy. It just is. It's a bunch of puckerbush, not an English garden. But Sarah is your girl. You know it and I know it. Deep down, she knows it, too. Don't let things slip away. If you want her, you better find a way to tell her. And fast."

"Any suggestions?"

"Not a one. I don't even remember what I just said."

"That's a convenient little dodge you have now with this memory stuff."

"Isn't it, though? Best I've come across." He tapped the top of the truck again, this time softly, and before he slid inside, he said, "She's your girl."

29

IT SNOWED AFTER DINNER. It began in the late afternoon, quiet and lovely, and in no time the ground took on a thin dusting. "A deer snow," my mother said at table. When I left the house, my mother wrapped up a few plates for Sarah and her family. They had gone out for dinner, but they would be hungry again later, she knew, and she placed the dishes in a small basket she used for pies. She pitied them that they had no leftovers.

"Who said I was going to see Sarah?" I asked her in the kitchen as she wrapped up the food.

"You're a smart boy, where else would you go?"

"I want to show her the film from up north."

"Whatever gets your foot in the door. She's not in love with this other boy, Allard. I'm sure he's perfectly nice and suitable, but he's not part of her story. You are. I know Sarah. She belongs up on that land with you. The Patricks know it, too, although they're bending over backward to be diplomatic. Just go see her. Remind her what you two are."

"I'm not sure it's as easy as you think. I let her down."

"Yes, you did. But a woman is always forgiving a man over something. We must like doing it, is what I've finally concluded. Bring her to see Billy. She won't be able to resist that."

I put the food beside me and drove to Sarah's. Charlie's Jeep Cherokee was parked in the driveway, its tire tracks fresh in the snow. I lifted the food out and went to the door and knocked. No one answered. I knocked harder, but still no one came to the door. I was trying to figure out what to do with the food when someone spoke from behind me.

"Who comes tap, tap, tapping at my chamber door?"

I turned and saw Sarah. She had been out walking. Snow stuck to her barn jacket and to her gray hat. She wore Bean boots and heavy socks that went up over the shins of her jeans.

"Dad's asleep in front of a football game," she said, her voice deliberately quiet, "and Mom's upstairs watching a movie. I felt so full I had to get out of the house. What do you have there? You look like Red Riding Hood with your basket."

"Mom sent it over. More food."

"Oh, good grief." She put a hand on her stomach.

"I wanted to see if you would take a ride with me up to the barn. I have the narwhal footage and I have someone you might like to meet."

Sarah looked at me. "Really? Just like that?"

"Yes, Sarah Crabby Pants. Maybe this time you just go along with me."

She smiled. I loved her smile.

"It's been a little while since anyone called me anything like that."

"Come with me. It's a pretty night. It's snowing."

She studied me carefully. I felt as if the whole thing could tip either way. Then she held out her hands for the pie basket.

"I'll put this inside. Let me leave a note for my folks."

"I'll warm up the truck."

She took a little while inside. I listened to two radio hosts talking about the Patriots' last game against Indianapolis. Snow continued to fall and melt on the windshield. Finally, Sarah slid in beside me. Her perfume filled the cab of the truck.

"Dad says to thank your mom," she said. "He woke up for thirty seconds to ask what she had sent over. He'll dive into it later, I promise."

"She sent over the works."

"That's what I told him. Then he went back to sleep."

We drove to the barn. The snow made getting up the dirt road difficult and we fishtailed twice, both times the rear end shivering until it caught. We did not see the creek, but the trees beside it had turned brilliant with snow. When the headlights swept over the barn, Sarah spotted Billy.

"Who's that?" she asked, her voice excited. She sat forward on the truck seat.

"It's Billy. He's a horse I brought back from the West Coast. Don't rush right up to him. I need to introduce you. He's got a little history."

"What kind of history?"

"I'll tell you when we feed him."

I parked facing down the hill in case the snow deepened. Then I shut the engine off. As soon as we stepped out, I was reminded of the silence that had always hung close to the barn. We heard no sounds; we saw no lights. I dug in my pocket and gave Sarah a headlamp. She put it on over her wool hat. I put on a headlamp, too. Then we walked over to see Billy.

"He's blind," I said softly. "Some boys squirted acid in his eyes. And I guess he ran and foundered in some barbed wire. He was a mess when they found him. Morgan's wife rescued him and kept him behind her cottage. She admired his courage."

"The poor sweetie. Acid?"

"In a squirt gun. They thought it would be funny. They offered him carrots and when he came over, they shot him. He stays in one place because he can't see. He's still sedated, but I'm beginning to think he's going to be okay here. She used to sing to him and he would come over and put his head over her shoulder. Morgan did, too."

"Can we turn off our headlamps so our eyes can adjust? There's enough light tonight. The snow is reflecting everything and I want to see him."

We flicked off our lights. We didn't move. Gradually Billy's outline became more visible. He was a beautiful horse despite the cruelty that had marked his body. His large, tufted forelock looked white and soft in the snow-light. I grabbed a hay bale from deeper in the barn and broke it apart for Billy. He didn't move to it.

"You need to sing," I said.

"You're joking, right?"

"Give it a try."

"I'm embarrassed to sing in front of you."

"Come on, Sarah. I've heard you sing before. He needs the sound of a woman's voice."

She looked at me. Then she turned back to Billy and began to sing softly. Her voice was sweet and low, and as soon as it began, Billy's ears flexed and turned to us. I whispered for her to sing a little deeper, and she did.

Billy followed her voice and came forward. When he reached the stable fence, Sarah reached up and put her shoulder under his massive head and nested it against his throat. She stopped singing and simply held him, her hand smoothing his neck, his eyes looking out at the snow he couldn't see.

"Wow, DOES THIS PLACE bring back memories?" Sarah said, looking around the barn office we had used all those years ago with Ed.

I had the woodstove going and the generator running. We had a lamp connected to the generator, and the woodstove—an old Vermont Castings Defiant—threw heat from the corner. Sarah sat on the couch in front of the woodstove. She had kept the fire going while I fussed with my Apple Mac Pro, getting the film ready.

"We spent a lot of time in here," I said. "We lived in here, more or less."

"Was Morgan pleased with the shoot? I mean, I heard the basics, but I didn't know his final word."

"Yep, he liked it a lot. They should have it ready to go this spring. They want to time its release with spring in the northern hemisphere. I guess it's a marketing idea to tie the arctic melt in with our own spring. And your article is going to run, too, right?"

"They're going to run it a month after as a kind of follow-up."

"That's terrific."

"I've seen some of this, Allard. I should tell you."

"I know," I said. "But these are different cuts."

I sat next to her. The stove had finally taken a stand against the barn chill. We had the stove doors folded back so it acted as a fireplace. Sarah had pulled an old afghan off the back of the couch and spread it over her legs. The wood smelled good in the fire.

"So Dad says you and your father are going to build a cabin up here? Dad's excited about it. He plans to be part of the work crew."

"We'll take any help we can get, but, yes, we're going to lay it out tomorrow."

"That's wonderful. Your dad must be so happy to have you back."

"I hope he is. My mom, too. It's good to be home. Thank you for helping me realize that."

"What kind of cabin will you build?"

"Simple lines. We'll do post and beam, of course, with Dad in charge. Maybe two bents, maybe three. We may run electricity up here, but not at first. That's what we're going to talk about tomorrow."

"It's a beautiful spot."

I nodded. I couldn't take my eyes off Sarah. She met my eyes, too, but just as quickly turned away. She stared at the fire.

"You ready for the film?" I asked.

"Sure. Fire away."

I put the laptop on the small crate we used for a coffee table and started the DVD. I turned off the lamp. Sarah settled back in the couch. Light from the fire flickered and made long shadows on the ceiling above us. The computer emitted a small whining sound, then began to read the DVD. The film opened on a small, shaky image of Sarah throwing Sky Top into the air. Her hands went up and Sky Top fluttered away, his wings clapping. Then the camera panned down to Sarah's excited face, when she said, *"Did you see it? Did you see him go?"*

"What is this, Allard?" Sarah turned quickly to study me.

But she knew. It was a film about her. I had collected all the films we had made, all the shots we had taken, and spliced them together. Sylvia Match, Morgan's film editor, had helped me edit it and put it in a narrative form. It followed Sarah's life. Sarah as a young girl riding her bike behind her dog, Natasha. Sarah being a character in Ed's obsession with Indiana Jones. Sarah swimming in the Baker River and running through the forest behind the barn; Sarah rock climbing in Rumney; Sarah turning to the camera and pretending to be a grand lady, using a stick as a pretend cigarette, vamping and goofing; Sarah graduating high school. Sarah and her mom, Sarah and her dad, Sarah sitting at our kitchen table, my mom at the sink behind her. A hundred images. A thousand shots. The final shot was a still Andy Bottom had taken of Sarah up on the ice. She was caught in profile, her eyes off on the horizon, Rope beside her. It was the most beautiful portrait of Sarah I had ever seen. The film faded afterward.

"That was lovely, Allard," Sarah said after a moment. "Thank you. I wasn't expecting that."

"I wanted to do it. For me as much as for you. I wanted to remember you, all of you."

"I'm engaged, Allard. Did you know that?" she said, her voice breaking a little. "A man I've been seeing . . . even before I went up for the narwhal shoot and saw you again I knew we were heading that way. I guess I needed to see you to make sure of my heart. That probably wasn't fair, but I had to do it. And when I came back, he was there. He's a nice man, Allard. He works as a lobbyist on global warming. He's smart and kind and he doesn't go away to places I can't follow. You'd like him."

"Congratulations," I said when I could.

"Don't say that, Allard. Don't say anything. The last thing I needed was to find you here waiting like this. Corey . . . that's the man who asked me to marry him . . . he's coming up to meet Mom and Dad. Tomorrow we're going out to see people, and I wanted to have it settled, you know, out on the table and tidy somehow. You're like Peter's bear, Allard. You're following me through dreams and time."

"I didn't plan it to be like this."

"I know you didn't. You don't have a mean bone in your body, Allard. You never did. That was one of the things I loved about you. I guess our timing just got bollixed up. Who knows why? Ed died and things changed. I know that now. I feel sorry for that boy and girl, for us, but I can't go back to it. You'll go on and do fine, Allard. Somehow, after the surprise of seeing you calms down a little bit, I think it will be better to know you are home. I won't have to worry about you now. And I won't be under your feet reminding you of Ed or anything else. In the end, it makes sense, really, doesn't it?"

"I want you to be happy, Sarah."

"Well, there, see?" Her eyes glittered. "We can all be happy. I made a resolution after I came back from the narwhal shoot that I couldn't wait any longer for things to fall in place. I didn't even know what I wanted from you anymore. You're so deep down in me, Allard. You don't even know. I didn't breathe without thinking about you for so many years. . . ."

For a long time neither of us moved. She looked at me.

I reached to the side of the couch and lifted the green metal box we had buried on Ghost Island all those years before.

"Oh, my," she whispered, and began to cry.

"Your canoe wasn't there, but I found a boat that was unchained and rowed out at first light this morning. I didn't have the map so it took me a little while to remember where we had buried it, but it was there, safe. I guess we should open it."

Sarah nodded and looked at me. She shook her head softly. Then she lifted the box onto her lap. She took a little time to get her breathing even. She slowly raised the lid. She put her hand in and drew out a length of clothesline and a photograph.

"Do you know what this is?" she asked, and showed me the clothesline. "I think this is the rope you and Ed used to pull me out of the river. She must have retrieved it . . . as a keepsake. And then she put it in here."

My mother had tied a pink ribbon around it to keep the line coiled. Sarah touched the coil of line to her lips. Her eyes glittered with tears.

"That's the clothesline we used," I said, amazed. "She wouldn't have faked it or substituted anything."

"No, she wouldn't. Not your mom. There's a photograph, too."

She lifted out a photograph and examined it. I could tell she recognized the picture. She nodded, as if remembering. When she turned it for me to see, I recognized it, too. It had been snapped of us shortly after we had first met. It had been in my mother's scrapbook. *Allard and Sarah,* it said. *Baker River, July.* It gave no year. Instead of a date, she had written a small verse. The words had faded with time, but they were still legible.

No sooner looked . . . but they loved . . .

"Do you know the quote?" I had trouble keeping my voice even.

"No, but the rest is here on the back . . . she copied it out. It's from Shakespeare. Your mother probably knew it by heart."

Sarah read it quietly, her eyes letting large drops fall.

> *No sooner met but they looked;*
> *no sooner looked but they loved;*
> *no sooner loved but they sighed;*
> *no sooner sighed but they asked one another the reason;*
> *no sooner knew the reason but they sought remedy . . .*

"What's our remedy, Allard?" she asked when she finished. "What are you doing to me? Why did you bring me here? This film, this box . . ."

"Marry me, Sarah," I said, and I felt my body give way, my spirit rise up. "Nothing makes sense without you. If I'm being unfair right now, I'm sorry, but I can't let you go without trying to keep you. Marry me. We belong together. We always have. 'No sooner looked but they loved,' Sarah. My mother is right. She knew."

She studied me a long time. She reached a hand out and touched my cheek. Her eyes shimmered.

"Sweet Allard," she whispered, her hand soft on my cheek. "You're my sweet, sweet love. I'm so thankful you were in my life . . . I'm so grateful I learned about love from you. Your gentleness, and your kindness . . . you're a good, good man, Allard. I know you are. But we can't go back. There's no remedy for us. That land we lived in, Allard, my sweet Allard, that land is gone."

"I know it is."

"I love you, Allard. I always have and I always will. But that country, we can't go there anymore."

"I don't want to go back there, Sarah. I want to be with you now. I want to go forward. I want us to live here beside the water. You're everywhere. You're in every thought. You're with me when I wake up and when I go to bed. You're never gone from me, Sarah. It's not back or forward."

She stared at me. Slowly, with great care, her eyes still on me, she leaned forward and kissed my lips. I tasted tears and felt her head nod against me.

"Be mine again, Sarah," I whispered. "Please. Be mine. Everything I have, everything I am . . . it's all tied up with you. All that I am is yours."

She nodded twice. Her lips brushed mine and it was the same kiss, the kiss we had shared under the ice a million minutes before. Then it was warmth, and the fire reflecting on her skin, and snow falling far away in the great land. I kissed her. I kissed her until the fire breaking the logs was the only sound and the trees moved above us and the stars sometimes got hit by the leaves and were erased from the sky. I kissed her neck and her shoulders. We kissed until our lips filled every molecule. We kissed constantly, madly, her body finding new angles, her hands everywhere. The chill of the barn left and then she was no longer merely Sarah, but part of something larger, part of everything, and I held her until I lost what outline remained mine, or hers, or where Sarah gave way to the air around us. The only remedy for love, I knew, was to love more.

30

WE MARRIED ON THE SHORE of the Baker River in the spring, exactly where Sarah and I kissed beneath the ice all those years before. Charlie Patrick commissioned a tent and hired a caterer, and for the reception my mother contacted the local fiddle band that had played at the barn raising. Mom scoured the riverbank for wildflowers and stole or borrowed every vase or container she could find. The house filled with flowers and the scent of growth, with wands and buckets of osier and beech. The first leaves had begun to appear on the oaks and maples, and Sarah made a bower of twisted branches near the opening of the tent, conning my father into building an understructure to serve as a lattice. Charlie promised a generous bar and suggested we open the wedding, after the ceremony, to most of the citizens of Warren. He hired three local college kids to bartend and appointed Lester Hawkins liquor commissioner.

Standing in the kitchen at two o'clock on the appointed day, my parents and I heard a bell begin solemnly ringing. That was our cue. The peal of the bell climbed the hill from the river and filled the house. I glanced at my father. He smiled and nodded. Mom simply unplugged the coffee, rinsed her hands under the kitchen faucet, and pushed at her hair. She wore a green skirt and a boiled-wool jacket. My father wore clean carpenter pants and a new flannel shirt. I wore jeans, a white shirt, and a tweed jacket.

Before we stepped outside, we gathered together and put our arms around one another. Here in our old kitchen, where my mother had produced a thousand, thousand meals, where her light had gone out to us on cold winter days to pull us back inside to warmth and brightness and safety, we held one another as a family. No one remarked on Ed's absence, but it was in our hearts. We pulled tighter together and listened to the bell calling us. My mother began quietly to cry and I pulled out a handkerchief and my father whispered that he loved us all. Then Mom shook herself, laughed, and said it was time to go.

We stepped outside. Down the river, two houses away, we saw Sarah's family begin toward us. When I saw Sarah, I felt my heart lift. She wore the white dress, *her dress,* that she had promised to wear all those years before. The sky above her was gray and dramatic, and rain might be in the forecast, but in that moment, with light and clouds mixed, she was a white bird, an exquisite flame impossible to ignore.

Because I could not take my eyes off Sarah, I did not at first see the line of basses arranged in a wide *V,* one end extended toward Sarah, the other toward us. A conductor stood halfway between our houses and raised her hand, and on the downstroke the basses struck a first note. The music came not through the air, but through the earth and trees, and we stopped for a moment to listen. Then one note built into a second and the conductor—I did not recognize her, but my mother did and whispered to my father her name—began leading them through the opening stages of the score, and the basses, my father's work, sang in a single voice, loud and powerful and gentle at once.

"I didn't have to ask any of them twice," my mother whispered to us—but especially to my father—her eyes full. "All of them volunteered, a tribute to you, sweetheart."

"The music of trees," I told my dad.

And it was.

The music rising, we walked slowly past the musicians, my father smiling and nodding at each one, my mother's arm through his. With each step, Sarah took more of my sight. Every bride is beautiful, but Sarah looked truly radiant, her smile wide, her flowers—she carried simple irises with daisies mixed through the bouquet—shaking a little with nerves. We walked directly toward each other, and the people gathered under the tent came out to watch. Then my mother and father stepped forward and took an arm on each side of me, and the Patricks took Sarah's arms, and our families gave us away. One house from two. Two families to one.

I held out my hand to Sarah.

Her hand settled into mine and our eyes locked, and the world went away. It was Sarah, the girl of the always, the girl who had never left me. I took her in my arms and we stayed together for a moment, the only point of stillness in the entire congregation, and the music gathered force and broke through and a single ray of sun hit the tent and turned it white. The river flashed brightly below us, and huge sheep-clouds ran above us, and both our families, our community, formed a loose line guiding us toward our marriage. Sarah held me close. And for the slightest moment the past and the present mingled, and Ed filled my heart. And I thought of the river running beneath the ice all winter, and of my father building a cabin, and of the map, the map of Canada, and the magnificent northern whales running through ice, and the great land calling us north. I thought of the look on Sarah's face all those years before as she drew the bow across the strings of my father's double bass. One sound, one sharp and lovely echo, and that sound became the fierce call of the geese arriving in spring, and of the hermit thrush, pure and lovely, asking us to go deeper into the woods, to find it, to keep our eyes upward.

EPILOGUE

ON A WINTER DAY SIX YEARS LATER, I took my son skating on the Baker River. It was December and dark and snow had not yet arrived. The smell of woodsmoke covered everything except near the riverbanks, where pine and earth replaced it. Sam—we gave him Ed as a middle name, of course—pushed off on his small double blades, trying to master the side-to-side motion. His cheeks, molten red with cold, pulled back in the way they did when he concentrated. He wore a blue snowsuit and thick mittens, and his mother, my Sarah, had wrapped a scarf around his neck. He held his arms out for balance and his small feet scraped quickly at the ice, his better sense telling him ice was too slippery to walk on. Now and then, at unpredictable moments, he gained a ghost of the necessary rhythm, and then I saw joy enter his eyes.

"Nice job, Sam," I said.

He nodded. He kept concentrating, furiously balanced, his arms reaching toward me as he entered my orbit. I stayed on one knee and let him crash into me, and I held him steady for a second. He looked beautiful standing there, the evening light around him, his skin flawless, his lashes, Sarah's lashes, long and slightly iced with cold.

"Do you think," I asked him quietly, "that we could skate this river to another river and then keep going, farther and farther north, until we could skate away to where the polar bears live?"

He nodded at me.

"Your uncle Ed once thought we could," I told him.

He nodded again.

"Do you want to go ahead of me and show me how you can skate?"

He pushed away. He took a series of choppy steps but managed to glide afterward. For an instant he was my brother skating, and he was my young self, and he was all children going forth. Then he hit a button of ice and it turned him and he swung halfway around, looking at the riverbanks, the water humming beneath us. The moon chose that moment to clear the mountains and I saw him outlined in light, my boy, my darling son, and I skated to him and held out my hand.

Acknowledgments

Everything about publishing with Simon & Schuster/Gallery has been a joy. I am especially grateful to Kathy Sagan, my editor at Gallery, for her patience in teasing out the scenes and themes of this novel. This is our second novel together, and my admiration continues to grow. Thanks, too, to Andrea Cirillo, who makes all the difference, and to Christina Hogrebe, whose insightful, close reading informs my work more than she might know. Thanks to all the many people at Gallery who have taken me under their wing: Louise Burke, Jennifer Bergstrom, Jean Anne Rose, Ayelet Gruenspecht, and many others too numerous to name. I have been met with enthusiasm, kindness, and generosity every step of the way. I wish every author I've ever known could have the experience of publishing with you folks.

THE
WORLD
AS WE
KNOW IT

Joseph Monninger

Introduction

As adolescents in rural Maine, Ed and Allard Keer save the life of Sarah Patrick, their new neighbor, who has fallen through a thin patch of river ice. As a result, a kind of special bond is formed among the three, but especially between Allard and Sarah, who eventually fall in love. The three of them grow up together, with the dream to work someday together at their own nature film production company. It seems that nothing, including jealousy or separation, can part them—until Ed's accidental death mere days before Allard and Sarah's wedding. Unable to make sense of or reconcile himself to his brother's death, Allard buries himself in his work, avoiding his family and his fiancé, until two years later, when an assignment brings them back together. Reunited with those most important to him, he is finally able to put the memory of his brother to rest.

Topics and Questions
For Discussion

1. Nature acts as a main character in this novel. How does the setting influence the course of the book? How much of what happens is a result of the setting?

2. Allard and Ed's father believes that owning land is salvation. Do you agree? If you could own a piece of land in any part of the world, where would it be?

3. Allard's father tells him that "the heart is always inexperienced." Do you agree with him, or do you believe that we take what we learn from one relationship to the next?

4. While reading, did you experience a sense of foreboding regarding Ed and Allard's trip? Did you see Ed's death coming? Or were you surprised?

5. When Ed dies, Allard loses his best friend and only brother. How would you have reacted if you were Allard? Would you have gone through with the wedding? Why do you think he needed to isolate himself? Do you think he was overwhelmed with guilt that he survived and Ed did not?

6. Even until the very end, Ed remains an optimistic person. How do the two brothers complement each

other? How would the story have been different if it had been Allard trapped in the rock instead of his brother?

7. Were you surprised when Sarah and Allard part ways at the end of Part II? What kind of advice would you have given Allard in this situation? What about Sarah? Do you think they had to split up in order to ultimately be together?

8. What did you believe would happen between Allard and Sarah when he proposes a second time? How do you feel about the ending?

9. In the end, Sarah forgives Allard and accepts his second marriage proposal. Do you think she was right to forgive him for abandoning her? Would you have been able to forgive Allard?

10. The Baker River plays an integral role throughout Allard's life. How is Allard a different person when he visits the river later in his life?

11. Sarah, Ed, and Allard show a true passion for nature and wildlife. How were you impacted by the conservationist message in the book? Do you share a similar vision?

12. The dangers inherent in working in the wilderness hit Allard and Sarah hard, but their desire to continue in their chosen field does not seem shaken. Knowing the sacrifices people in this line of work make and the dangers they face, do you believe the end product is worth the risk? Why?

ENHANCE YOUR BOOK CLUB

1. The Keer brothers are set on making the Baker River Film Company a reality from a very young age, and both work in film as adults. The Discovery Channel's *Planet Earth* series is an excellent example of nature films. Rent the DVDs with your book group or watch clips online at http://dsc.discovery.com/tv/planet-earth to get a sense of the Keer brothers' dream profession.

2. PBS Now has also shown a documentary called *On Thin Ice*, about the rapid rate of glacier melting, which mirrors the topic of the documentary Allard and Sarah help produce in the novel. Watch it at http://www.pbs .org/now/on-thin-ice.html, then discuss.

3. Wilderness is central to the lives of the characters in *The World as We Know It*, but many of us rarely spend much time in the outdoors. The National Park Service has a "Find a Park" section on their website (http://www.nps .gov/index.htm) that can help you plan an outing for your group. Or check out your local state parks.

4. Sarah Patrick not only takes part in the Baker River Film Company but becomes an acclaimed nature writer. To learn more about the experiences of living in harmony with nature, read Joseph Monninger's critically acclaimed memoirs *Home Waters* and *A Barn in New England*.

A Conversation with Joseph Monninger

1. What was the inspiration for this story/novel?

I live in Warren, New Hampshire, where the novel is set, so the inspiration for this narrative is all around me. My wife, Wendy, and I raised a son here, so it wasn't difficult for me to imagine what growing up in this town might have been like. From that beginning point, Allard and Sarah's story developed naturally. As someone who has moved around a fair amount, I wondered what it would be like to stay rooted to one place, one community. The joy Sarah and Allard experience is the joy of knowing where you belong in the world. Ultimately, this is a story that echoes the loss of Eden. Luckily, Allard and Sarah catch themselves before they are banished forever.

2. Have you yourself ever been, like Allard and Ed, lured by the map of the great north? What was that like?

My inclination has always been to go north. I'm not sure why. I once owned a home on an island off the coast of Cape Breton, Nova Scotia. I've taken a mail packet boat along the southern Newfoundland coast and spent some time on St. Pierre and Miquelon watching the seal colonies. I like pine trees. I like cold rivers. So for me, adventure has always pointed north, and I suppose I transferred that impulse to Allard and Ed and their dad.

3. Do you have a position, like Sarah does, on animal rights?

Oh, this is a tricky one. I love animals, and I have been a vegetarian at different times in my life. I struggle. I always think, gosh, I love my dog and cat, so why should I kill other animals when it isn't necessary? I won't even get into all the ecological questions about raising livestock, but those concerns are considerable. Add to that the ultimate question of animal intelligence, their capacity to suffer, and so on, and you have an entire bundle of issues. So I suppose Sarah is espousing views that represent part of my mental state. At the very least, I believe those important questions should be part of our consciousness. They are worth asking and exploring.

4. As the author of fiction, nonfiction, and memoir, do you find one easier to write than the others?

Not really. They all require the same set of muscles. Nonfiction is a bit more time-consuming because it requires verification and research. Fiction permits us the luxury of making things up. But I like doing both.

5. Does nature play a big role in your personal life?

Absolutely. My wife and son are avid kayakers, and we try to take a river trip once a summer at least. We also live beside a river—the Baker River, from the novel—and we fish in it, swim in it, and canoe it. I'm also a lifelong fly-fisherman, so I am on the water a good deal during the spring, summer, and fall. So yes, nature is an everyday part of my life.

6. Do you believe in fate?

Not really. The idea of fate is an intriguing one, but I don't quite buy it. Dramatically, though, it's an important concept. Romeo and Juliet are "fated." So are many tragic heroes. Readers, I think, feel the need for things to come right . . . to have consequence and inevitability. Maybe that's fate.

7. What is your favorite moment in this book?

I like the sequence when Allard has a dinner for Sarah up on a meadow. That little rift in the relationship is important to the novel, and I think it's true to life. I enjoyed writing those scenes. I also like the opening because it represents my initial engagement with Allard's voice. For a writer, it's pretty special when a character begins whispering his or her story.

8. Do you fly-fish or do woodworking?

As I mentioned, fly-fishing is one of my passions. I always tell friends that it is "the only thing I do that is the only thing I do." Meaning, it wipes my hard drive clean and lets me think about nothing. And again, I won't even go into the animal rights issues associated with fishing.

I'd love to do more woodworking, and maybe will someday, but I wasn't brought up in that environment. My wife is better at woodworking, and most around-the-house skills, than I am. I'm learning, though. It actually seems to rely on the same thinking patterns as fishing. It engages me when I do it and it takes me away.

9. How do you relax at the end of the day?

Scotch! Actually, we have a bell on our porch that we ring at cocktail time. But I also love movies and sports, so sometimes I'll watch something. My wife insisted some years back that we buy a hot tub, and I thought she was crazy. I figured it would end up like an exercise bike with clothes draped all over it. Not so! Turns out we take a hot tub four to five times a week. Winters in New Hampshire require a plan for heat and relaxation!

10. Who are your favorite authors or authors who may have influenced your writing over the years?

Oh, probably too numerous to give any kind of meaningful list. I've loved certain books at certain times, and I am grateful to those authors. One of the earliest memories I have of reading revolves around Stuart Little and *Charlotte's Web*. And *Lord of the Rings* was awfully important to me during high school. As a Peace Corps Volunteer in Africa, I loved the big, fat nineteenth-century novels because they provided another world to visit. But I love books, plain and simple.